To the Nez Perce Tribe, whose gallant reclamation of their ancestral lands at Am'sáaxpa in 2020 inspires a continued legacy of strength, honor, and healing that resonates in these pages and will echo throughout history.

PRAISE FOR
IN THE WRATH OF LEGENDS

"David Buzan transports readers into a world cloaked in mystery, suspense, and terror. 'In The Wrath of Legends' adds more depth, richer characters, and lighting quick action which culminates in a rewarding sequel sure to satisfy even the most discerning reader."
–Eric P. Bishop (author of the bestselling *THE BODY MAN series*)

"David Buzan has crafted a sequel that is every inch the peer of his international best-selling *In the Lair of Legends.* This is literary fiction at its best – the words are poetry, but for this novel it's a vehicle for delivering action, drama, and plot to the highest degree. A thriller of incredible dimension, *In the Wrath of Legends* is a masterpiece."
–Karen K. Brees, Amazon #1 best-selling author of the *Katrin Nissen WWII series* and *The Esposito Family Chronicles*

"This rollercoaster sequel of literary excellence must be devoured in one sitting. Its recurringly clever narrative draws from a vast cultural and spiritual palette and unexpectedly releases into whitewater descents of action that leave you breathless."
–Tom McCaffrey (bestselling author of *THE CLAIRE SAGA*)

THE WINTERHAWK SAGA: BOOK TWO

IN THE WRATH OF LEGENDS

DAVID BUZAN

Black Rose Writing | Texas

ISBN: 978-1-68513-719-9 Paperback, 978-1-68513-720-5 Hardcover
LIBRARY OF CONGRESS CONTROL NUMBER:
PUBLISHED BY BLACK ROSE WRITING
www.blackrosewriting.com

Printed in the United States of America
Suggested Retail Price (SRP) $19.95 Paperback, $24.95 Hardcover

In the Wrath of Legends is printed in Garamond Premier Pro

*As a planet-friendly publisher, Black Rose Writing does its best to eliminate unnecessary waste to reduce paper usage and energy costs, while never compromising the reading experience. As a result, the final word count vs. page count may not meet common expectations.

IN THE WRATH OF
LEGENDS

PROLOGUE

Elkhorn Peak
Carson Mining Company
La Grande, Oregon
1875

The dawn sky blushed.

The bleak winter landscape had started to encroach upon the remote terrain of Elkhorn Peak with the same fearlessness of an alpha predator staking its claim upon territorial hunting grounds. The vista was rife with the vestiges of isolation as the distant outline of the mining community presented itself as a mirage of humanity.

After the first blanket of snowfall had appeared this month, it was now only weeks before 100-inches of accumulation would transform the grandly majestic chorus of the Blue Mountain Range into a mournful tune of inhospitality. By then, the gold miners stationed at Camp Carson would have already traveled east to La Grande to rejoin their families until the warm thaws of spring beckoned them back.

By the 1870s, seventy-five percent of gold extracted in Oregon came from the Blue Mountains. While most of that gold was mined from orogenic gold veins and associated placer deposits, mines like Camp Carson utilized gravity dumps of water excavated from underground rivers in the spring and summer months to reach the precious mineral deposits buried underneath the mountains.

But not everything of value buried at Elkhorn Peak was gold. Floyd Hunsacker had accidentally stumbled upon this truth while prowling around the network of caverns that pockmarked the mountain's base. The rest of the Camp Carson miners preferred to spend their downtime socializing in the saloon shacks, but old man Hunsacker had always enjoyed the solitude of exploration.

And that's when he'd first discovered the pioneer treasure.

Because heavier loads increased the risk of injury and death for the mules and horses climbing the rugged terrain, the settlers navigating through the Blue Mountains decades earlier had made the decision to lighten their wagons. Personal possessions of all sorts had been abandoned within the network of caves in hopes of returning someday to reclaim what had been hidden. Hunsacker often wondered if those pioneer secrets held more than silver—perhaps something the mountains themselves guarded.

In any event, it was a grand testimony to the pioneers' faith, tenacity, and—

Stupidity, Hunsacker had thought grimly.

The first cave discovery he'd made had been nothing but a disappointing assortment of rotted clothing sacks and trunks of worthless pottery, but Hunsacker had kept searching until he had found enough silver cutlery, gold-etched porcelain dinnerware, and jewel-encrusted family heirlooms for it to feel like a small treasure.

It wasn't going to yield him the same kind of riches that those bung-tongues at Carson Industries made from their miners' blood and sweat, but he reckoned the bounty from the last several months of scavenging was more than enough to keep him supplied with cold beer and cactus whores until the end of his days.

Hunsacker thought that made him a *very* rich man, indeed.

Given the worsening weather conditions and his age-related physical ailments, Hunsacker knew that the unexplored cave he was entering today would be the last one until the springtime thaw. Of course, the pioneer treasure hidden in this cave might ensure that he would never have to return.

Hunsacker felt a surge of excitement at the thought as he stepped into the unexplored cave. He hefted a burning kerosene lantern with arthritic fingers, swinging it back and forth like a talisman warding off evil spirits.

Spiderweb remnants of the overnight snowfall had been blown ten feet inside the cavern, crunching loudly beneath his lumbering footfalls. The splash of light from the kerosene lamp illuminated the craggy walls as the entirety of the cave came into full view under his light. As he walked, Hunsacker passed a discarded pickaxe etched with Chinese characters. It was a relic of those mining cohorts of his who had already been driven from these hills.

He stopped abruptly. His heart hammered.

There was something *glinting* in the back of the cavern. His mind raced with all the possibilities of such a find. The glinting objects could be gold coins; perhaps a collection of priceless diamonds, or even—

Bones.

Hunsacker stepped closer to see what the lantern had revealed. It was a large group of skeletal remains, piled high on the cavern floor. He reckoned the bones were from pioneers who had sheltered from a storm and succumbed to the elements.

Hunsacker frowned as the lantern picked up something else now.

He swallowed hard, feeling the thick clump of saliva tickling the back of his throat like porridge. The glinting he'd seen earlier had come from a large bone pile, but he had been mistaken in thinking they had been remnants from the settlers.

What he was staring at now was the skeletal remains of just a single creature.

The cave had been the final resting place for something of absolutely massive proportions; bigger than any animal he'd ever seen. The skull of the creature was immense, each hollowed-out eye socket looking like it could fit a harvest moon inside it. The jaw of the animal had clicked open, revealing rows of humongous teeth, each one as big as a shot glass.

Hands shaking uncontrollably, Hunsacker dropped the lantern, nearly tumbling over the rocks at his feet. The glass from the lantern shattered, bathing the cave once again in total darkness. Panic unspooled inside of him like a rattler unfolding itself in his guts.

Whimpering with fear, he turned away from the monstrous skeleton, moving quickly towards the cavern exit.

He stopped in his tracks; breath hitched sharply in his lungs.

A pungent, animalistic odor enveloped the cave. Hunsacker sobbed, realizing something was in here with him now.

Thundering footfalls crunched through the cave, followed by a snort that echoed with animalistic excitement. Crimson eyes pierced the blackness, staring hungrily into his own.

"God, please help me…"

Hunsacker felt his bowels loosening as his head was sucked into a gigantic mouth. His body jerked wildly as he batted his hands against the creature, fists pounding uselessly against thick fur and dense muscle. He screamed as the monster's tongue slimed across his face, agony searing as its jaws crushed down.

His final thought was that the sickening crunch was his own skull being chewed to pieces.

PART I
MY FIRST BLIMP RIDE

CHAPTER 1

Blue Mountain Range
Umatilla, Oregon
1905

Hope dies last.

Chenoa Winterhawk understood that to be the mantra of every warrior. It was a shared belief among soldiers of every generation, and of every nationality. The cause might have been what propelled you to put boots on the ground, but it was the undying embers of hope that brought you through to the bloody end.

Chenoa thought that to be true in war, but she believed that was also true in life. To extinguish hope is to experience what the Apostle John described as a sin unto death. Just as blaspheming against the Holy Spirit is a spiritual condemnation the Creator cannot forgive, losing the last vestiges of hope is a mortal trespass where the heart cannot find any absolution.

Chenoa understood this to be true, but she understood something else, too. The harbinger of lost hope is apathy. To accept the unacceptable is to have shed your core humanity, to have traded it in for cheap cynicism that crumbles under the weight of shifting moral defenses that become systematically uprooted.

Anger is the strongest anchor in these moments. It hides in the deep recesses of the subconscious, ready to defend. In many instances, when such anger does appear inside a warrior, it results in a fight to the death.

Very much like what she had just experienced.

The man she had been tasked to protect on this dirigible mission had just asked her a simple question. The man undoubtedly felt himself to be innocent—they were just words, after all—but the innocuous question itself was a spectacularly ignorant display of his inciteful intentions.

Chenoa rolled the moment back in her mind, knowing the man's question was tantamount to a war of words. To her, it was shots fired. And so, with a withering look of hostility, she took careful aim at her combatant and fired back.

"Honor?" Chenoa answered him coldly. "I've buried more honor than you'll ever know." As she spoke, Winterhawk touched an antique silver locket fastened on a chain around her neck. There had once been a picture inside of it, but it had long ago faded away the way some memories eventually do.

The locket had belonged to Chief Jolon Winterhawk; now, it was the only thing of her father's she had left. It was dented and scratched, as were all of the memories that still compelled her to hold onto it. More of a war medal than a family heirloom, over the years it had come to symbolize duty more than anything else.

"Duty doesn't have a sweetheart," her father had once told her. "It only has a mistress. She's unfaithful, and she'll ditch you the second you're no longer useful. Just like love is only a word until someone comes along and gives it meaning, the same thing applies to duty. Only it's not another person who'll give it meaning, it'll be you."

Chenoa felt the shifting eyes of her travelling companion as the man nervously cleared his throat. "I intended no disrespect, Winterhawk."

Seated across from her in the open-air gondola of the Signal Corps Dirigible, Major Quinn reflexively held up both of his hands to her, showing his age-weathered palms in a gesture of muted cordiality. He wore a permanent expression of bluster etched on his craggy features. Thinning strands of red hair curled downwards in a greasy clump, the wispy follicles acting as punctuation against the deepening furrows of his pinkish brow.

"I was only referring to your uniform," Quinn continued, "and wondered if you wear it to honor Chief Winterhawk."

Chenoa glanced down at her clothing. Dark blue shirt, light blue pants, red neck bandana. Standard government-issued uniform for the Army Indian Scouts. It was adorned with a specialized shoulder patch: two crossed arrows intersecting with a bow. She frowned at the insignia.

Why are you pulling a face, Pocahontas? That's the cross of your calling. If there's one thing that Chief Joseph made clear after his surrendering at Bear Paws Mountain, it's this old chestnut: If you can't beat 'em, join 'em!

It was her father's voice sounding off in her head. And as usual, Chief Winterhawk was right.

After the end of the Civil War, Congress had authorized President Andrew Johnson to enlist a select handful of Native Americans to serve as U.S. Army Scouts. Their job was to be wilderness guides, protect soldiers against the threat from hostile tribes, and begin a concerted indigenous assimilation into the United States military. By the turn of the twentieth century, two thousand men and nine women had already served in the unit.

What could possibly go wrong? As it turned out, plenty.

The indigenous soldiers were identified by their tribes, and in many cases, inter-tribal animosities were long standing. In some instances, after the Army suppressed one tribe, it turned around and offered those same tribal members an opportunity to serve as scouts against enemies from another tribe.

Years ago, her father had encountered the very same thing.

After he'd returned home from the Civil War, he had discovered that a faction of Nez Perce elders had strongly disapproved of his U.S. Cavalry service. In their eyes, he betrayed his people by wearing an American uniform. Luckily, Chief Joseph had believed something else. In a show of deep respect, Joseph had officially given him the title of Chief Jolon. But her father had never sought after that leadership. Instead, he had turned to the simple life of a farmer.

Jolon had left behind the war while never forgetting about the warrior.

In his eyes, it was possible to be two people at once as long as both halves honored the same reflection. The difficulty arose when a person attempted to conceal their true nature; being someone they aren't can only last as long as what's hidden remains dormant.

James, the half-brother of Jesus, spoke about this in Scripture. He cautioned that denying those parts of themselves is akin to staring at yourself in the mirror, and immediately forgetting what you look like.

Sin wants you to forget it exists, until it doesn't.

In a way, that's what serving as an Army Indian Scout represented to her. The sins perpetrated against her people couldn't be easily forgotten as long as she was there to constantly show her face to the people who had perpetrated them.

Keep telling yourself that, Chief. Maybe the Nez Perce won't be ground to dust beneath the wheels of injustice this time just because of you. And if a bullfrog had wings, it wouldn't bump its ass a-hopping.

Sighing, Chenoa returned her gaze to Major Quinn. He was the senior military man whom she'd been tasked with escorting safely. Her orders had been to deliver him to a pair of First Sergeants—McNichols and Bryce—with the Army Corps of Engineers stationed at a base camp located on the Wenaha River.

Quinn was in possession of an old Chinese mining map that revealed the location of the largest underground river in eastern Oregon. It was a treasure map of the new age. Quinn had been ordered to protect it with his very life.

But from where Chenoa was sitting, she doubted Major Quinn was capable of protecting a warm mug of piss. Frowning, she studied him closer.

The soldier was distractedly flicking at the unruly red hair splayed across his forehead with plump sausage fingers. He was taking great pains not to gaze down at the scenery whisking past below them. Given the immensity of his girth, the man was obviously comfortable sitting at heights no greater than the elevated heels of his combat boots.

"You asked pointedly about my honor," Chenoa finally answered. "The truth is that I don't need to wear a uniform to honor my father."

Major Quinn fired off an apologetic nod. "I only meant well."

"People like you always do," Chenoa said. "Some of us traverse this world by actually *doing* well, and not just *meaning* well."

Splotches of red slowly crept up from beneath the collar of his immaculately pressed uniform. Tendrils of embarrassment snaked along the fleshy jowls of his neck like a dab of rouge on a slaughter-bound sow.

Nice bit of emasculation there, Chief. Why don't you just accuse him of being hung like a gnat, and call it the end of a perfect day?

Quinn had just fumbled the last of his cordiality with all the untested skill of an anxious groom unfastening his bride's brassiere. While he had obviously never mastered the tricky balancing act of interracial politics, Quinn was faring even worse in the arena of gender acceptance. No matter how much he longed to walk under the warm light of twentieth century enlightenment, ethnic discourse would never cast a shadow on him. Among his own people, it probably never would.

That kind of thinking is nothing more than a case of selective amnesia. Your father might have served in the Great Rebellion, but he never carried the weight of enlightenment around with him. There's right and there's wrong, and everything else in-between is just that old river in Africa: denial.

Chenoa sighed at her father's voice, but once again, he was right.

Selective amnesia was especially true within factions of her own culture. While nearly a quarter-million Native Americans had served during the Civil War to end the propagation of African slavery, the intervening decades had brought a harsh light onto a shameful aspect of tribal relations.

The truth was that indigenous slavery had long predated the arrival of Europeans to the Americas. Archeological evidence of monuments and codices, alongside accounts from settlers and soldiers, provided tangible evidence of widespread Indian slavery throughout the nation. It was estimated that as recent as 1880, there were over two million Native American slaves still held captive within dozens of tribal territories.

It's the dawn of a new century now. You don't have to be clanging around in rusty leg irons to be a slave these days. People are held against their will by false beliefs, false hopes, and false promises. As for your father, he put on that uniform and became shackled to something else altogether: false advertising.

During the Civil War, Chief Joseph had sent ten of his greatest warriors as a way to show solidarity between the Nez Perce and the United States. Joseph had been brokering a peaceful truce between the two nations for years, offering unconditional support in exchange for an agreement that his people would remain on their land.

Her own father had been one of those ten warriors. Jolon Winterhawk had become a lieutenant in the U.S. Cavalry, becoming the most highly decorated indigenous soldier to have ever served during the Great Conflict.

You know what all that bunk really means, amiga? Your Poppa was the healthiest person in the leper colony. That's all that war really is: a disease. Most men find death is the only cure from it. But Chief Winterhawk had you and your mother. That was the antidote that saved him. The question we have before us now is this: what's gonna save you?

The aircraft shuddered violently.

Chenoa snapped quickly out of her darkening reverie. Her first thought was that they had just come under enemy fire. She cursed herself for allowing the Zieg-8 rifle and her weapons satchel to have been stowed out of arm's reach.

But a fast glance off the starboard side of the blimp proved that her fears were unfounded. The aircraft was simply changing its course, now flying against the powerful wind gusts that were so prominent in the Blue Mountain Range.

Chenoa recalled the briefing she'd received days earlier about the dirigible.

The enthusiastic aviation sergeant inside the hangar giving the briefing had cautioned about encountering mountain wave turbulence during the flight. He had explained that these waves were generated whenever strong winds encountered mountain ranges. As the winds struggle to rise above the peaks, a strong inversion causes the winds to be redirected back toward the surface. This can cause an excessive amount of low-level turbulence and unpredictable wind gusts.

"In other words," the aviation sergeant had elaborated, flashing a spectacular set of rotting buck teeth, "it can feel just like a cloud rodeo up there in the blimp."

"Cloud rodeo," Chenoa had echoed.

The aviation sergeant had nodded so emphatically that she was momentarily concerned that one of those rotted teeth would come dislodged and drop from his mouth like a piece of black licorice.

"Only you wouldn't want to get bucked off this mother-scratcher. If you find yourself kissing dirt during a cloud rodeo, you'd better hope God kills you quick."

Chenoa had understood that sentiment perfectly. In this life, prayers or otherwise, sometimes hope is all that you can ever cling to.

And hope dies last.

CHAPTER 2

Chenoa Winterhawk held tightly onto the wooden gondola for support as the 90-foot Baldwin-class dirigible banked sharply through the air. The compartment continued to shake with turbulence as the dirigible resumed its maneuvers hundreds of feet above eastern Oregon's Malheur River.

This blimp was the latest in state-of-the-art military reconnaissance. Although the Army Balloon Corps had been decommissioned and systematically dismantled after the end of the Civil War, military interest in utilizing strategic air travel had not abated over the intervening decades.

After being impressed by a flight demonstration by Thomas Scott Baldwin at the St. Louis Air Show after the turn of the century, the Army had commissioned him to build a small fleet for the newly created Aeronautical Division of the United States military.

Captain Baldwin built all the dirigibles with four principal parts: a cigar-shaped balloon filled with hydrogen gas; wooden open-air gondola slung beneath the balloon for holding the crew and passengers; Curtiss lightweight motorcycle engine that drives the large propeller; and horizontal and vertical rudders to steer the craft.

Offered up to the Army Corps of Engineers for use in the west, this particular blimp had officially been named the Signal Corps Dirigible No. 4. However, the lieutenant who had been first trained to fly it had popularized another name for the contraption: *Lathos*.

The word was taken from the ancient Greek, where it translated to "error."

Those Army boys sure know their way around Clever Avenue, don't they? But you don't need an ancient text to read the writing on the wall these days. No, ma'am. It's the same white-man's motto today as it was yesterday: What's mine is mine, and what's yours is mine.

Chenoa shook her head. It wasn't supposed to be like this; not this time.

The Newlands Reclamation Act had authorized the federal government to commission emergency water diversion, retention, and transmission projects in arid lands. When President Theodore Roosevelt had signed the so-called U.S. Reclamation Act bill in 1902, he paid particular interest to the arid lands found in eastern Oregon and Washington. These specific areas were targeted because agriculture in these parts of the country had reached untenable levels. Lack of sustainable farming meant an economic demise in the west that would eventually cause an industrial imbalance in the United States.

"No nation has ever achieved permanent greatness," President Roosevelt had remarked in his appeal to Congress, "unless this greatness was based on the efforts of the farmer and rancher. Their livelihood, and that of our entire nation, now rests in the immediate diversion of water resources."

To this end, Roosevelt had turned to the Army Corps of Engineers and given them the unenviable task of moving mountains. The undertaking of creating new waterways and diverting rivers would largely be achieved through the creation of dams. And to do this, several tribes who had previously relocated along these same rivers would need to be misplaced all over again.

Including the Nez Perce.

For millennia, thousands of Native Americans had lived in villages located along numerous Oregon river shores. In these areas, salmon fishing was central to culture, sustenance, and trade. But after the Reclamation Act went into effect, the Army Corps of Engineers spent the next several years relocating the tribes of Umatilla, Warm Springs, and Nez Perce off those rivers where dam construction would soon begin. Those displaced tribal members were sent to hastily constructed villages, and promised electricity to offset the major loss of land heritage and economic hardships.

The Malheur River, which had been second only to the Snake River in terms of providing sustenance to the Nez Perce people, had been forced to move all over again. Chenoa had experienced this once already as a young girl, where she learned firsthand that broken promises can resemble weaponized threats.

She curled her hands into fists of anger at the thought.

Seated behind the controls of the Baldwin-class dirigible, Lieutenant Misciso watched her. "What's wrong, Winterhawk? Does flying make you nervous?"

She levelled her hard gaze at him. "This is my first blimp ride."

Misciso licked his lips, allowing his eyes to travel across her body with wanton abandon. Although beautiful, Chenoa displayed the toughened physicality and daunting muscle of her warrior lineage. Her waist-length black hair was in a braided ponytail, with an unusually shaped hair clip fastened in the back.

Although she found him repellant, Winterhawk kept her eyes on him.

Lieutenant Misciso was fielding a triple deficit: half her age, half her intellect, and half her height. He had buggy eyes as green as river rock, with blonde eyebrows so unruly it was like he attempted to grow a beard on the wrong end of his face. His cracked lips had formed into a perpetual sneer, offsetting the row of crooked teeth which shone like a picket fence besmeared by years of bird dung.

Misciso chortled. "First time, huh? Well, don't fret, teepee tits." He sat up with exaggerated straightness before attempting to mimic a white man's cliched-and-ugly rendition of a Native American speech pattern. "God of wind...in big sky...protect chief's daughter."

Chenoa nodded. "Perhaps you're right," she said. "Or it could be that this airship operates on the Principle of Archimedes: a lifting force which is equal to the mass of the displaced fluid. The envelope bag of the Signal Corps Dirigible No. 4 is filled with hydrogen. It's also equipped with a Curtiss lightweight motorcycle engine that drives the large propeller, while rudders pilot the direction of the craft. That sound about right, Lieutenant Misciso?"

Misciso's sneer melted off his face. "Congratu-fucking-lations. You read a book once. Doesn't prove a damn thing, Winterhawk."

"I think it proves one thing."

"Yeah? What?"

"It proves that without fools there can be no wise men."

Chenoa saw him absorb her words like a knife. It was a deep wound that would leave a lasting scar. One of many, probably. Misciso was a man who carried personal slights the way camels carry their humps. It was built into the very fabric of his nature, not given a second thought because it was his constant reality. That was usually the case with burdens, anyway. That was their danger, too.

People tend to grow up believing what's said about them. The slights received as children can warp adult thinking. School taunts can dull critical thinking skills until they've been replaced by an apathetic self-esteem. That's when a person's reality shifts in accordance to another's perceptions. That's when you begin to believe the worst about yourself. When it comes to a negative self-image it's always the bigger the lies, the greater the truth they conceal.

Maybe si, maybe no. It could also be that some people are just born bad. We don't like to think of that as being true, do we? We like to flatter ourselves with the belief that our destination comes from the result of our decisions. But when framed against the vast cosmos, that idea seems like a rather arrogant supposition. Men like the good lieutenant here ride the rails of destiny after having their tickets punched while in the womb. It doesn't excuse who they are; it just is what it is. Think of it this way: don't plant a garden, then blame the bunny for hopping off with a carrot. There are some things designed by the Great Spirit with a distinct purpose in mind. Some men, too.

It was something that Chenoa had heard from her father many times before. While she didn't fully believe that, there was no denying that the world she inhabited wasn't set into motion by mere happenstance. Coincidence should never be an excuse for ignorance; fate never an alibi for bad judgement.

Manifest destiny was a belief held by many of the early settlers in North America. They had convinced themselves that they had been divinely ordained to fulfill a sacred mission to expand westward and remake the tribal lands they found into the very image of the agrarian East. They believed it was their destiny to succeed.

Just like Roosevelt's Newlands Reclamation Act. It had been put into motion as a means of protecting the nation's best interests, but you could paint anything with that brush. A web might be beneficial to the spider, but the fly would rightfully disagree.

She figured that's why President Roosevelt himself was coming to Oregon this week. He'd planned a photo-op at the site of the newly constructed Owyhee Dam in order to drum up public support in a region that had proven incredibly hostile towards his irrigation policies.

Chenoa wished him luck.

Behind her, Major Quinn cleared his throat apprehensively. "How much further until we land, Lieutenant?"

Misciso pulled his hateful gaze off of Chenoa just long enough to glance down the river. "Another few miles, I reckon."

"And then where are we going, Major Quinn?" Chenoa asked.

"The mine at Elkhorn Peak," he answered. "It's abandoned now, but some of the Chinese miners mapped a location of an underground river somewhere inside there. They figured there had to be a rich gold vein running through that hidden river, so they meant to return in secret someday. But the Snake River Massacre happened. For many of those Chinese workers, someday never came."

Chenoa nodded grimly.

The Snake River Massacre was a legendary injustice. It happened in 1887 along the border of Oregon and Idaho when a gang of seven white men ambushed two camps of Chinese miners. They shot dozens of them before mutilating the bodies and leaving them in the Snake River. The eventual indictment listed 34 counts of murder. Only three of the seven men were ever caught and tried for the massacre, and they were found innocent by an all-white jury.

The Snake River Massacre ignited a much broader pattern of racism and violence against Asians. In Oregon, anti-Chinese sentiment, along with the belief that Asian laborers were stealing white jobs, led to the passage of the

Chinese Exclusion Act. This temporarily banned Chinese immigration to Oregon, Washington, and Idaho. At the turn of the century, it even became illegal in Oregon for anyone of the white race to marry someone of Chinese nationality.

"Snake River Massacre." Misciso shrugged with indifference. "Shit happens."

Chenoa briefly wondered how the Army Corps of Engineers found out about this Chinese map. How did it end up in the care of Major Quinn?

Chenoa looked once again at Quinn's large hands, the plump fingers drumming restlessly on the uncomfortable wooden gondola perch he rested on. There was some obvious detail she had missed. She was certain of it.

And then she saw it.

On the fourth digit of his left hand. The creased indention against the flesh. The mark of where a wedding band had once been.

Chenoa stared intently into Quinn's face. For all his puffy bluster and uncomfortable social manners, there was an unmistakable kindness that shone in his eyes. There was a hint of sadness in them, too. It was like when the winter winds blow at the very end of fall, reminding you that everything in this world was locked into an inevitable cycle.

She thought once again about the questions about her father. And then, she understood why he must have asked them.

"How old is she?"

Major Quinn looked momentarily bewildered. "I don't quite understand—"

"Your daughter," Chenoa said. "How old is she?"

CHAPTER 3

Major Quinn glanced nervously at Lieutenant Misciso, but the man was focused on steering the dirigible. He had one hand on the swiveled hydrogen valve, and the other on the rear rudder control. His eyes were set on a point somewhere up ahead on the Malheur River.

They must be nearing their destination point.

Satisfied that Misciso wasn't listening, Major Quinn leaned forward, his tone almost conspiratorial. "Huan is twelve," he said quietly. His words were quickly snatched by the rush of air around them. They scattered into the wind like flower blossoms.

"Huan," Chenoa said. "That's lovely."

"It means 'happy' in Chinese," Quinn explained. He glanced down at his left hand, eyes lingering on the cleft of skin where a wedding ring once resided. "Li always made me happy. Before she passed, I swore Huan would never want for joy."

Chenoa nodded. "Happiness is a worthy commitment, especially after you've lost someone."

Or in her case, several people.

Chenoa's father and her mother had entered into glory within a year of each other. Her *Pik'e* had gone first, succumbing to a lingering cough that had eventually snatched away her final breath in her sleep. Chief Winterhawk had followed his wife soon after. Her father's illness had been much more pronounced. It was almost as if he'd been carrying a collection of hidden wounds that had decided to surface all at once.

Quinn read the sadness etched in her face. "Husband?"

Chenoa shook her head. "No, but there used to be somebody…once."

Once.

Chenoa doubted that a word with a heavier connotation had ever been invented. It implied the untethering of dreams, where our memories became like a kite yanked from our hands until it vanishes into the dark clouds of time.

Nearly half a lifetime ago, Sonsela had been her *once*.

He had been the proud eldest son of a salmon fisherman within the Nez Perce. The type of young man who wasn't a warrior, but showed strength in his commitment of upholding the family lineage.

Chenoa and Sonsela had fallen easily in love. It hadn't taken much incentive from either of them. Just that first look; later, that first touch. It hadn't taken much to end things, either. Just death.

Sonsela had drowned in the Snake River. He had been found by Chief Winterhawk in an overturned canoe: face marred by vascular marbling, and crawdads skittering from his mouth. 'Peacefully,' her father had said about his passing. Chenoa found no comfort in death, especially for the living.

Chenoa pulled herself away from those memories; forced herself to return to the present moment.

"Sonsela was his name," Chenoa finally said. "He died many years ago."

Major Quinn offered her a pained look. "Parents?"

Chenoa shook her head. "Both my mother and father died three years ago." She motioned to the Army Indian Scout emblem. "What I do in the name of this uniform, I do now for my *Tota* and my *Pik'e*."

Quinn absently touched the breast pocket of his uniform. She guessed that's where he kept the Chinese map hidden. "I believe that to be the greatest battle each of us ever has. How hard we fight for those whom we love. To never surrender on what we have promised them."

Chenoa felt a wave of sadness brush up against her heart. How Major Quinn had met his late wife would undoubtedly be an interesting tale. A United States military officer falling in love with a Chinese immigrant is the fertile soil that poetry springs from. But his wife had died, leaving him alone to raise their daughter.

Winterhawk thought once again of promises. And of the map. It was then that she finally understood. "It's amnesty, isn't it? That's what the map will bring your daughter."

Major Quinn nodded solemnly. "The only blessing that came with Li's passing was that she wasn't alive to see our marriage deemed illegal. The map belonged to Li's grandfather, and now I'm using it to trade for Huan's future. The Army Corps of Engineers gets their water, and my daughter doesn't get deported."

The sharp click of a revolver's hammer being cocked echoed.

"Touching," Lieutenant Misciso said. The Colt Model 1905 handgun in his hand was pointed at Chenoa. "Unless you want to see this flying heap redecorated in arterial red, I recommend that neither of you make any sudden moves."

Chenoa's muscles tensed, eyes flicking to the far end of the gondola. Her weapons satchel and the Zieg-8 rifle had been stashed there. Her gear was less than ten feet away, but it might as well have been a mile. She wouldn't be able to make it a single step before she was cut down by the Colt.

"What the hell is going on?!" Major Quinn sputtered. "I demand an explanation for this outrageous act of aggression!" His hand twitched toward his pocket, as if shielding Huan's future from Misciso's treachery.

Misciso laughed. "Cut out the horse hockey, gramps. The mission has been altered. We're going on a little detour."

Chenoa narrowed her eyes. "Where?"

"No need to concern yourself with the details, teepee tits. This is strictly on a need-to-know basis. All *you* need to *know* is that there's a man waiting down there who is mighty anxious to see you."

"My parents taught me to never talk to strangers."

"He ain't no stranger." Misciso nervously licked his lips. "Not to *you*, anyhow."

Chenoa resisted the urge to crush his larynx with a closed fist and wrestle the gun away. She would twist the barrel into his eyes and pull the trigger until his head looked like gushing pulp from a rotted apple.

She could certainly do all those things, but there was one thing she *couldn't* do. She couldn't fly the Signal Corps Dirigible No. 4. And without a pilot, the *Lathos* would spiral downward hundreds of feet and kill them all.

Chenoa took a calming breath as the dirigible began to descend.

CHAPTER 4

Hermiston Brothers of Charity Orphanage
La Grande, Oregon
1905

There are times in life when God turns His back on you.

Lexington Tass believed that every bit as much as he believed that the Lord caused the donkey to speak to Balaam. That was his favorite Bible story, after all. In fact, he had recently asked Brother Tobias about its meaning in Scripture.

Of all the monks at the Hermiston Brothers of Charity, Brother Tobias was the kindest. He was not in the habit of striking the boys at the orphanage, and seemed to have no qualms about giving his dinner away to whomever might have been starving after a weekend punishment without food. And perhaps the best part was that Brother Tobias never treated Lexington like he was *only* fourteen. In his presence, you felt like an equal and that was a priceless gift.

"That passage is about divine appointments," Brother Tobias had answered. "Balaam shows us that God uses the most unusual circumstances to speak to us, and the donkey shows how the Lord uses the least among us to bring forth His wisdom."

That made sense. No wonder he loved the story of Balaam so much. Lexington understood what it was like to be thought of as less.

His teen mother had abandoned him at a rail station in Gallatin City, Montana when he had been five. "I can longer take care of you," she had said.

"Now, God will have to." She had left him at that train station with only the clothes on his back, and a wad of dollar bills.

That's how he had become a member of the Great Orphan Train.

Between 1854 and 1899, an estimated 250,000 American children—some orphaned, others abandoned—traveled west by rail in search of new homes. Of those, less than ten-percent eventually found themselves taken in by new families. The vast majority became laborers in mills or ranches, or succumbed to disease and starvation.

Lexington always figured that the Hermiston Brothers of Charity Orphanage was a combination of all those things. Every child here toiled in the fields, most went to bed each night hungry, and some died of ailments that couldn't be prayed away.

Lexington had been among them for eight years now, and he'd experienced everything at the orphanage except for the Coffin. Of course, he'd known all about it ever since his first day. Being sent to the isolation pit was the biggest punishment the monks ever bestowed on anyone there, so the Coffin was something every boy had learned to fear.

And because of last night, it had become Lexington's turn to experience the isolation pit for the first time. The trouble was that Royce had been asking for it. He'd stolen bread from Lexington's dinner plate. When Lexington had demanded that he return the food, Royce had defiantly popped the bread into his mouth and swallowed it whole.

And so, Lexington had punched him right in the face. It had been a hard hit, too. He could feel the cartilage of the other boy's nose folding beneath his fist before the loud crack reverberated throughout the stunned dining hall. Royce had yelped loudly with pain, pressing his hands against his face as blood seeped through the cracks in his fingers.

A disappointed-looking Brother Tobias hauled Lexington out of his seat and dragged him into the hallway. "Seven times seven," Brother Tobias had said. "That's how many times our Lord said to forgive those who trespass against us. You'll learn that tonight!"

WHILE THE ORPHANAGE had been around for decades, the isolation pit was a much later addition to the property. Built a mile away from the orphanage and located an hour's walk south of Elkhorn Peak, the Coffin was befitting of its nickname: a ten-foot-deep hole dug into the same stretch of forest that had once been used as a horse graveyard by the Carson Mining Company. Local legends told the story that the graveyard had stopped being used by the miners because the horse carcasses had begun to mysteriously vanish from the camp before the animals could be buried. Rumors began circulating, some of them wild conjectures about a man-eating demon that lived among the network of caves deep inside Elkhorn Peak.

For most, it was absurd conjecture. But for the monks, it was a way to instill fear into the orphans. When you're bad, you get punished; but when you're *really* bad, you get sent to the horse graveyard. And once you're that unlucky, spending the entire night in the Coffin is the reward.

Having just spent his first night of punishment in the isolation pit, Lexington was shivering with cold. His stomach rumbled with hunger, and his throat was parched. The need for food and drink had now consumed his every waking thought.

Sitting in the cold mud of the forest pit, Lexington's knuckles throbbed. He had a pang of flickering guilt for Royce's pain, though he shoved it down. He knew he was supposed to feel penitence about what he did to Royce, but the truth was that he did not. The boy had stolen from him, and he'd gotten exactly what he deserved.

Then, a loud voice startled him.

"Despite Israel's rebellion, God graciously provided a way for them to live near His holy presence in the tabernacle."

Lexington jerked his head up. Brother Tobias was staring down at him from the lip of the hole; arms folded across the front of his dark robe. The morning sun was framed just beyond his shoulder.

"Brother Tobias!" Lexington had cried out with as much surprise as relief. "Please get me out of here!"

"God offers grace despite rebellion, Lexington. Do you truly repent?"

"Yes."

"Do you?" Brother Tobias sounded unconvinced.

"Yes! I feel really bad about what I did!"

(He honestly didn't.)

"And what else?" Brother Tobias asked.

"I asked God to help me to never do anything like that again!"

(He would definitely do it again.)

"Very well." Turning, Brother Tobias slid down a five-foot rusted iron ladder that had been fastened to swivel bolts to the top edge of the pit. "Climb."

Lexington didn't need any prodding. He jumped up onto the lowest rung and began climbing quickly. As he reached the top of the ladder, he saw Brother Tobias whirl around. Something had just moved out from behind the trees and caught his attention.

The boy frowned in momentary confusion. He smelled a putrid, rotten odor wafting over him. He brought up the back of his hand to cover his nose. "Brother Tobias, what is that—?"

"Run, Lexington!"

He saw it first from out of his peripheral vision. It moved with a speed that seemed impossible for its massive size; torso thickly muscled and matted with two sharply contrasting shades of brown. The unblinking eyes were crimson red; gleaming with hunger. When it opened its maw to emit a savage growl of rage, rows of jaggedly pointed teeth flashed, hungry spittle dribbling out of the sides of its mouth.

Lexington screamed.

Brother Tobias raised the silver crucifix chained around his neck as the creature charged him. "In the blessed name of the Holy God—!"

The creature walloped both massive hands down on his shoulders. The force of the blow was staggering. With a sickening succession of snapping bones, the monk's upper body was driven downward. The creature struck him again, this time using the palm of its massive hand to mash his head down through his shoulders, where it vanished under a geyser of splattering blood.

Spinning around, Lexington began to run as fast as he could. He could hear the horrifying sounds of Tobias being devoured behind him. Wet flesh ripping and tearing as—

Lexington caught a quick flash of fur and teeth before a second creature barreled into him sideways like a runaway locomotive. He was launched airborne, flying through the air for several seconds before landing hard. With the wind knocked from his lungs, he writhed on the ground, painfully attempting to swallow air.

High above him, the sun had inexplicably turned red. Then, he realized what it *really* was. It wasn't the sun. It was the eyes of the second monster

The right arm of the creature reached down, clawed fingers flexing. Lexington felt a searing pain as the hand closed tightly around his head. The boy batted helplessly against the massive arm as he felt himself being jerked upwards.

"Please, God!"

The breath of the creature snorted against the back of his neck. Seconds later, he felt the agonizing daggers of teeth chewing methodically through his spinal column before his entire world was consumed with agony.

CHAPTER 5

Baxter Mines Peak
Blue Mountain Range
Adrian, Oregon

Built near the Malheur River, the three-tiered Baxter Mines had once been the epicenter of the largest sustained gold rush in Oregon history before becoming exhausted. Although the Baxter Mines had remained inoperative for the last two decades, one of the most impressive feats of technological engineering ever built had remained there.

The aerial tramway had been constructed as a means to efficiently transport gold ore from the top level of the mine. Its twin lines of steel cable stretched 500 feet down to the shores of the Malheur River, functioning as a continuously circulating ropeway system. Suspended fifty feet in the air, a massive stone-carved transport bucket was still hung at the midway point along those cables.

At its operational peak, the tramway ran over 50 times a day, where waiting hopper barges took the ore to smelting plants for refining and purification. Now, it stood alongside the Holbeer Mini Steam Donkey and the Grafton Crane as a symbol of Oregon's contributions to America's Industrial Age.

Looking down at it from her vantage point in the *Lathos*, Chenoa recalled a Nez Perce proverb: 'The river chooses your path, but you choose your strength.' She thought it was apt whenever contemplating the individual responsibility of navigating modern life between the mechanical and the natural worlds.

As if proving her point, a lumber barge rattled noisily along the Malheur River below the blimp. It was shepherding a flotilla of tree trunks towards the lumber mill located on the shores of Adrian near the newly constructed Owyhee Dam. A three-man crew could be seen traversing along the deck. They were gawking up at the unusual sight of the floating dirigible.

Good, Winterhawk thought as she glanced down at the crew, *we'll be remembered.*

She looked at Misciso to see if the appearance of the barge had rattled him. It hadn't. It was almost as if he had expected to see it. She found that deeply troubling.

"I don't know what you're planning," Major Quinn said, interrupting her thoughts, "but there's still time to do the right thing."

"Do the right thing." Misciso snorted. "Sunday School ethics don't mix very well with these uniforms."

"What would you know about ethics?" Chenoa asked disgustedly.

Misciso grinned. "Only that you must learn to do unto others before they have the chance to do unto you." He swiped a spittle off his lip with an excited flick of his tongue. "Conquered races like yours learn that part too late, Winterhawk. You don't understand that, so you don't know what's coming next."

"What's coming next?" Quinn asked.

"The end of the beginning, and the beginning of the end. There's a man waiting for us down there who understands everything perfectly. You'll see."

Chenoa felt a small balloon of fear burst in the pit of her stomach.

The ends set up the beginnings. That's how things invariably change in this life. The consistent predictability of the world is itself nothing but a cosmic sleight of hand. What seems constant and forever might well someday turn into the yesterdays and the forgotten.

It can be like crossing a swaying suspension bridge that's being buffeted by the wind. Sometimes it's all you can do just to hang on lest you find yourself toppling over the side. You have to hang on or risk losing everything.

Some things we experience are poetry, but other things are just graffiti. Those are the moments that have desecrated our hearts. Those are the memories that have been scratched into our very souls. It's pain that takes us there. And sometimes, it leaves us there, too.

You hold onto that pain, amiga; you hold on real tight. Strength doesn't come from letting go, it comes from holding on. You fight to hold on because it's the pain you're avoiding that gives things perspective. If you let go of some of it, then you really let go of all of it. You just need the strength to hold on.

Chenoa thought briefly of the scars that her father had brought home with him after the Civil War. The ones he talked about, and especially the ones that he didn't. Those were the scars that he had kept carefully hidden. She didn't think it was because he had been afraid of talking about them; rather, he had thought that perhaps talking about them would have somehow lessened all they represented.

Some experiences define you. Not just in what you went through, but in how you went *through* it. You encounter the worst this world has to offer and come out on the other side, completely changed.

Or you don't.

That's life. Everyone gets pushed through the rapids of painful experiences; some paddle, some drown. And the ones who drown, they never rest until they can pull as many people down with them as possible.

The *Lathos* began to descend more rapidly toward the clearing on Baxter's Ladder, giving the large suspended tramway cables a wide berth.

There was a group of three soldiers and a giant man standing on a clearing near the peak. Two of the soldiers were wearing Army uniforms. The giant man standing in the middle of them wasn't wearing any military attire, but he exuded absolute authority. He wore industrial denim pants, with an oversized cotton shirt that did nothing to conceal his otherworldly musculature.

Chenoa's heart began to gallop as she got a full look at the big man. What she saw made her gasp aloud with shock.

She was now staring directly into the face of her father.

CHAPTER 6

Malheur Indian Reservation
Eastern Oregon
1883

"Life is like chess," Chief Jolon Winterhawk said. "Once you make a move, it stays on the board."

Her eyes stinging from sweat, Chenoa gripped tightly onto the rock face. She had already given up trying to convince herself *not* to look down. The temptation was just too overwhelming. And besides, it was a good way to chart her slow progress up from the banks of the Malheur River that stretched out below them.

Twenty-five feet had already been cleared; now, another twenty-five feet of the rock face left to go. Her father was climbing closely behind her, fingers finding handholds with the same methodical intensity as his conversation. He had obviously wanted her to concentrate on his words with as much focus as the rock wall she was clinging to.

As usual, she was finding it difficult to grasp either.

Chenoa glanced down at him with mild irritation. "*Tota*, you promised that I could begin weapons training when I turned sixteen. That's *today*, Poppa."

Jolon nodded. "I remember."

"Arrows?" she sighed. "Rifles? I'm never going to be a warrior unless I know how to properly use them."

"It's not the weapon that saves you, it's the training."

"Then *why* aren't we training?"

Jolon motioned with his chin towards the rock face in front of them. "Before you wield a weapon, learn to wield yourself."

Chenoa aggressively rolled her eyes. "Come. On."

Jolon grinned. "Stop stalling and start climbing. If you worked your legs as rapidly as your mouth, we could be scaling up the Owyhee Canyon instead of this river pebble."

Chenoa gawked. "Pebble?! *Tota*, if we fell from here—"

"We would survive. As we lost our grip, we would push our legs against the rocks, then kick out as hard as possible. The momentum would be enough to propel us over the sandbank and drop us safely into the river. Now, climb."

With a sigh, Chenoa resumed the climb. Her fingers traced the patterns of rock above her head, finding secure places to grab, pushing upwards until she reached the next handle hold.

"Every soldier knows that the environment around them is a weapon," Jolon continued, patiently trailing behind her on the rock wall. "What is directly behind you and what is directly in front of you, both of those things can kill you. But they can also save you, Chenoa."

In the years following, Chenoa would become a strong mountaineer. She would develop an uncanny sense of the mountains, possessing a nearly supernatural ability to find vertical paths when things appeared all but insurmountable.

But on *this* particular day, she had found herself struggling. The skin on her fingers hadn't yet developed the rough calluses that would protect her hands from the bite of the rocks. She wasn't yet comfortable in the placement of her feet, which kept her feeling unbalanced. Her breath, which would later become measured and controlled, came out in quick gasps and fast gulps.

Chenoa looked up and saw the safety of the cliff's outcropping still over a dozen feet away. The muscles in her limbs burned with defeat. Plus, she was afraid.

Her left foot slipped from its perch, rocks crumbling as she clung desperately to the wall. Utter panic consumed her. "Poppa...!"

She felt her father's hand on the bottom of her foot, firmly cupping her heel. She felt the strength in his fingers, and the immense power behind the arm that held her steady.

"Everyone slips," Jolon said gently. He hadn't raised his voice, yet she could hear him clearly above the din of the raging waters below. She would eventually come to realize how important that was in life. The ability to focus on the voices of the ones who matter will always drown out the noises of the things that don't.

"The strongholds are always there," he continued. She felt him gently pushing up against her heel, allowing her to extend her arm enough to grab tightly onto an outcropping of rock. "The Creator has built them into the design of this world, and He also placed them inside of you. Life can be jagged; it can cut us just like these rocks. Experiences can weaken us, and there are times when we might feel ourselves losing our grip."

Grunting with exertion, Chenoa held tightly onto the rock. She felt the comfort of her father's hand move off from her foot, leaving her once again dangling in the air. She refused to panic this time, biting her lip hard to keep her mind away from the fear. Instead, she stared directly into the rock wall inches from her face.

She brought her leg forward, nearly yelping with triumph as her foot pressed down on a secure section of the cliffside. She had once again regained her balance.

"We find the question of where our strength resides answered by the very rocks we find ourselves climbing. That's true on the mountain, but I also believe that's true in life."

Bolstered with confidence, Chenoa pushed upwards with both legs, surprised to find herself now gripping onto the edge of the outcropping. With a renewed burst of strength, she pulled herself safely onto the flat stone. She now lay on her back, panting with exertion, feeling the sun's warmth drying the sweat on her face.

Her father stood beside her. He wasn't tired, and he wasn't breathing hard. For him, the climb had been no more challenging than pulling himself up onto the saddle of his horse.

She looked up at him with gratitude. "Thank you, *Tota*."

Jolon reached a hand down, helping her up to her feet. "Your grandfather believed in the power of the *Weyekins*. He would tell my brother and me that the invisible world was one of incredible spiritual power, and that the *Weyekins* would not only protect a warrior from harm, but that they could also become a protective spirit."

Chenoa scrunched her brow. "Like a guardian angel, Poppa?"

"Yes."

Chenoa couldn't help but notice the distant look in his gaze. Her father was juggling a memory again. It was one of the ones that he always seemed on the cusp of sharing, but never did.

But he surprised her on that day.

"I once met a man," Jolon said, his eyes focused somewhere on a point in the distant horizon. Chenoa understood that he was fixated on something that had nothing to do with the present. "It was after the Civil War ended. We were both on a military train. This man died to protect what was on it."

"What was so valuable on the train?"

"Me," Jolon answered. "This man was a soldier, but he didn't lay down his life because of duty. He sacrificed himself for two people he had never met, and knew that he never would."

"Who were they?"

Jolon stared at her for a long moment. "You and *Pik'e*."

Chenoa felt the weight of his words pressing down against her heart. It seemed to her at that moment that the entirety of the whole world was held together by the strands of sacrifices. Some were made for the greater good, but she'd seen plenty of others that were meant for wanton destruction. The frightening part was realizing that there were some people in the world who didn't know the difference.

"Colonel Smythe was a guardian angel," Jolon continued. "He was a *Weyekin* in the same way that my father was. Some of them we encounter in this life are spiritual protectors, and others we meet will become physical ones. I'll always be *both* of those things to you, Chenoa. Do you understand?"

"Yes," she answered. But she really didn't understand at all. Her father had an odd way of looking into both the past and the future. It was an unusual gift she didn't believe that she'd ever possess. It was something uniquely his own, seemingly growing in power with each new birthday she celebrated.

But Chenoa didn't like to think about that very much. It was because she understood that as she got older, her father got older, too. That didn't seem like such a good tradeoff for that particular gift of his. Truth be told, it felt more like a sacrifice than a privilege...and one that neither of them had made willingly.

There was a heavy stillness in the air between them now. Chenoa sensed it. Her father had been waiting to talk with her today about something very important. She felt a pang of anxiety in her stomach wondering why.

She didn't have to wait very long for the answer.

"This man Smythe once told me that the Devil also answers prayers. Do you believe that, Chenoa? Because if you don't, then I suggest that you'd better start."

Chenoa let that thought bounce around in her head for a moment. "That good things happen to bad people? I know that happens. But those people don't pray for those things in the same way we do; they *can't*, Poppa. They don't pray for the end of sickness, or the safe return of a tribal warrior. I think the worst of people look only at what's in this life for them. And if they *do* pray, then they only really pray to themselves."

Jolon smiled. It seemed that the gesture was more out of weariness than of joy. As if he had once thought the very same things, but had found out something completely different.

Even at her young age, Chenoa had understood that's what experience really was. It was knowing the difference between expectations and reality; accepting of what *was* instead of what *wasn't*.

She wasn't at all prepared for her father's next question.

"Do you remember your *Piimx*? Do you remember Akando?"

"No," she replied quickly.

Jolon laughed. "You lie like a rug, Chenoa."

She felt her face growing hot. "I only meant that I don't remember him very *well*."

That was only a half-lie; or, perhaps, a half-truth. The difference between them might appear to be inconsequential; arguably only a matter of perspective. But there was a wide chasm indeed between half-truths and half-lies. In the end, it comes down to what you wanted to believe and how badly you *didn't* want to believe it. Because engaging your spirit in halves of anything would ultimately be deceiving yourself. And that, she understood, was when people allowed themselves permission to become the person they never wanted to be.

Chenoa shook her head in correction. "I remember him, Poppa. I remember *Piimx,* but maybe not in the way that an uncle should be remembered." She pursed her lips at that, trying hard to grasp onto the meaning. "He was young, wasn't he?"

"He was old enough," Jolon answered. "Akando was eighteen when he was banished from the Nez Perce."

Chenoa had been three when it happened, but she vividly recalled that particular day. Swathes of memories began to suddenly unfurl within her.

There had been a kaleidoscope of butterflies swarming around a bush, colorful wings fluttering against the backdrop of the setting sun. The horse her uncle had been riding had violently trodden over it as he galloped across the meadow.

Akando been placed backwards on the saddle with his hands tied. He'd been forced to wear a hollowed-out cow's head, which symbolized shame within the tribe. Soon after, the dark woods had completely swallowed him up, seemingly forever.

Akando had never been mentioned by her father again, until today.

"Not everyone within the Nez Perce valued the guidance of Chief Joseph," Jolon explained. "He was attempting to build a peaceful understanding between the white settlers and our people. But there were some tribal members who didn't want a truce with the white man, they wanted a war. And these men shed a lot of innocent blood hoping to get it."

Even with the warmth of the noonday sun casting down upon her from atop the high cliffside, Chenoa felt a sudden chill run across her body. "What did those men do, Poppa? What did...*he*...do?"

"Unspeakable things were done to women and children."

"Unspeakable things," she echoed.

Chenoa knew that sort of evil didn't just spring up after one single act of sinful rebellion. It has blooms and deep roots. It festers inside the heart and takes hold in the mind. It grows because we water it with our actions, and fertilize it with our thoughts.

"After our father was killed by their hand, Akando wanted nothing more than to make the white man suffer. My brother led violent raids and slaughtered settlers' families. His rage acted as a poison against Chief Joseph's peace, while his hatred consumed his entire soul."

"What about those other men, Poppa? Were they banished, too?"

Jolon shook his head. "Joseph had them executed. It was only in honor of my father that Akando was spared the knife. He was banished forever from the Nez Perce for his crimes."

"Why are you telling me about this today?"

Jolon motioned towards the rock face they had just scaled. "The best climbers know it's all about the footholds. In the end, that's how we survive, or how we fall. It's about what we trust to hold us up when we feel ourselves slipping."

"Footholds," Chenoa echoed.

"Akando didn't have any. When my brother fell, he tried taking me down with him. He begged for forgiveness, and pleaded for mercy. I wanted him executed for what he had done, but Chief Joseph spared him. Our father's blood sacrifice paid his debt."

"Do you think he's dead by now?"

"Dead enough," Jolon said. His voice was heavy with regret, not certainty.

Chenoa searched his face for a long moment. "There's something else, isn't there?"

Jolon nodded slowly. "I need you to understand something. There are monsters in this world, Chenoa. *Real* ones. They behave purely on instinct, driven by hunger and self-preservation. I know because I've seen them up close."

"Monsters," she said.

"There are human monsters, too. And they're even worse. They know the wrong that they do, but they choose to inflict harm, anyway. Those types of men are self-created, blaming the world for their behaviors and actions. To them, the sin justifies the means."

"Can men like that ever change?"

"No. They can only be stopped."

"Then, what if my uncle is still alive?"

"If he is, and if he ever tries to find you, then you don't bother asking any questions. You shoot him first and when you do, you shoot to kill."

"Why, father?"

"Because Akando would murder you just to get revenge against me. He wouldn't hesitate for a second to spill your blood." Jolon placed a firm hand on her shoulder. "Promise me, Chenoa; promise me something right here, right now."

Her eyes went wide. "What, Poppa?"

"If you ever encounter Akando, you drop him like dirt on a coffin."

"I promise," Chenoa whispered.

She squeezed her eyes closed. Visions of monsters...and monsters among men began to pollute her thoughts.

Chenoa wondered if she would ever meet one. She also wondered if she'd be able to tell the difference between them when she did.

CHAPTER 7

Baxter Mine Peak
Blue Mountain Range
Adrian, Oregon
1905

"They say that blood is thicker than water," Akando Winterhawk boomed, eyes dancing with sheer delight. "I don't know about that, but I do know this: blood is a lot harder to clean up."

"You would know, of course," Chenoa said.

The man-mountain standing before her had a jagged knife cut that stretched from the bob of his Adam's apple and extended around to just beneath the lobe of his left ear. The skin of his upper chest and lower neck had been permanently scarred by fire. He was obviously no stranger to pain.

Akando wasn't wearing a holster, but there was a massive knife sheathed on his belt. She recognized the weapon immediately. It was a Razorback, the two-bladed swivel machete knife used to take down massive crocodiles in—

"Australia," Akando said, reading her thoughts. "Their hunters use the Razorback to take down rampaging crocs. One of the blades goes through the top of the jaw, while the other goes straight into the brain."

He placed one hand atop the Razorback, his fingers gently caressing the handle. "You can see if a man's a gardener just by looking beneath his fingernails. True passion is hard to conceal."

Chenoa turned away from him in disgust.

The landing party greeted the *Lathos* several minutes earlier, with Quinn and Chenoa being ordered by Lieutenant Misciso to disembark ("Carefully! Slowly!") from the dirigible.

After they had set foot on the ground, two of the men wearing Army Corps of Engineers uniforms had immediately brandished .45 Colts at them. Chenoa recognized them immediately: Ferro and Ivers. The last she'd heard, they'd been tasked with transporting supplies to the Owyhee Dam. She wondered what had turned them into traitors.

Chenoa shifted her gaze to the other soldier standing among the group.

He was a tall, lanky man who was loosely holding a Parker 12-gauge shotgun cradled in the crook of his arm. He had all the markings of an Army 1st Lieutenant. The uniform pattern displayed a Cavalry officer's tunic with shoulder straps, while he wore his trousers over his boots as prescribed for garrison duty. 'Briggs' was embroidered on a fraying insignia patch just below his left shoulder.

His eyelids jittered as he took his precious time looking her body over.

"I heard stories about your old man," Briggs croaked, his grotesquely large Adam's apple pushing hard against the flesh of his neck. "And about *you*, princess. I reckon you inherited your daddy's balls."

Chenoa shrugged. "Somebody in my family needed to have some."

Akando laughed heartily. "You remember your *Piimx*? I'm honestly surprised, Chenoa. You were barely out of moss nappies the last time we saw each other."

"I have an advantage because I have a gift."

"What gift is that?"

Chenoa steeled her gaze. "I never forget assholes."

"You've got a mouth on you," Misciso said. He had climbed out from the *Lathos* and was approaching the group. Chenoa saw that the hydrogen flame on the dirigible was now capped, but still live. The blimp was on temporary standby, ready for takeoff at a moment's notice.

That meant that whatever was happening next, it would be happening soon. But what *was* going to happen next?

She thought about President Roosevelt's manufactured photo-op at the Owyhee Dam that was scheduled tomorrow. He was attempting to muster up public support in this region for his unpopular irrigation policy.

The location of the underground river and President Roosevelt's visit were somehow connected. They were both part of Akando's plans for revenge.

Chenoa took notice that Misciso was now standing much too close. She could smell the sour stench of his breath, and could feel the heated wantonness of his flesh. He licked his lips like a parched sow staring at his own reflection inside a puddle of mud. "I've dipped my wick in a lot of trim, but squaw pussy's always the best."

Chenoa turned her head sharply. "I'm sure the only time you've been inside a woman is when you toured the Statue of Liberty."

Misciso's face noticeably darkened.

Anger was a universally understood reaction; it didn't need to be explained. It only had to be observed. But this wasn't anger, but something much worse: primal rage. You could see it reflected in his eyes; could hear it in the guttural noise he made somewhere deep down in his chest.

It was also in the way he held his gun, and in the ferocious way that he suddenly pointed it at her.

"Shit happens," Misciso growled. He pressed the barrel of the Colt directly into the center of her forehead.

His finger danced on the trigger.

CHAPTER 8

Misciso ground his gun hard against Chenoa's forehead.

The other soldiers were caught off guard by the sudden escalation of anger, but Akando appeared completely relaxed. His expression was neutral, and he even wore the faintest semblance of a wry smile.

"You really must learn to control that temper," Akando said. He bound forward with more speed than should even be possible for a man of his size. He unsheathed the Razorback even faster. There was the sound of steel slicing through the air. This was followed by a loud clicking noise as the mechanism releasing both 10-inch blades, which Akando now held directly behind Misciso's neck.

"Let's not lose our heads here."

Misciso gulped. After a tense moment, he carefully holstered the handgun and stepped away from Chenoa.

In her peripheral vision, she noticed Major Quinn's hand had hovered briefly over his pocket. She understood how protective he was. He needed to fiercely guard the map because not only was it Huan's only chance at a future, but it was also his only shield against Akando's wrath.

As if on cue, Akando dramatically re-sheathed the Razorback. "What is it with men? We see a woman with a problem, and we can't help but give her a dozen more."

Quinn's frightened eyes fixed on her. He motioned at Akando. "How exactly do you know this man, Winterhawk?"

"Chenoa is the daughter of Chief Jolon," Akando said, "Her father is my brother—"

"Was." Chenoa corrected him sharply. She tried to keep the anger out of her voice, but failed. "Even when my father was still alive, you were always just a *was* in our family."

"Jolon. Dead." Akando smiled. "I'm not *at all* sorry for your loss."

Chenoa inhaled sharply at that.

She had breathed in the stench of loss many times. It splinters the heart, leaving future hopes and dreams scattered like fallen limbs in the forest after a storm. Feeling a great personal loss is akin to a stopped clock. It becomes our primary focus because that's where we continually cast our gaze, and wonder why time doesn't ever move. But to move on means putting distance between you and the pain. That's a long journey. Nobody can walk those steps for you.

The truth is that you'll never be the same person you were after a loss as you were before it. You move from who you *were* directly into who you *are*. You may not even know it's happening, but pain doesn't need your permission to change you. It just does it.

"Jolon was an apple," Akando continued. "He was white on the inside, red on the outside. My brother betrayed our tribe when he chose to fight in the white man's war."

"*Our* tribe? Are you talking about the same Nez Perce tribe that disavowed you because you murdered innocent women and children?"

"Innocent?!" Akando scoffed. "British General Thomas Gage purposefully gave smallpox-contaminated blankets to the Shawnee and Lenape people as gifts. When the European descendants expanded across this continent, they mindlessly destroyed one indigenous tribe after another. The Governor of California proclaimed that a war of extermination needed to be waged against our people until our entire race becomes extinct. President Jackson referred to us 'savage dogs.' The colonists acted out their hatred towards us without any restraint or shame.

"Did you know that the first way of war within the United States included the doctrine of killing Indian women so they couldn't sustain tribes through childbearing? The shared American identity is genocide; yet, you dare slander *my* name for waging a similar war against them."

Chenoa felt a rush of seething anger. "Tuekakas told us that light and darkness cannot dwell together. Well, Old Joseph was right. You cannot avenge murder with murder. You cannot kill a child and declare it righteous in your own eyes."

Akando waved her off with mild irritation. "An old Cheyenne proverb states that a nation hasn't truly been conquered until the hearts of its women are on the ground. By wearing that American uniform, you've sacrificed your heart to them."

Chenoa gestured at the soldiers. "If you believe that, then what justification do you have for consorting with these men?"

"They've declared an allegiance only to their pocketbook," Akando explained. "Pacific Knight gold funds my revenge to flood the Nez Perce lands that my brother betrayed."

The Pacific Knights...

Chenoa had encountered them previously when the Army had fought during the Great Rancher Rebellion in Oregon. Pacific Knight members had been among the ones trading gunfire with her. It was a bloody conflict that resulted in the loss of eighty-five lives on both sides.

The Pacific Knights had been the northwest sect of the Knights of the Golden Circle, that infamous group of Confederate soldiers who had banded together after the end of the Civil War. They had never accepted the loss after the Great Rebellion; instead, they had schemed to bring about the financial ruination of America. They had hidden millions in cash throughout the west in hopes of financing another war effort among the politically fractured states.

And Akando claimed to have gotten his hands on some of it.

Chenoa was dubious. "You found Pacific Knight money?"

"Some, yes; not *all*."

"How much?"

"Three million," Akando winked. "Give or take a brothel visit or two."

"And you just happened to know where this money had been hidden?"

"Yes."

"I don't believe you."

"I said the exact same thing to Alvinston after he told me about it."

"Alvinston?"

"He was my cellmate at Alcatraz," Akando explained.

"You were at Fort Alcatraz?"

"Yes."

"Why?"

"Because I was a Sheepeater."

Chenoa shook her head. "Bullshit."

"Sheep shit." Akando corrected.

Sheepeaters. Winterhawk had certainly heard about them.

The Sheepeaters were a notorious band of Western Shoshone that had integrated warriors from the Columbia Plateau and the Snake River Plain in 1878. They were named after their primary food source: bighorn sheep.

Two years after the Nez Perce War had ended, the Sheepeaters began embarking on violent raids across ranches and settlements throughout eastern Oregon and southern Idaho. They were also responsible for dozens of murders of American and Chinese miners. Then, the group had become hunted by the military. In 1879, Capt. Reuben Bernard and Troop G of the 1st Cavalry finally confronted the band of Sheepeaters in Grangeville and defeated them.

"I thought the Army hadn't taken any Sheepeaters prisoners."

"They took some. The lucky ones ended up at the Fort Hall Reservation in Southeastern Idaho and were forced to die. The unlucky ones were sent to Fort Alcatraz and forced to live."

Chenoa shook her head. "No Indian sent to Fort Alcatraz ever returned."

Akando narrowed his eyes. "*I* returned."

CHAPTER 9

There were no coincidences in this life, only planned accidents. Destiny oftentimes appeared as a single strand, but perspective was being able to examine those things from afar. It's when you do that you'll discover that particular strand was always attached to a huge tapestry. That's when you finally see that life is nothing more than an interlocking weaving of experiences.

The strands of Chenoa's family had somehow led her here today. Akando had somehow orchestrated it, but it was the Creator's fingerprints that had touched each event leading up to this moment. She just needed to find out why.

She knew that Akando had gone to a great deal of trouble in gaining information about this particular mission. He'd recruited these men to help him carry out his plans of stealing the map and kidnapping her. But why exact his revenge now? With her father dead and the Nez Perce people scattered, what value did Quinn's map hold for him?

Chenoa once again thought about the upcoming visit from President Roosevelt. She didn't know how he was connected with the map, but she knew that he must be somehow. She needed to find out more. She had to keep Akando talking.

"My father once told me that the largest harvest of lies always contains the smallest grains of truth."

Akando smiled broadly at her. "Jolon was right. The subjectivity of truth gives seasoning to the fabric of the lies."

"Seasoning."

Akando waved his hand in mild annoyance. "People want to believe, Chenoa. They want to be told that things are the way they are. We don't believe with our eyes; we believe with our ears."

"That sounds like someone trying to justify their actions."

"Consequences justify themselves, Chenoa."

"All of *this* is justified?!"

"All of what, exactly?"

Chenoa gestured to Major Quinn. "Kidnapping." Then, she touched a hand to her heart. "Murder."

Akando narrowed his eyes. "Martyrdom should appeal to you."

"Why?"

"Because it's untainted morality."

"Morality," Chenoa said. "Men like you have morals that are like the last snowfall in spring: there one day, and gone the next."

Akando laughed. "You amuse me, Chenoa."

"The feeling isn't mutual."

"We've wasted enough time," Akando said abruptly.

Chenoa stiffened with momentary panic. She was still too much in the dark about everything. She needed to know more about what he was planning.

Akando might be one of the scariest looking men who ever put one boot in front of the other, but he's still just a man. And like most men, Chief, there's one favorite topic in the world he enjoys above all else: himself.

"Akando, tell me more about your imaginary friend."

He looked puzzled. "Imaginary?" Then, a wide grin cracked his features. He had understood her jab. "My cellmate at Fort Alcatraz? I'm afraid that Alvinston was flesh and blood."

"Who was he?"

"A decrepit Confederate soldier," Akando answered. "After the end of the Great Rebellion, Alvinston had fled to the west to save his neck from being stretched in the east. When he reached Oregon, he joined the Pacific Knights. Became one of their chief treasurer officers. Found himself handling a great deal of their money; found himself skimming it, too. He buried everything he stole in a secret location right before the Army managed to capture him."

"The Army never found the money?" Chenoa asked.

"Nobody knew there was any money to look for." Akando rubbed his chin. At first the gesture looked contemplative, but it was more akin to unconscious excitement. "Anyway, as luck—*my* luck—would have it, Alvinston was a lunger. Those coughing fits would always hit worse at night. The cruel irony was that it kept *me* awake, not him. The old fool would be hot with the fever; delirious, and talking in his sleep.

"On the last night of his life, the old man had a premonition of his demise. He cried out for a confession. Mistook me for a priest. For absolution, I asked him to confess where he'd buried that money. And so, he did."

Chenoa thought back to that time with her father on the cliffside when she'd just turned sixteen. She remembered something important that Chief Winterhawk had once told her. His words bore great weight today.

"Sometimes the Devil answers prayers," she repeated from memory.

Akando's eyes lit up. "Indeed!"

Chenoa tilted her head, thinking. "You know it's impossible, though."

"What is?"

"Escaping from Alcatraz. Nobody's ever done it."

Akando pinched a smile. "Nobody's ever done it...*alive.*"

She sensed that Major Quinn was startled by this latest revelation. His body stiffened, and he was staring at Akando with more than a hint of suspicion. "You were on the *Wavecrest*, weren't you?"

There was a flash of surprise behind Akando's eyes. "Was I?"

Chenoa scrunched her brow. She searched her memory for any recollection of the *Wavecrest*. She came up short.

Major Quinn noticed her confusion. "The *Wavecrest* was a prisoner barge," he elaborated. "When the Army Corps of Engineers were tasked with beginning construction of a massive bridge project in San Francisco, they needed to clearcut several hundred acres of forest. For this, they turned to prison labor from Fort Alcatraz. The *Wavecrest* was the ship that ferried those workers to the job site."

"Workers." Akando chewed at the word like it was a piece of leathered jerky. "Workers indicates a *quid pro quo* arrangement. We were slaves."

"What exactly happened, Major Quinn?" Chenoa asked.

"Late one afternoon, there'd been an explosion in the engine room of the *Wavecrest*. Sixteen prisoners and 8 military personnel had been onboard. There were no survivors. The investigation revealed that it had been—"

"A tragic accident," Akando quickly interjected. "Nothing more."

Chenoa stared at him. "Accident."

Akando shrugged. "It was in all the papers."

"What *wasn't* in the papers?"

Akando clucked his tongue scoldingly at her. "I believe we've gotten too far off the trail with this tall tale. I'm afraid we could stand around and discuss the incompetence of the United States Army all day, but we do have a schedule to keep."

Chenoa looked over at the traitors. "Have you boys gotten your dirty hands on any of that treasure yet? I'll wager none of you have gotten a cent of that money."

Lieutenant Ivers shook his head disapprovingly. "We aren't fools, Winterhawk. Akando has already paid us an advance; lots now, and lots more later."

"That's right, princess." Ferro's bluster was obviously hiding a deep-rooted fear. "We've all sworn allegiance to the United States of Akando."

Chenoa looked at the soldiers with venom before turning her heated gaze back on Akando. "I'm surprised you haven't heard."

"Heard what?"

"That soldiers loyal only to money are just like foreskin: they vanish whenever things get hard."

CHAPTER 10

For a moment, Chenoa wondered if she'd just pushed him too far.

"I could feed you to them, Chenoa," Akando growled. "These bastards would spend hours tearing your body apart as they satisfied their lusts in every imaginable way."

"Then why don't you?" Chenoa tasted hot bile in the back of her throat as she pushed those grotesque images of his threat out of her mind.

"Because," Akando said carefully, "I want you to experience something even *worse*. After I unleash the underground river with explosives, you're going to watch helplessly as it floods the entire eastern valley. By delivering the map to me, it will be you who brought destruction upon the Nez Perce. I'll tell the survivors it was Jolon's daughter who failed them."

"Leaving you to be—"

"The real Chief Winterhawk." His eyes briefly flickered with the memory of old emotional wounds. His hand grazed the scar on his neck, a reminder of Chief Joseph's harsh judgment. Banished, he'd wandered the wilderness as his heart hardened more with each step he had taken away from his Nez Perce home.

Jolon's loyalty to Chief Joseph had been the final betrayal, a wound cutting deeper than any blade that scarred him.

Watching him wrestle with his memories, Chenoa seethed at the audacity of Akando's plan. The Nez Perce had been uprooted before; rivers stolen, and promises broken. She wouldn't let him drown their future, too.

"Chief Winterhawk," she muttered.

"Well," Akando shrugged, "since the office of the President of the United States is already occupied, I chose the next best thing."

"What exactly are you planning for President Roosevelt?" Chenoa asked.

"Just a welcoming committee."

"Teddy is just a bonus," Briggs elaborated. "He's become blinded to the real needs of the American people. Roosevelt fucked his loyal soldiers with a hard-on for the ranchers, so we're going to fuck him right back."

Akando relished her pained reaction to what Briggs had just said. "I understand that you and President Roosevelt have broken bread together."

Chenoa nodded. That was true.

Years ago, Chenoa had been hired by President Roosevelt to be his bear hunting guide during an Oregon trip. They'd become good friends. After she had taken him to visit her father's grave and explained his military history, Roosevelt had been the one to suggest the Army Indian Scouts as a way to continue with Jolon's service. "Leave the grizzlies to their dens," Teddy had remarked, "and go live the quiet life."

Thanks for the advice, she thought grimly.

The abandoned mine loomed large behind the group. The wind howled through the skeletal tramway, its cables swaying over them like hangman's nooses.

"You don't have the hardware to pull this off," Major Quinn finally interjected. "You'll need more than a few sticks of dynamite to blow up the Carson Mine."

"Thanks to my good friends with the Army Corps of Engineers," Akando motioned at the traitors, "there's enough ordnance stashed inside Elkhorn Peak to launch Paul Bunyan to the moon." He locked his fiery gaze onto Major Quinn. "Give me the map. NOW."

Quinn took an involuntary step back. "No-can-do."

Chenoa admired his bravery; foolish but undeniably brave.

"No-can-do," Akando repeated with awe. "Is that some kind of favorite Chinese dish your dead wife cooked?" He chuckled at the joke. "But while on the subject, it's a tragedy that so many Chinese female orphans end up dying in American whorehouses. It makes my heart sick thinking of Huan ending up that way."

Chenoa was amazed at how deep Akando's pockets must be. Presidential itineraries, knowledge of secret missions, and even the name of his captive's children. Money could buy anything these days.

Quinn's upper lip began to tremble. "No, please! I'll give you—"

"Don't you dare give him that map!" Chenoa snapped.

"I admire your bravado," Akando said, "but you're no soldier. Examine the tactical situation, Chenoa. Just look around. You've already lost."

"That's not how I see it."

Akando pinched a smile. "And what do you see?"

"Three things: big men, big guns...and big mistakes."

Chenoa quickly eyed the Lathos's flickering hydrogen flame; muscles tensing.

It's time to do what you do best, Chief, but do it bloodier. When this is all over, Akando will be like the skinny blind man at a fat people's orgy—he won't know what hit him.

With a yell of rage, Chenoa flung her body into the air.

CHAPTER 11

Chenoa Winterhawk collided against Major Quinn with bone-rattling force.

He carried tremendous girth, but she had caught him completely off guard. The impact against his upper torso buckled his knees, and he collapsed backward.

Chenoa rode atop his body as he fell, fists repeatedly hammering blows against his chest as he crashed to the ground. When they landed, she began to furiously claw at his face. Her fingernails drew blood. He shrieked with pain, hands batting against her.

Chenoa brought her lips close to his ear. "I'll come back for you," she whispered. "Just stay alive!"

Quinn's eyes widened; a spark of hope amidst his despair.

"Get her off of him! NOW!" Akando boomed.

It was Corporal Ferro who reached Chenoa first. Still holding on to the .45 Colt, he reached down with one spindly hand. His fingers wrapped around the thick mound of her ponytail. He viciously yanked her off of Quinn.

Chenoa allowed herself to be pulled backwards by Ferro, feigning helplessness, arms wildly pinwheeling. She made an exaggerated motion with her right arm, pretending to bat away Ferro's tight grip on her ponytail.

But she had used the movement as a ruse, allowing herself the opportunity to pull off the clip from the back of her head.

"No..." Akando whispered, eyes going wide. His attention was focused solely on her left hand, eyes intent on something she was now holding.

It was the Chinese map.

Chenoa had pulled it out of Quinn's uniform pocket during the momentary confusion.

And it wasn't the only thing she had done in those few seconds.

The pin she had taken off of her hair...

The talon was an adornment that had been worn by Native American women warriors for centuries. This particular pin was given to her by her mother on her eighteenth birthday. It was four-inches of carved grizzly breastbone, with two pincer-like bear claws grafted onto it by dried muscle tendons.

The talon slid easily across her knuckles.

Corporal Ferro flashed a look of astonished incredulity. He took a step back, mouth twisted in surprise, raising the Colt.

"What—?!" Ferro sputtered with confusion.

"Life's a bitch," Chenoa yelled with fury, pulling back her right arm, "and so am I!"

She rabbit-punched Ferro's left eye with extreme force. He squealed shrilly as the bear claws punctured his eyeball, the visage popping grotesquely like a bursting rotten apple.

Chenoa ground the talon hard against his skull, twisting her wrist savagely as the claws scraped mercilessly along the inside of his ocular cavity. She pulled her hand back. The talon slipped off her fingers but remained deeply embedded in the gushing eye socket.

Ferro's surviving right eye locked onto her, lid quivering wildly with fear as—

His upper cranium noticeably shifted, two halves of his skull momentarily sliding in opposite directions as the flesh of his forehead suddenly vanished in an explosive blast of crimson powder.

A deafening boom reverberated across the peak.

Briggs.

The shotgun.

Chenoa jerked her body down into a crouch, shoving the map into her pocket as a cloud of brain matter splattered through the air.

While the powerful buckshot from the Parker 12-gauge finished ripping the entire upper portion of Ferro's skull into minuscular bone fragments, his right eye had been miraculously unscathed by the blast. It dropped straight downwards into the jagged open cavity that used to be his skull, landing with a sickly plop onto his still-writhing tongue. The detached eye rolled slightly forward like a marble, then fully backwards, vanishing down his exposed throat as he swallowed it whole.

Even in death, Ferro's nerve sensors were still firing; legs taking a solitary step forward, hand still clutching onto the Colt.

Five seconds had now elapsed since the first shot.

Major Quinn was still lying prone on the ground. His face was bleeding, chest heaving from the adrenaline of her assault. He was staring up at her with wide eyes.

Chenoa could sense movement from behind Ferro's sagging corpse as the men instinctively moved away from the splattering gore.

She heard the distinctive sound of the racking of shells from the shotgun. Briggs was preparing to fire off another blast with the 12-gauge. He would have already compensated for the first shot. He would have lowered the shotgun barrel, probably now aiming squarely at Ferro's back.

At this range, the buckshot would tear the rest of his body to pieces…and her right along with him.

I've got an idea, Chief. Let's stuff it inside a peace pipe and see if anyone smokes it. Are you ready to hear it? It's called: Move. Your. Ass. NOW!

Chenoa spun on her heels. She slammed her body backwards against Ferro's collapsing corpse. His lifeless arms flopped across her shoulders, her own body temporarily propping him up. She reached up with her right hand, her digits sliding across his dead flesh until her fingers rested firmly atop of his.

With their fingers now intertwined around the trigger of the Colt, Chenoa twisted both of their bodies around. She felt the heavy pressure of Ferro bearing down against her as she forced her arm to guide his lifeless limb in a wide arc.

The shocked features of Briggs came into full view. He had the Parker cradled against his shoulder; barrel aimed low. He hadn't yet fired the second shot. The hesitation would cost him...plenty.

Chenoa pulled Ferro's trigger finger, firing the Colt.

The shot impacted with the barrel of the shotgun. The slug nicked against the iron, ricocheting wildly upwards. Briggs cried out in surprise, blood splashing against the side of his face as the bullet opened a flap of flesh on his neck.

He dropped the shotgun and staggered back in pain.

Chenoa swept Ferro's arm sideways, unloading another volley of lead.

Ivers and Misciso immediately flattened themselves on the ground as the bullets passed harmlessly above them.

Chenoa kept Ferro's gun arm moving, tracking the weapon towards Akando until he was standing dead center in front of the Colt. He stood absolutely still, his face a stoney mask of resolution. Only his eyes betrayed any hint of emotion. They were simmering rage.

Chenoa used the dead man's finger to pull the trigger.

Akando dove forward, hitting the ground hard. He somersaulted sideways as lead from the .45 punched wildly into the dirt all around him.

The Colt clicked empty. The echoes from the gunshots boomed loudly across Baxter's Mine. Then, there was nothing but deafening silence.

Akando rolled quickly to his feet, his breathing measured and controlled. He whipped his head around, eyes searching.

Chenoa was nowhere to be found.

He then noticed two things simultaneously.

The first was the sight of Corporal Ferro splayed out on the ground, his bloody corpse looking like a flesh-stuffed scarecrow whose upper torso had been ground up in the gears of a wheat combine.

The second was the *Lathos*. The cap restraining the hydrogen flame had just been removed. And even more incredibly, the dirigible was now rising into the sky.

Yelling, Captain Misciso had regained his footing. He charged towards the ascending blimp.

Clutching a hand against his bleeding neck, Briggs stared at the sight of the *Lathos*. "What the fuck?!"

Corporal Ivers looked over at Akando with an expression of complete shock. "What the hell is she doing now?"

Akando frowned. "Chenoa is now playing hard to get...rid of."

CHAPTER 12

Combat doesn't change who you are; it reveals who you are.

Adversity has a habit of doing that. The best laid plans and the most carefully thought-out endeavors become nothing but ashes in the burn pile once the unexpected strikes. The most skilled pugilist understands that in-ring tactics vanish once the first punch lands on your chin. That's when the pain wakes you up. That's when you realize reality tastes a whole lot like blood. Sometimes, the blood you taste isn't even your own.

Winterhawk could certainly attest to that. The coppery taste of Ferro's blood was still fresh in her mouth as she flung her body into the dirigible. She landed hard, rolling forward until she faced the capped hydrogen valve.

She understood that she only had seconds before Akando would realize exactly where she was, and what she was doing. He would unleash his traitorous soldiers to retrieve the map at any cost, forgoing all his previous revenge schemes against her in the process.

Plans could be altered; but in the end, dead is dead.

Chenoa grabbed the valve handle and twisted it sideways, uncapping the flame. She felt a jolt at her feet as the hydrogen pushed up against the envelope bag with a loud snapping sound.

The *Lathos* began to quickly ascend.

She glanced at the Curtiss motorcycle engine that drove the large propeller of the aircraft. While she had doubts about being able to actually pilot the dirigible, she understood that the rudders were operated by a pair of foot pedals.

She would have to worry about that later. She couldn't be in two places at once; first, she needed to get to her weapons satchel. For the moment, the dirigible would get some much-needed distance between her and her enemies. She would concern herself with how to steer it once she was at a safe distance from the soldiers.

Chenoa stumbled quickly across the rocking wooden gondola of the *Lathos*, eyes fixated on the Zieg-8 placed atop the weapons satchel. Her eyes darted overboard, heart hammering. The dirigible had only lifted ten feet off the ground. It was ascending much too slowly.

She had reached the Zieg, her hand curling around the stock—

The *Lathos* suddenly dipped sharply, throwing her off-balance. The weapon dropped from her grasp, clattering onto the gondola floor, skittering across the wood. It wasn't turbulence that had caused the aircraft to shift dramatically because it hadn't achieved enough altitude.

No, this was something else. It was a momentary weight imbalance. The shifting weight indicated that someone else was mounting the *Lathos*.

The weapons satchel also began to slide, but she stopped it with her boot as she regained footing. The dirigible rocked sharply again, but she was prepared this time. She absorbed the haphazard movement with her knees.

"Winterhawk!"

The yell came from behind directly her. It was Lieutenant Misciso. He had reacted quickly enough after the gunfire to have reached the aircraft first. He'd been able to grab onto the gondola and heave himself upwards into the craft.

Chenoa flicked her eyes down. A leather strap was poking up from inside the satchel. She hooked her right foot inside it, jerking up with her leg. The object flew upwards. She caught it deftly with one hand.

Chenoa whipped around.

Misciso was standing ten feet from her. He was framed in front of the hydrogen spout, legs spread wide for balance. His crooked smirk betrayed his overconfidence. The massive steel cables of the tramway were framed behind him as the dirigible now passed the height of the suspended stone bucket.

Misciso edged his hand toward the holstered Colt. "Hope you're hungry because it's time to eat a bullet!"

Suddenly, the triumphant look had vanished. It was because Misciso had glanced down. He saw what she had just grabbed from the weapon's satchel.

Chenoa was holding a weather-worn shepherd's sling. It had an elongated grip crafted from the nearly impervious wood of a Hornbeam tree. The sling itself was a thickly corded flattened piece of coal-stretched turtle's neck. When the dogbane cordage was stretched out to its full two-foot length, the sling was even durable enough to hold the suspended weight of a man.

Misciso wore a grin of disbelief. "What are you planning to do with that, King David? Fling a stone?"

"No," Chenoa answered honestly. She feigned a lunge forward with her shoulders, giving the impression that she was planning to move towards him.

Misciso brought his hand across his waist, rapidly unholstering the Colt and aiming. In a flash of the eye, he was already pulling the trigger.

Chenoa wasn't faster than a bullet, but she didn't have to be.

Misciso had anticipated a center mass target stepping directly towards him across the unsteady dirigible. He had reflexively aimed at precisely where he knew her next steps would be. At this range, he knew that the slug from the Colt would eviscerate her breastbone and slice her lungs into ribbons.

But instead of a target, all he got was a blur of motion.

Chenoa had guessed that after pulling his weapon, Misciso would aim fast and fire faster. She had drawn his complete attention by the exaggerated lunge with her shoulders; his reflexes automatically targeting the exact spot where that movement should have taken her.

But instead of stepping forward, Chenoa had lunged sideways and launched herself airborne. Her right arm was extended high over her head with the sling.

The blast from the Colt reverberated loudly, the bullet missing its target by mere inches. The slug impacted with a section of the gondola, shearing off a fist-sized section of wood with a loud crack.

Misciso reacted quickly, shifting the gun sideways, tracking the moving target, finger curling around the trigger.

Chenoa, still airborne, swung her arm down in a controlled, savage arc. The sling made a distinctive snapping sound as its payload was released. She landed hard on the floor of the *Lathos*, rolling into a crouched position.

The Colt fired again, but this time the noise was drowned out by Misciso's savage scream. The shot went wide as the soldier flung both arms backwards, reacting to the horrifying impact of the object flung at him from the slingshot.

What had hit him directly in the center of his throat hadn't been a stone. It was a five-inch falcon beak.

Bird beaks had been utilized by indigenous warriors for centuries, and across several different continents. While a sharp or heavy stone was used when engaging shielded targets with a sling, beaks were optimal for deadly close-quarter attacks.

The falcon's beak had hit dead-center in the bottom of Misciso's neck. It had torn a jagged hole through the flesh as it had passed completely through his trachea. Now, a perfect shaft of sunlight shone through the bleeding, gaping hole.

"What a pain in the neck," Chenoa muttered.

Misciso dropped the Colt, wrapping both hands around his throat. He gasped loudly for breath, lungs already wheezing. He fell backwards, his upper torso landing directly onto the burning hydrogen spout. The white-hot metal cylinder impaled him through the abdomen.

Misciso pounded his arms and legs helplessly against the gondola as the hydrogen spout pushed flames through his body. The flesh of his stomach began to blacken under the relentless heat, the flesh rippling uncontrollably like a large stone being tossed into a tranquil pond. In the next few seconds, his lungs began to melt as the hydrogen lit him up from the inside-out.

His mewls of anguish faded sharply into grotesque wet sounds as his heated ribcage pushed its way completely through his chest. In that same moment, his uniform caught fire. Soon, the flames were licking against the wooden frame of the gondola.

There was a wet popping sound as Misciso's heart exploded inside his chest, killing him instantly. His legs began to spasm in the final throes of muscle reflex as the flames engulfed his entire body.

Winterhawk secured the slingshot against the belt strap around her waist, scrambling to her feet. She glanced at the Zieg-8 lying nearby. She would need to grab it fast before the entirety of the *Lathos* was consumed with fire. In just a few minutes, the entire blimp would detonate in a massive hydrogen explosion.

She felt the winds pushing against her face as the dirigible was rocked by turbulence. Smoke was now billowing off the *Lathos*, concealing the skies all around her.

Reaching down, she scooped up the Zieg-8.

Then...

Instincts.

The hair on her arms stood at attention.

She felt as if she was standing in the crosshairs.

Her eyes darted quickly over the railing. The twin steel cables of the aerial tramway filled her immediate vision. And thirty-feet below that stood Akando. He had shouldered a Winchester sniper rifle, aiming it directly at her.

She noticed the flame emanating from the barrel a millisecond too late.

Akando had already fired.

Chenoa felt the savage impact of the bullet walloping into her chest as the echoing blast sounded loudly above the crackling flames. She felt an intense blast of pain pressing against her heart. Her arms were flung backwards, the Zieg-8 spinning out of her hands. It flew over the edge of the gondola, dropping into oblivion.

Chenoa careened backwards over the railing, her body tumbling helplessly from the *Lathos*. She felt the immediate pull of gravity. Then, her entire world went black.

CHAPTER 13

Chenoa fell.

CHAPTER 14

Higgins Haven
Blue Mountain Range
Eastern Oregon, 1905

The day had turned into night and turned right back into day again.

It was the very monotony of predictability that shrouded everything in the universe. Once understood, that realization was what cast the greatest aspersions on those living with blind faith. It didn't take a theologian like Jonathan Edwards to come to terms with the reality that things in this world, once they are set in motion by a Sovereign God, would never be altered by Him until the end of days.

While Ricco Traff understood that brimstone was a biblically sound doctrine, he had always thought Hell itself must be constructed in such a parallel way as to be recognizable to those souls cast into the Lake of Fire. Those subjugated to eternal torment would forever be beholden to universal truths: days would always turn into nights. The punishment of Hell could be found in its repetition.

"Why should the fires of Hell be different than the hells on earth?" Ricco muttered aloud from his perch on the rolling wagon. His scratchy voice sounded like a dull knife striking a wet stone as his words echoed soullessly between the mountain ranges.

Trudging on ahead of him, Nathaniel brayed loudly in response as he pulled the wagon over the uneven mountain terrain. The aged mule understood the banality of repetition, having been a water hauler alongside Ricco for the better part of two decades now.

With Ricco now pushing 60 years of age, this loyal mule had now become the only family he had. Truth be told, Nathaniel was his only friend, too. Years ago, Nathaniel had pulled him through a terrible blizzard and saved his life.

Traff knew that other people wouldn't understand that sentiment, but he didn't give a damn about any of that. This animal was his only companion in this life; something he was truly blessed to admit. He and the mule had traveled a lot of miles together over the decades, and it hadn't always been easy.

Traff had started out in adult life engaging in the lucrative freighter business. As a freighter, he would typically transport all manner of merchandise to small towns across northern and eastern Oregon. He'd travel long distances to deliver consumables to settlements that lacked the necessary stores and supplies.

It wasn't a noble profession, but it was a steady living.

Until it wasn't.

As towns grew in population, so did the local commerce. General stores began to multiply within communities like jackrabbits, catering to every whim and fancy until the novelty of the traveling freighter became obsolete.

Luckily, Ricco had stumbled upon a niche business that would ultimately become even more profitable than his tenure as a freighter.

Water hauling.

Because of the arid landscape, eastern Oregon mining communities had found themselves in dire need of water. The supply in and around the mines was oftentimes scarce, and sometimes required an operation to shut down for months before a water source could be rerouted or sufficiently replenished.

For huge operations, even a temporary shutdown would have been financially disastrous. Not only would the miners migrate to competing camps to seek other jobs, but without a large workforce community, the mines themselves were left vulnerable to theft and hostile takeovers from other mining companies.

Haulers became the solution. Their business was to transport water to places that didn't have enough of it, or couldn't sustain the little amount they had at their disposal.

In a bit of serendipity, one of Ricco's best ammunition clients in La Grande had become employed as a security guard at the Carson Mining Company. After listening to one of the owners grumbling one day about the severe lack of water resources, Traff had been recommended by him for the job.

It had been a lucrative gig that had lasted for years.

The mine located inside Elkhorn Peak was the third largest in the entire region. It had a steam-powered elevator, three levels of winding mine cart tracks, and powerful boiler-fueled quarry water hose used for placer mining.

But eventually, the water supply needed to power the steam engine and boiler became larger than the resources that were available. By the end, Rico was just one of ten haulers delivering water before the mining camp had to be shuttered for good. It was the same fate delivered to other mines in the region.

This was exactly why President Roosevelt's Newlands Reclamation Act was going to both revolutionize and stabilize this part of the country. While the federal government's commission for emergency water diversion throughout Eastern Oregon was an economic lifesaver, for many people, it was simply a case of too little, too late.

Much like it was for Rico Traff himself.

He reckoned that this run to the cabin of Colonel Higgins would be one of his final water deliveries. He certainly wasn't getting any younger. Neither was Nathaniel, for that matter.

Shifting on the seat, hands gently holding onto the reigns, Rico glanced again at his mule. Nathaniel was pulling the four wheeled express delivery wagon up the mountainside with little sign of his advancing age. He seemed content to do his job; nothing more, and nothing less.

Lack of self-pity was the gift that God gave all animals. Traff wish that was something that he could jettison from his own life with the ease of snot deposited into a rag on a frosty morning. Feeling sorry for oneself became a full-time job for too many folks, and more than a few of them put in plenty of overtime hours. He understood because he'd personally punched the clock on self-pity many times.

When his water hauling business first started waning, the impending financial plight was all he could think about. He'd spent his life surviving on limited means, never splurging and always saving, but the thought of having no money coming in filled him with fear. That's when he realized that living with blind faith wasn't some abstract concept; no, far from it. There were moments when God whispered things gently in your ear to get your attention, while other times, He grabbed you by the shoulders and shook you like a rag doll.

That's what happened to Rico. In His divine providence, God had used this faltering business as a way to refocus his spiritual priorities.

Besides, life was just too short. The reality for Traff was that it was getting shorter all the time. Once you understood that you're living with more yesterdays than tomorrows, priorities shift. When it comes to ageing, the skill finally becomes stepping over the bullshit instead of always stepping directly into it.

Nathaniel began to bray shrilly, getting his attention.

The Blue Mountain Range loomed on the horizon, its pine-thick slopes whispering secrets of ancient spirits. Shadows danced in the underbrush, hinting at unseen eyes.

A large wood cabin could now be seen less than a quarter-mile up the horse trail they had been traveling on for the last several hours. They were finally nearing Higgins Haven.

Ricco snapped the reins, coaxing a burst of speed from the mule. He could hear the jostling of water from the four large barrels stacked behind him in the wagon as it began rolling faster.

The delivery in the back was for Colonel Higgins. Another shipment of filtered water for his cabin retreat: Higgins Haven. After he retired from active duty, Higgins had bought this property and was spending his retirement operating as a bear hunting guide. His grizzled beard and war-scarred hands spoke of battles won, and many more lost.

While there had been quite a few people staying at this cabin over the years, but none as famous as the one arriving soon. Rico shook his head at the thought.

He never imagined that his journey through life would have led him here, where he would be providing his services to the President of the United States.

It was all to be kept very hush-hush, of course. While Colonel Higgins and Theodore Roosevelt had served together during the Spanish-American War, they hadn't actually seen one another for a great many years since.

"We're old friends," Higgins had explained to Rico earlier in the week. "Being on the battlefield binds men together, Traff. Family background and social status are completely levelled out when you're standing shoulder-to-shoulder in the trenches. Uniforms have a knack of becoming life's great equalizer."

Rico had nodded in affirmation. To him, it *sounded* good; yet, he thought it was probably a falsehood. People believe what they wanted to believe. He certainly had never encountered an equalizer in life that brought balance to inequality. Only death did that.

But even so, he gave Higgins the benefit of the doubt. He had never served in the Army like the good Colonel had; perhaps the rules are different when bullets are involved. Or maybe it's just that people needed those different rules to make peace with the very things they could never control.

"Teddy is coming *here*?" Traff had inquired.

Colonel Higgins had nodded. "Directly after his Newlands Reclamation Act speech at the Owyhee Dam. That's going to be proceeded by a controlled blast deep inside the old Carson Mines at Elkhorn Peak. The Army Corps of Engineers have supposedly discovered an underground river there that will feed the dam and irrigate this entire region."

And run me right out of business, Traff had thought.

Surprisingly, he wasn't bitter about the notion. Years ago, he'd gambled by spending his life's savings to purchase a pair of filtration units from the Jewell Pure Water Company. Installed beside Nathaniel's corral in the back of his homestead, these large units utilized sand filters for treating water strictly for drinking purposes. The Jewell operated on specialized filters that used gravity to allow water to percolate through columns of sand inside cylindrical cisterns.

Fed by a constant supply of resources from the Malheur River, the Jewell filtration units had produced some of the best tasting drinking water in all of eastern Oregon. And after word got out about it, those filters had made him a tidy sum.

However, it hadn't taken long for his competitors to get wind of his methods. Soon, there were Jewell's scattered all over the region. But by then, Rico already had a steady supply of loyal customers.

Colonel Higgins was one of them.

"How many barrels will you need for the visit?" Traff had asked.

"Four should do it," Higgins had answered. "There's Teddy and I, then there will be two Secret Service boys hanging around the cabin for protection."

Traff reckoned that four barrels was two too many for such a small group, but he had wisely kept his mouth shut. Men of property and standing understood the intrinsic value of silence. A priest had once remarked to him that God's chosen should keep their mouths shut so they could always hear the voice of Satan.

He figured that was as apt a description of business as there ever was.

Now, Rico glanced over his shoulder at those four barrels of filtered water in the back of the hauler wagon. After that underground river fed into the Owyhee Dam, he wondered if this to be the final trip he'd be making to Higgins Haven.

He figured that it probably—

Nathaniel.

The mule had suddenly stopped on the mountain trail. He began whimpering loudly, his head began whipping back and forth. There was a slight tremor running through his body, the fur pulsating noticeable beneath the constant gaze of the hot afternoon sun.

He was scared of something. No, there was more to it than just that. Nathaniel was absolutely *terrified*.

Heart hammering, Rico reached beside him for the Winchester Model 1901. The weight of the shotgun felt comforting in his hands he rapidly dismounted from the driver's seat of the hauler wagon.

He quickly made his way towards Nathaniel, eyes nervously scanning the forest that surrounded them. "What is it, boy? Did you hear something?" The mule whimpered in response; teeth bared as he brayed loudly back at him.

Rico glanced towards Higgins Haven. They were so close to the cabin now. Perhaps Nathaniel had heard something coming from inside—

Movement. Coming from the south, directly behind him. Like the wind, only it moved with purpose.

Traff whirled around on his heels, raising the shotgun.

A massive shape rumbled through the dense underbrush of the forest. It looked like an enormous trunk had sprung legs, only this tree had white bark covering it.

Traff squinted harder.

He was staring at a strange creature with streaks of light-colored fur. Whatever the animal was, it was impossibly fast. In the span of seconds, the creature had cleared the edge of the forest and vanished deep inside the shadows of the woods.

A pungent odor sudden filled his nostrils. The overwhelming muskiness of it nearly made him gag. He reflexively brought up the back of his hand and covered his nose. "What the—?"

Nathaniel brayed shrilly behind him. It sounded almost like a scream. It lasted only seconds before the noise of his braying was drowned out by a horrifically wet tearing sound.

Then, absolute silence.

His heart thundering, Traff jerked around in panic.

Nathaniel was standing ten feet away from him. All four of his hooves shuffling in place on the dusty ground. It was like the mule was attempting his own version of a Mark Time March.

It probably would have even been comical if it wasn't for one horrifying detail: Nathaniel's head was missing. It looked like the mule's neck had been pulled taut and twisted, then the head pulled clean off like it was nothing more than a stem of an apple. Globs of viscera flowed from the savage hole that had been created in his body, slithering to the ground with a sickening splat.

Rico took a stumbling step forward, his mind overwhelmed with what he was witnessing. Grief and rage coursed simultaneously through his body.

"Nathaniel!"

His mule began to shake uncontrollably as the final nerve pistons fired off inside his dying body. Free from the wagon harness that had been strapped around his neck, Nathaniel toppled forward, rolling until he was laying completely on his back. With his legs now sticking up in the air, the mule gave one last involuntary shudder and was mercifully still.

Traff could hardly wrap his mind around what he was seeing; could barely comprehend what could have possibly happened. That *thing* he had seen in the woods must have done this. Whatever massive animal it was had just killed Nathaniel.

And now, it would be coming back for him.

Enraged, he raised the Winchester, wildly swinging the barrel around in a semi-circle. He frantically peered into the deep shadow of woods crowding all around him. "Come out and get me! Come on out, you hairy tree fucker!"

Rico saw a flash of sudden movement in his peripheral vision. Something was moving towards him, coming from the direction of the cabin. Whatever it was, it was running fast in the shadows.

Yelling with rage, Traff swiveled his body towards the movement. Operating purely on a hunter's instinct, he levelled the shotgun and pulled the trigger.

For one horrifying moment, he realized that it wasn't the creature that he had seen in his peripheral running towards him. In fact, it wasn't an animal at all. It was—

Colonel Higgins took the full force of the Winchester directly in the chest. His face wore a mask of shock as the blast knocked him completely off his feet. His arms flailed wildly in the air as his entire breastbone was savagely ripped open by the powerful .35 centerfire cartridge.

Higgins was dead before his body hit the ground.

Traff felt his gorge rise; vomit filling his mouth and dripping from his nostrils.

Then, he heard something charging up fast behind him. Its footsteps were thunderous, impacting against the ground like cannon fire. He knew immediately that it was the creature. He gripped the shotgun tight, knowing that he needed to turn around. He needed to shoot it before—

With his shoulder hunched low, the monster rammed into his back with all the force of a locomotive. Rico cried out in agonizing pain as he felt his hips shatter on impact, could hear the tortured wrenching of his spinal column as it bent sharply before snapping cleanly in half.

He was flung fifteen feet in the air before crashing back to the ground, his arms and legs akimbo as he rolled helplessly to a stop. He felt fire deep in his lungs, his broken body unable to draw any more breath. The pain was everywhere; then, he felt a merciful calm enveloping him. His vision was blurred, but he noticed that the sun was temporarily blotted out as dark storm clouds appeared to blanket the skies. He felt rain droplets splash against his pupils, but he was unable to blink.

Traff could suddenly see the sun again. The storm clouds must have moved.

He then heard a deep, guttural growling.

And then, Rico finally understood.

It wasn't clouds that had momentarily hidden the sun, it had been the monster towering over him. And it wasn't rain that had splashed against his eyes, it was saliva dripping from the hungry mouth of the creature.

He heard the sound of his own flesh tearing; could see the creature gorging on the innards that were now oozing out of a rip in his stomach.

Traff's eyes fluttered closed. He felt the wind ruffle his hair one last time. And then, mercifully he felt nothing at all.

CHAPTER 15

Malheur Indian Reservation
Eastern Oregon
1888

"Every battle is different, and every battle is the same." Jolon Winterhawk looked over at Chenoa, his eyes gently probing into her mask of grief. "Just as every death is the same, yet every death is different. Someday you'll understand."

"Someday." Her voice sounded gravelly; vocal cords raw and hoarse.

They were standing together at Sonsela's gravesite. The soil beneath their feet was freshly disturbed, darkened in that distinctive way of something recently dug up, or freshly buried.

She turned her face away from the grave. "Poppa?"

Chenoa despised how weak her voice sounded. It cracked sharply like bark falling from a wind-ravaged tree that was unable to hold on to itself after a heavy storm. But trees took solace in knowing that it was the roots that were keeping it alive. She'd do well to remember that. When the worst storms threatened to take everything away, it was those roots that saved you. And sometimes those roots were all you really had.

"Yes?"

"On my sixteenth birthday, you spoke to me about grandfather; about guardian angels. Do you remember that?"

Jolon nodded. "I remember it."

Chenoa swallowed hard. It was difficult to continue, but she needed to. When the answer you know you'll receive isn't the one you want, that's when it becomes even more important to ask the question.

"Sonsela…"

"What about him, Chenoa?"

"Is it possible—I mean, do you think he might…?"

"He's not coming back." Jolon shook his head with sadness. "The invisible world is one of incredible spiritual power. The *Weyekins* are protective spirits, shielding a warrior from harm. They become like guardian angels guiding us through the tribulations in this world. But in His wisdom, the Creator hasn't given everyone that privilege."

"Privilege." Chenoa's eyes welled up with hot tears. She thought she'd run completely out of them, but her sorrow produced as many as her heart felt she needed. And over the last few days, she had needed a lot.

"You know, after your grandfather was killed, our mother did her very best to raise Akando and me. She was all alone, and gave up so much of her life to take care of us. She was angry at the Great Spirit because of what had happened."

Chenoa felt his words worming uncomfortably through her head. She had only the faintest memories of her grandparents. Like so many of that generation within the Nez Perce, they hadn't lived very long after the forced relocation. It was as if having their homeland taken away had caused a mass terminal illness.

"She didn't like being a momma?"

Jolon brushed a hand beneath his chin, as if absently feeling for stubble that he'd forgotten wasn't there. "*Like* has nothing to do with it. When people become survivors, they have to be strong. And sometimes they have to be strong for all the wrong reasons. If you don't learn anything else during war, you'd better learn *that*. And you'd better learn it right quick."

Chenoa searched his face. "Which war, Poppa?"

"I fought in the Great Rebellion, but your grandfather fought another type of war. My father was protecting his family against the men who tried to kill us."

Chenoa thought back again to that day on the cliffside. She remembered her father telling her about Akando, and how his twisted ideology led to the bloody betrayal of his people. Her uncle had sworn retribution against everyone who he felt was responsible for the death of his father.

Both her father and her uncle had seen her grandfather murdered; yet, the brothers had each responded vastly differently to it. One had found everyone outside of the Nez Perce to be guilty; the other had protected those same outsiders because he felt a sense of duty.

Jolon stared hard at her. "You were thinking about Akando, weren't you?"

"Yes," she admitted.

"My father put himself directly in the line of fire in order to protect his family. Because of his sacrifice, Akando and I lived. The Great Spirit honored him in death, and that's how he was chosen to be a *Weyekin*."

Chenoa's eyes went wide. "You saw him as one?!"

"I saw enough." Chief Winterhawk had a distant gaze now.

Chenoa looked down at her father's left leg. The slashing wound was now covered by his pants, but she'd seen it plenty of times over the years. Long, deep claw marks that stretched along his hamstring and calf. He'd always explained the wound as being the aftermath of a bear attack, but she'd long suspected that the savage claw marks had come from something else.

Jolon noticed the focus of her gaze. "The world was once nothing but flesh and teeth. The elders speak of such things; they tell us about the legends that have roamed our lands."

"Legends," Chenoa repeated.

She thought of the Nez Perce tales about the Nu'numic. Vividly recounted stories about fierce protectors of the forest, with variations of these monsters shared among every native tribe in North America.

Even the mountain-dwelling people of the Arapaho and Shoshone nations believed there was a species of the Nu'numic that prowled hungrily among the snow peaks and ice caves. Those tribes referred to them as Sásq'ets or the Kala'litabiqw.

Within the Nez Perce, those terrifying man-eating creatures were known as the Wen'ey'ti: mountain monster.

She felt a brief shiver of fear course through her. "Monsters," she whispered.

"*Legends*," Jolon corrected. "What gives those legends meaning is the belief we ascribe to them." He held out his right arm, something clutched in his hand. "Do you know what this is?"

She recognized it immediately: his treasured silver locket, her father's closest thing to a family heirloom. "That is your *minopaniwin*," she explained. "Your totem that brought you good luck when you were a soldier." She knew that it had once held a picture of her and *Pik'e* inside of it, but the photograph had long since faded.

"It's not a totem, Chenoa. This locket was a gift handed down to your *Pik'e* on our wedding day. It had originally been given to her family by a white man."

Chenoa couldn't contain her surprise. "It was?"

Jolon nodded. "Your grandfather, the one on your mother's side, had been one of the brave Nez Perce warriors who saved the Corps of Discovery from starvation in the Bitterroot Mountains. To show his gratitude, Captain Meriwether Lewis bestowed this locket on your grandfather. It was a gift that he gave your *Pik'e* after we were married. Before I went off to war, your mother gave it to me as a way to keep both of you close at heart. And now, I'm giving it to you."

He pressed the locket firmly into her hand. She stared down at it with incredulity. It was battered and scratched, and emanated a peculiar warmth. She placed the chain around her neck carefully, feeling it pressing against her chest.

"That locket isn't some Nez Perce rabbit's foot. You wear it to protect your heart, Chenoa. I know how it works because it protected mine."

Struggling with emotion, she placed a hand firmly against the locket. "I promise to always wear it." Her tears began to flow again. She watched as they dropped from her cheek and splashed down upon Sonsela's grave. The soil quickly soaked them up, as if they were badly needed to nourish the memory of what was buried underneath.

Then, even more tears splashed down onto the grave. But these weren't hers. Standing beside her, Jolon was weeping with her now.

Chenoa wasn't sure if he was crying for her loss, or if perhaps it was because of something that ran much deeper. Grief often took the hand of other emotions and walked them carefully out into the light. Whatever the reason, she reached out her hand and clasped his tightly.

They stood there for a long while, weeping together as the sun slipped behind the trees and covered the woods in a shawl of deep shadows.

CHAPTER 16

Baxter Ladder Peak
Blue Mountain Range
Adrian, Oregon
1905

The locket had protected her heart.

Chenoa realized what had saved her the moment she felt the thundering impact against her upper body. The blow had hurtled her helplessly backwards over the gondola railing, and had sent her careening through the air.

It had been Akando...

The slug from his Winchester Model 1905 sniper rifle had impacted against her chest with deadly accuracy. It would have punctured her flesh and completely eviscerated her heart except the locket had dangled in its path at that precise moment.

Luck threatened to make a liar out of the Creator, her father had once said.

She had blacked out a second after the bullet struck her, but the whipping of the wind had snapped her back into full consciousness.

Now, Chenoa gulped lungfuls of cold wind as she fell backward away from the *Lathos*. The dirigible was now totally aflame, the fires licking steadily upwards towards the hydrogen-filled envelope bag.

The ground had been 100-feet below her when the bullet's impact had flung her over the side. Now, it was 80-feet away.

...75...

Certain death was now seconds away.

Winterhawk made out something coming up at her quickly. It was the twin steel cables of the aerial tramway. Fastened between the steel ropes was the stone transport bucket.

Chenoa twisted her body in mid-air, positioning herself forward, arms splayed out. Dipping her head, she glided through the air.

The heavy cables would slice her body clean in half if she miscalculated the trajectory by even a single foot. Her target was the heavy-duty tram bucket placed directly between the twin tensile cables of steel that stretched from the peak of Baxter's Mines to the bank of the Malheur River.

She knew that if she attempted to land inside the bucket, the force of the impact would result in a dislocated knee or a broken leg. That unforgiving stone would be unyielding against the fragility of her body.

The only chance she had would be to grab the side of the tram bucket. But at this speed and trajectory, grabbing on to the lip would result in her shoulder being wrenched completely out of its socket, dropping her back into the air.

Then, if the fall didn't kill her, Akando would make sure another hail of bullets would.

50-feet.

Winterhawk was positioned directly above the bucket now. The next two seconds of the fall would decide whether she lived or died. There was absolutely no room for error now. Even a miscalculation of a single foot would surely result in her death.

Just breathe, amiga. As you fall, look down; carefully spot the exact landing point. Keep your feet splayed out, knees slightly bent. Your hands should be up, elbows bent. Grab the bucket ledge, then immediately straighten your arms. You'll slide for a moment, but let your legs absorb the impact.

Chenoa fell directly between the heavy-duty tram cables, her body missing the steel by inches. The dangling stone bucket was an arm's length from her now.

Keeping her elbows bent, she grasped the rim with both hands. She planted both feet against the swinging stone, pushing hard. Immediately straightening her arms, she pulled her head back, feeling her feet sliding down the bucket. Her body stopped with a sudden jerk, and she felt a severe tugging against her deltoids.

Chenoa was now dangling 50-feet above the ground as she held tightly onto the swaying tram bucket. She gasped with the exertion, lungs screaming for air.

Winterhawk tensed her body for the inevitable spray of bullets that she knew was coming next. Akando and his traitors would be firing at her any second now. But strangely enough, those shots never came. Feeling a sudden wave of heat wash over her, she understood why.

The dirigible was directly above her now, floating only several dozen feet away. The fire had completely overtaken the balloon envelope. She frowned because she knew what would happen next.

Hydrogen is extremely flammable in high-altitudes because of the dense concentrations of air. When fully mixed with the thinning components of oxygen from a fire, a fast-reacting chemical reaction takes place. When this occurs, hydrogen will detonate, immediately followed by a massive explosion.

With a loud ripping sound, the envelope covering the canopy of the dirigible tore into two pieces as the fire finished eating away at it. The hydrogen flame began to burn a bright blue as it became fully exposed to the high-altitude oxygen.

The *Lathos* would fully detonate in seconds.

She heard panicked yells from the men below. The soldiers hadn't fired at her because they were too busy scrambling for cover.

The *Lathos* had now become a bomb. And now, it was in a terrifying freefall. Without the balloon envelope for buoyancy the blimp had nowhere to go but straight down.

Spiraling out of control, the dirigible was now on a crash course for Winterhawk and the stone bucket hanging off the tram cables.

CHAPTER 17

Chenoa dangled helplessly from the stone bucket. She had no choice but to hang on because a drop from the tram cables from this height would pulverize her bones.

She could already feel the painful bruising beginning to form around the left side of her chest from Akando's rifle shot. The locket saved her life, but it hadn't shielded her upper body from the bullet's impact.

She glanced over her shoulder and watched the lumber barge making its way down the Malheur River. It would soon be passing the sandbanks where the tram cables reached the end of the line. Perhaps, those men aboard might be able to help her. The trouble was, the barge was five hundred feet away.

Chenoa looked at the tram cables running down a 45-degree slant towards the river. An idea flashed through her head on how she could possibly reach the barge. It was desperate and it was futile, but she was out of options.

Bad plans were all she had left.

Grunting with effort, Chenoa pulled herself up and climbed inside as the bucket rocked precariously between the cables.

Just then, a strong headwind swept across the peaks. The burning dirigible was caught up in the sudden gust. Incredibly, the *Lathos* lifted upward, spinning 180 degrees as it briefly floated in midair.

Ducked down inside the bucket, Chenoa's eyes went wide with shock as she saw what had just happened.

The wind had altered the blimp's trajectory. It was no longer coming down directly on top of her; now, the *Lathos* was hovering over the cables directly behind the bucket.

The headwind vanished.

The blimp was momentarily frozen in midair.

And then, it began to fall straight down. The burning dirigible spun wildly as it rapidly descended, on a collision course directly between the tramway cables.

A second later, the blimp slammed hard against the tensile steels with a wallop, flames shooting out in all directions.

Chenoa pulled her body down, throwing her arms over her head as fire blanketed the bucket.

The wooden gondola cracked on impact with the cables, tipping the blimp completely over onto one side. The underside of the flaming blimp faced the direction of the river, while the burning hydrogen spout was pointed towards the upper peak of the Baxter Mines.

Chenoa hopped into a crouch, hands grasping the heated stone edges of the bucket as the cables heaved wildly from the impact.

The near-skeletal remnants of Misciso's corpse still remained impaled on the white-hot hydrogen tube, which rattled dangerously as fire completely ravaged it.

Winterhawk realized that the hydrogen was only moments away from complete detonation, but that was actually the least of her worries. The current positioning of the blimp itself was far more alarming.

The aerial tramway had been constructed so that its steepness was measured by its slope length compared with the vertical rise ratio. When designing it, the engineers had erected the cables to be disproportionately slanted at 40-degrees in order to move transport bucket more easily from the peak to the shoreline.

When the *Lathos* had crashed, it had balanced itself on two sets of steel cables placed on a steep downward angle. The blasting hydrogen tube had reacted like a reverse propeller, which pushed the dirigible *forward* from its stationary position.

"Oh, hell..." Chenoa muttered as she saw it.

Propelled into motion by the hydrogen spout, the flaming blimp was now sliding down the steel cables directly towards her. It would collide with the bucket in three seconds and cook her alive.

It was time to move!

Chenoa climbed precariously onto the edge of the bucket, her heels wobbling as she briefly squatted.

...two seconds...

The blimp screeched like a banshee as it moved rapidly down the tramway.

Winterhawk yanked the shepherd's sling from her belt. She gripped it tightly in her right hand, unfurling the two feet of dogbane cordage.

...one second...

"This is a very bad idea!"

Letting out a yell, she launched herself off the stone transport bucket and soared into the air.

CHAPTER 18

Winterhawk was fully extended in the air before she swung her right arm around. The thickly corded dogbane of the sling wrapped expertly around one of the cables. Still holding tightly onto the Hornbeam grip with her right hand, she reached out with her left and grabbed the coal-stretched neck of the weapon.

She bobbed briefly beneath the cable, legs kicking in the air. For a terrifying moment, she thought the sling wouldn't support her weight...but it did.

It also began to move.

Fast.

She swung hard with her legs, adding a burst of speed as the shepherd's sling began sliding down the aerial tram cables.

Directly behind her, the *Lathos* impacted against the stone bucket with a loud crash. Splashes of fire flung out in all directions.

Chenoa held tightly onto the sling as it began picking up more speed.

The fire-branded dirigible bounced over the stone bucket and continued traveling down the tramway cables behind her.

The fast-approaching sandbank of the Malheur River became larger as she continued her perilous slide. Although still over two hundred feet away, she could now clearly make out the name of the vessel: *Sulaco*.

The sight of the flaming blimp had caught the men's attention aboard the barge; they began shouting loudly, pointing with exaggerated hand gestures.

Chenoa prayed that she would be able to reach them in time.

As the flaming carcass of the dirigible continued its thunderous slide, a high-pitched whistle began emanating from the blimp's hydrogen tube.

It was getting ready to explode.

Winterhawk was one-hundred feet from the Malheur River.

She needed to go faster, or she was going to die.

Fighting against the pain, Chenoa pulled both legs up against her chest. The aerodynamic position coaxed more speed from the sling's slide.

The water was fifty-feet away.

Barreling down nearly directly behind her, the blimp emanated a loud metallic shriek.

Twenty-five feet to the shoreline.

The metallic shriek had now turned into like a tortured scream.

Fifteen feet from the river.

NOW!

Chenoa jerked against the hornbeam handle of the sling, unfurling it. She felt her stomach lurch as she executed a flying drop from the cables, throwing both arms backwards, sailing over the shoreline.

The hydrogen tube detonated with a deafening thunderclap.

Misciso's skeletal remains mixed with hundreds of wooden shards as the gondola exploded. The fiery detonation was massive, pushing out tremendous shockwaves and heaps of fire.

Chenoa dove headfirst into the river, her boots vanishing under the water as a roaring wave of flames blanketed the water only inches above her.

The three men aboard the *Sulaco* threw themselves onto the deck as the blast rocked their boat. As the barge shook violently, the logs it had been herding rolled against the waves, bouncing off each another with loud cracks. The collision of logs forced sap leakage, fluid oozing onto the surface of the water, several patches igniting instantly with the flames.

Winterhawk broke the surface near the bow of *Sulaco*, immediately gulping for air. She fastened the sling back on her belt, keeping clear of the burning patches of sap all around her.

She noticed that shrapnel consisting of several of Misciso's bone fragments had been pinned against a few of the logs as if they'd been fired by a marksman.

The aerial tramway had been completely ruptured by the explosion, both cables snapping like a porch flag whipped by the wind. The sheer force of the detonation had sent dangerous ripples along the cables, the steel throbbing like a guitar string plucked by the fingers of a giant.

"CHENOA!"

Akando. His enraged voice boomed like thunder from his position at the top of the mine. Even from this distance, she could see the anger etched onto his face.

"Give me that map!"

Chenoa reached into her uniform pocket. She pulled out Major Quinn's map. She opened it, quickly studying the locations of the three main tunnels, the main mouth entrance, and—

Her eyes narrowed. There was something unusual indicated on the southwest corner of the map. She recognized it immediately. It was an alternate entrance. Akando likely didn't know about it. She decided that would be her way in.

Chenoa held the map high above her head, dramatically waving her arm so Akando would be sure to see it.

"NO!"

Crinkling it up in her fist, she tossed the map into one of the areas of burning sap. Even damp, the map began to blaze quickly. In the next moment, the river's current whisked it away into oblivion.

Chenoa turned in the water and faced the men on the *Sulaco*. "Help me! Please, you have to help…"

She let the words die in her throat. The men on the barge were looking intently up the hillside, ignoring her completely.

Akando was staring back at them. His right arm extended, hand balled into a fist.

She realized why Misciso hadn't been concerned about the presence of the barge earlier. It was because those men on board weren't witnesses—they were conspirators.

Akando rotated his hand and delivered a thumbs-down gesture.

The men on the barge had just been ordered to kill her.

Chenoa whipped her head around, eyes darting. There was no escape.

The third man in the group was the one standing closest to the railing. He reached out, dramatically whipping off a black tarp that had been covering a large object on the deck.

It was deck-mounted Model 1893 Gatling Gun.

The other two men on the barge began to cackle wildly. The leader, a scar-faced man, grinned cruelly, while his partner adjusted the Gatling's crank.

Moments later, her world exploded with gunfire.

PART TWO
GHOST TRAIL OF THE LOCUST

CHAPTER 19

The Model 1893 Gatling was a nasty piece of fire-and-forget hardware. It was built with a state-of-the-art feed strip system, and equipped with a rotating cylinder to pull 200 rounds per minute. This allowed it to spit bullets at any speed and at any angle, even in elevations where other gravity-based systems could become unreliable. And at this close range, it couldn't miss.

Winterhawk knew she was a sitting duck, dead in the water in the next few seconds unless—

Her gaze fixed on the mass of floating logs nearby. She had an idea; grimaced hard. It seemed that bad plans had become her new specialty.

Kicking hard through the water, Winterhawk grasped tightly onto the edge of the nearest log. Pulling her body up out of the river and clamoring onto the trunk, she yanked out a large piece of Misciso's femur bone from the wood.

Upon seeing her movement, the third man slid behind the large frame of the 1893 Gatling Gun with astonishing speed. He wrapped his hands around the trigger handle and swung the swivel-mounted weapon towards her.

The first two men on the barge stepped away from the Gatling gun, but stayed close to the railing. Eyes searching for Chenoa, they were almost drooling with excitement for what they knew what would happen next.

I'll be happy to disappoint you, Chenoa thought. Grasping tightly onto the splintered hunk of femur, she darted across the floating trunk.

The third man opened fire on her.

With a thunderclap of ear-splitting noise, the log was relentlessly peppered with 58-caliber rimfire conical slugs. Huge shears of wood splintered off as the massive bullets ripped mercilessly into it.

Racing across the trunk, Winterhawk leaped into the air. The slugs exploded into the area of the log she had been standing on just a half-second before.

Chenoa landed deftly atop another trunk, continuing her crazed run.

The third man maneuvered the Gatling around, tracking her as he continued to fire. The slugs tore into the trunk; huge plumes of water splashed around it as the bullets hit the river like mini-mortars.

Still gaining speed, Chenoa jumped onto a floating third log.

Easing off of the trigger, the man repositioned the barrel. He aimed directly at her back. She'd gotten lucky so far, but the Gatling wouldn't miss this time.

The first two men on the boat began hollering with anticipation.

Chenoa tugged the shepherd's sling off her waist as she ran.

The third man fired, laughed gleefully as the stitch of bullets tracked centimeters behind her. In one more second, they would—

Chenoa flung her body sideways off the log, torso twisting in midair until she faced the bridge of the ship.

The bullets shredded against the end of the log beside her; splinters showered the air.

Enraged, the gunner took his finger off the trigger as he saw the woman fire something at him from the sling before diving into the river. The man braced his body for the sting of impact; instead, he felt absolutely nothing. She had missed!

Laughing, he centered the barrel of the Gatling onto the area of bubbling water he'd seen her disappear down into. This woman couldn't swim fast enough to escape what was coming next.

With an orgasmic cry of victory, he pulled the trigger, knowing that violent death would be unleashed in seconds.

And he hadn't been wrong.

He'd only miscalculated which one of them it was who would be doing the dying.

JUST SECONDS AGO, Chenoa had felt the sickening vibrations of the 58-caliber slugs pounding beneath her feet as the deluge of bullets hit the log.

The difficulty in navigating floating logs came down to a matter of simple balance. Where to place your weight with each step was compounded by how slick the trunks were; how each footfall could potentially shift the log in the water and cause a slip.

As agile as she was, her reflexes couldn't have compensated for even a small slip because of the second variable: the 58-caliber rimfire conical slugs.

While the deck-mounted Model 1893 Gatling gun was a formidable piece of hardware, its lack of accuracy was compensated by horizon shredding firepower. With a weapon like that, accuracy was a minor inconvenience tantamount to wiping your boot after squishing a spider before stepping onto a church carpet.

She knew that was bad enough, but things got worse.

Running across logs while being chased by bullets was the easy part; taking the shot with the sling was impossible.

Not only would she need be launching the bone fragment from a horizontal aerial position, she'd also be firing the sling at an upwards trajectory while targeting a bullseye approximately ten-inches in diameter.

It was a terrible plan, indeed.

Having reached the end of the third log, Winterhawk felt the bullets smashing inches behind her. She knew the gunner would keep firing from the same fixed position at her back because there was nowhere left for her to go.

But the shooter hadn't anticipated her leaping off the log; hurling her body sideways. Holding the sling close to her chest had allowed her to easily load the bone fragment just as her feet had left the bobbing trunk.

She caught the man's look of utter astonishment as she extended her arm, aiming for the Gatling gun as she felt gravity pulling her towards the water.

Of course, taking the gunner down would have been a much easier shot, but that still would have left the weapon operational for the other men. She needed to eliminate both threats at once.

She recalled her training as she pulled back on the shepherd's sling.

The tribal elders at the Malheur Indian Reservation had referred to the skill as: *cewce-wnim-iskit tex-ext'e.*: the Ghost Trail of the Locust.

To become proficient with a sling, young Nez Perce warriors practiced their aim on the invasive grasshoppers that ravaged the cornfields. They used pebbles to pick off the insects until skill overtook luck.

The bigger challenge was the locusts.

While most grasshoppers are solitary, locusts hunt for their food in formational swarm clouds. Locusts have stronger wings than grasshoppers, but are much smaller in size. They arrive in the fields in large groups; they can devour quickly. And they typically are always guided to feeding areas by the queen.

The queen is much larger than the rest of the locusts, with distinctive pincers used for burrowing into the ground to lay her eggs. Because the queen travels within the center of the swarms, she is an incredibly difficult target to single out with a sling. Only the nest deadeye shots could take her down; thus, they must follow as ghost path to display instincts that nobody else could see.

Chenoa had mastered the Ghost Trail of the Locust by the age of 12. By the time she turned 18, she was the greatest shot the tribe had ever seen.

Now, it was all muscle memory.

Fire and forget.

And so, she did.

The splintered sliver of the femur was launched into the air with a distinct whoosh of air. It streaked like a bolt towards its target. The bone glinted in the sunlight before being swallowed within the smoking barrel of the Gatling gun.

Just as Chenoa hit the water, the man was already aiming at the exact spot in the river where she'd hit. He had pulled the trigger.

It all happened in a split second.

The first 58-caliber rimfire conical slug entering the barrel from the shell feed impacted against the wedged sliver of bone. The slug skipped upwards inside the barrel before becoming lodged sideways. The entire feed strap system jammed. The rotating cylinder spun a quarter-turn before emitting a huge metallic spark that licked the coiled feed of shells. Then, hundreds of bullets exploded.

The third appeared to be completely vaporized from the inside-out as the exploding Gatling gun lit up the deck of the *Sulaco*. The man's severed hands were still gripping the weapon, but the rest of his body had been peeled open in a gigantic plume of chunky crimson spray.

The other men were blown completely off their feet by the force of the detonation. The first man was saved from instantaneous death by where the second man had been unluckily positioned.

The second man didn't even have enough time to emit a scream before the wave of exploding slugs peppered his torso. His skull was instantly cleaved into three sections, brain tissue popping into the air like birthday confetti. The concussive blast tore both his legs off, dropping the gruesome remains of his upper body onto deck. The force of the explosion spun his ragged torso around twice, just as if it was a children's top spinning its way across the hardwood floor.

With a groan of twisted steel, the fiery remains of the deck-mounted Gatling toppled forward and crashed through the railing. The gory remains of the gunner fell with it as man and machine sunk to the bottom of the river.

The barge survivor pulled himself unsteadily to his feet, his coat smoking from the blast. His eyes were wide with astonishment as he stared at the jagged hole in the deck, then at the twitching pile of meat that used to be his friend.

Sensing something, the man turned sharply.

The smoke from the explosion wafted across the deck, revealing the raised canoe hooked on the starboard side of the ship.

There was a figure standing on top of it.

Winterhawk was drenched from the river; eyes blazed with rage. She was holding onto the hickory oar from the canoe. In her hands, it looked like a formidable weapon.

The man reached for his handgun. "Holy Mother of God...!"

Winterhawk launched herself out of the canoe. "Wrong guess!"

Chenoa landed on the deck of the *Sulaco*, the oar raised above her head. The man had his hand on the butt of his weapon when the oar smacked against his elbow, cracking the bone instantly.

Chenoa swung hard again. The oar connected against the man's left kneecap, shattering it. Now completely off-balance, he pinwheeled his arms wildly as his body collapsed to the deck. He landed on his shattered kneecap, letting loose a high-pitched scream.

Chenoa drove the oar under his chin and hurled him backwards. Scurrying over his body, she pressed the hickory hard against his throat. Her face hovered inches above his.

"What did Akando want with this barge?"

The man sputtered for air. "...the Owyhee Dam..."

"What about it?!"

"Blow it up...during Roosevelt's speech."

She pressed the oar harder against his throat. "How?!"

He shook his left arm wildly behind him, gesturing towards the steering bay of the *Sulaco*. "Twenty cases...Ketchum grenades...and coal torpedoes."

Winterhawk's mind raced.

Coal torpedoes were powerful marine ordinances used extensively during the Civil War, while Ketchum grenades were nothing more than trench meat grinders used to devastating effect on the battlefield.

Chenoa looked up the steering bay of the lumber barge. There were multiple crates of Ketchum grenades stacked inside. She guessed the coal torpedoes were being held in the storage compartment below.

This was more than enough explosives to put a huge hole in the Owyhee Dam, as well as wipe out anyone unlucky enough to be standing too close.

Winterhawk felt utter rage consuming her. Akando's bloodlust apparently knew no bounds. Well, she would ensure to sink this floating death trap before it reached its destination. And after that—

A tremendous booming noise suddenly erupted from the top of the Baxter Mines. A second sound immediately followed; it was like a metallic wind.

Whatever it was, it was getting closer to the barge.

Chenoa looked up into the sky.

Her eyes went wide.

The double-roped steel cables from the tramway had just been launched airborne. The untethered cables were hurtling down from the sky.

They were now heading directly towards the *Sulaco*.

CHAPTER 20

The hydrogen explosion from the *Lathos* had completely altered the physics of the tramway. After the cables severed, they'd been pulled backwards like a snapped whip retracting. It had taken several minutes of additional strain, but the tramway's turnbuckle had eventually buckled from the force and created a catapult.

The process was called tensioning.

To offset the winds, the turnbuckle had been attached to the steel ropes in order to properly tension it. The engineering allowed adequate maneuverability for the wires to twist and pull without snapping.

But when the ferrules on the tramway had been demolished, the turnbuckle had been stretched to an extreme degree. The result had turned the tramway into a catapult that had just launched the steel cables upwards into the sky.

With a trajectory that would take them straight down onto the lumber barge.

Tensioning? Catapulting? You can call it any damn thing you'd like, Chief, but tomorrow's newspaper obituary will still read the same: "Chenoa Winterhawk Struck Dead by Bad Luck ...Over and Over Again."

Chenoa got to her feet and began sprinting along the deck.

The metallic whistling grew louder as the steel hurtled closer. The cables were falling at different speeds, but they would both strike the *Sulaco* in mere seconds.

The barge survivor looked up and saw what was coming down. His pockmarked face twisted in pain, eyes wide with terror. "Ulysses S. Grant on a cracker!" he cried out with shock."

Unable to stand because of his shattered kneecap, he began to drag himself across the deck in a feeble attempt to get out of harm's way.

Chenoa reached the starboard side of the railing. She swung the oar around. It connected forcefully with the canoe hook and dislodged it. She saw it drop from view, and heard it splash onto the river.

She rapidly pulled herself on top of the railing. Feeling the massive shadow of the first cable completely enveloping her, she jumped overboard.

The first cable smashed against the *Sulaco*. The vessel shook with the force of the impact, wood splintering. The crawling man found himself directly in its path. The steel sliced him in half as it plowed its way straight through the deck.

Winterhawk landed hard in the canoe, the oar flying from her grasp. She cursed with frustration as she watched it vanish into the water. She quickly scrambled around the boat, searching desperately for another oar. There wasn't one.

There wasn't any way she could propel herself away from the barge.

Chenoa knew that the first cable hadn't struck the cases of ordnance, but she wouldn't be so lucky when that second cable landed.

The eerie metallic wind of the second cable filled the air.

Winterhawk grabbed both sides of the canoe, taking in a huge lungful of air.

The cable landed on to the boat with a thunderous crash. It completely obliterated the cabin, plowing through wood and glass.

Chenoa threw her entire weight to one side, tipping the canoe completely over.

The steel slammed against the Army crates, shattering them into millions of pieces. The Ketchum grenades exploded upon impact. The massive fireball quickly engulfed the entire ship, spreading fifty feet out across the river.

The ship began to ferociously burn as the fire crept closer to the coal torpedoes down in the storage hold. Once those cases got hot, it was best to be somewhere else.

From beneath the water, Chenoa felt incredible heat blanketing the overturned canoe. The shockwaves rocked it away from the barge like a stone skipped across the river.

The canoe had shielded her from the fire, but it wasn't able to withstand the pressure from the explosion. Without warning, the canoe suddenly cracked in half. Still holding tightly to the upper end, Chenoa felt the lower half pull away from her and sink.

Winterhawk felt something scrape against her legs.

Lungs burning for oxygen, she opened her eyes in panic.

The fireball still arcing on the surface illuminated everything directly below the water. For the briefest of moments, she thought she recognized the shape that was looming just beyond her vision.

It was man.

Her heart leapt involuntarily.

Sonsela had returned! Her father had been wrong. Her long-ago love had become a *Weyekin*. He'd been sent back by the Great Spirit to guide her out of this hell.

Chenoa nearly reached out a hand to him, then stopped.

The frothing underwater turbulence had just pushed the man closer towards her. She could now make him out in every detail, or what was left of him.

The shape she had seen wasn't Sonsela, but the bullet-riddled corpse of the Gatling operator. His face had almost completely peeled off; strips of flesh flapped from his skull like seaweed. He'd had both legs blown off just below the knee.

Chenoa knew that's what she had felt earlier. It had been those jagged pieces of the man's tibia rubbing up against her.

The broken tail end of the canoe filled up her vision. Still sinking, it caught the man in the chest, pushing him away. She watched as the corpse was dragged deeper into the river.

"I almost had you," the dead man seemingly said. *"Why, we almost had each other. But I'll never really be gone, Winterhawk. You'll still feel me touching you in your nightmares."*

The bottom section of the canoe had now pushed the man nearly out of sight. She got a glimpse of his dark shape smacking hard against the river bottom. He rolled against a litter of jagged rocks before the boat piece pinned him in place. She saw one of his dismembered arms floating upwards, almost as if he was giving her a final farewell gesture.

"I'll be sure and tell Sonsela hello for you, Winterhawk. After all, we both live down here now."

Chenoa closed her eyes, forcing the voice out of her head.

If only some memories could die the way people do. That they could somehow be buried deep in the soil and forgotten. But memories are too powerful to ever really die, especially the bad ones. Memories like that have an appetite of their own. They bite you, and after they do, what flowed in them now flows through you, too.

The truth is that bad memories only die once we do...and sometimes, not even then.

Winterhawk's chest suddenly began to burn from lack of oxygen. Still gripping onto the surviving section of canoe, she kicked upwards, rolling the front half of the boat to the surface with great effort.

Inside the burning carcass of the *Sulaco*, the fire had finally reached the boxes of coal torpedoes stashed below deck.

Now perched atop the surviving portion of the canoe, Chenoa began to take in huge lungfuls of air. She tasted acrid smoke in her mouth. Glancing over at the barge, she was surprised to see how far the first blast had moved her away from the burning vessel. She was now dead center of the Malheur River, roughly sixty feet away from the *Sulaco*.

She also noticed that the cluster of tree trunks had ended up between her and the *Sulaco*. They looked like wooden predators just waiting for the chance to tear her completely to pieces.

That was probably true.

Everything imaginable had tried killing her today. And yet, here she still was. She had survived everything—

The coal torpedoes onboard the barge exploded.

The massive blast reduced the *Sulaco* to millions of pieces of splintered wood and twisted metal. Large chutes of fire arced through the air in every direction. The tremendous shockwave pounded into the river like a hammering fist, forming several large maelstroms with dangerous vortex downdrafts.

And then...

Waves.

When water flows along open channels at high velocities like what is found in rivers, it can oftentimes become highly unstable. Even the slightest of disturbances can cause river surfaces to abruptly transition to much higher levels than normal. When a shockwave is introduced into the environment, a hydraulic jump wave is formed.

Winterhawk could hardly believe what she was seeing. The tremendous blast from the coal torpedoes had created a wave of considerable size. In seconds, the swell had achieved a height of over thirty feet.

The powerful wave had also scooped up the massive trunks along its path, propelling them towards her with the speed of wooden rockets. Colliding with them would be fatal.

The giant wave was almost upon her now.

Chenoa crouched low on the upper half of the canoe, sliding her feet against the edges for maximum support. She stretched out her arms, elbows bent.

The wave charged into her at astonishing speed. She felt the water push up against the fractured canoe. One of the logs scraped dangerously against the left side of the boat, jostling it.

Chenoa kept her body compression low, throwing her hips to the right. The canoe cut sideways, moving rapidly away from the log. She began rising upwards from the trough of the wave.

She felt the force of another log bearing down directly behind her. Winterhawk shifted her weight back to the left. The canoe slid sideways atop the wave as the trunk shot through the exact spot in the water she was at.

Crouching down low, she shifted her body weight back-and-forth. The canoe began cutting a zigzag path atop the wave until it was perched just below the crest.

Looking downriver, she was surprised by how far she'd already travelled after leaping off the *Sulaco*. Glancing back, she could no longer see the peaks of the Baxter Mines.

She thought quickly.

From here, Elkhorn Peak was a full day's travel through the Qualen Pass. Given their current location, it would be the easiest route that Akando could traverse to reach the Carson Mine.

Easiest, yes; not the quickest.

Stretching over 190 miles, the Malheur River was a tributary of the Snake River that covered the vast area between the high deserts of the Harney Basin and the densely wooded Blue Mountains. Malheur was also heavily braided, with bifurcation splits occurring dozens of times throughout its length. These waterway splits created islands, deltas...and waterfalls.

Chenoa could see one from her vantage point atop the wave.

Looking Glass Falls was a 100-foot drop into a deep basin below, the waterway feeding into the braid of rapids that made up the Wenaha River. That particular river flowed east through the eastern side of the Blue Mountains and ran parallel to Elkhorn Peak.

Looking Glass Falls was 20-miles from the Carson Mines. Taking the path along the Wenaha River to reach the mine was the fastest route, which might give her an advantage over Akando if he was taking the Qualen Pass.

The problem was that the Wenaha River wasn't accessible by boat from any point along the Malheur River.

Unless...

Do you know how the snail reached Noah's Ark? Persistence. In this life, there's either finding a way *through or finding an excuse to* be *through. You might be tired, amiga; hell, you might even be scared. But there's one thing you ain't, and that's beaten.*

Winterhawk steeled her gaze.

The swell was lessening as it was absorbed into the breadth of the river. The canoe was already cresting off the shrinking wave. Just ahead, she noticed that two of the logs were being pulled by the flow of the encroaching rapids. But they were heading in different directions.

The right log was continuing its journey unabated along the Malheur River, while the left log was being guided towards the bifurcation split that would take it over Looking Glass Falls.

Winterhawk thought about the orders she'd been given before embarking on the mission. After taking the *Lathos* to the drop-off point, she and Quinn were supposed to have rendezvoused with McNichols and Troost, two Army combat engineers, at their base camp along the Wenaha River. That neither one had been with Akando back at the Baxter Mines offered her a small glimmer of hope.

It meant that those two combat engineers hadn't become traitors.

If that were true, she could locate their base camp and get help. She was outnumbered and outgunned, but getting those soldiers to fight alongside her would even the odds. Besides, she knew absolutely nothing about how to disarm any of the explosives already placed inside the Carson Mine. McNichols and Troost could take care of the bombs, and she would retire Briggs and Ivers from the planet. Then, fitting Akando for a pine overcoat would be her gift to the world.

The mission parameters had changed. Making sure that Major Quinn returned safely to his daughter, Huan, had become a moral imperative.

Akando and his men had tried to kill her today.

Tomorrow, she was going to make them wish that they had.

It looks like you're finally out of excuses, Chief. Time to make your move. It's now or forever.

Gritting her teeth, Chenoa positioned her body towards the left log and jumped off the canoe. The moment her feet left the boat, the canoe twisted sideways and spun wildly down the river.

Winterhawk landed on the trunk, her feet sliding on the slippery surface of the log. Her hands managed to locate a hollow in the girth of the trunk, which she held on tightly to as the log hurtled towards the waterfall.

Holding onto the edge of the hollow as a stabilizer, Chenoa pulled herself to a kneeling position. She stared straight ahead. She watched with fascination as this section of the Malheur River disappeared over the falls before becoming part of the Wenaha River.

It was something one moment, then it would become something entirely else in the next. Sometimes, it takes only a second to change something forever.

Like what was happening now.

Not only could a one-hundred-foot drop into the water kill you, but she also had to make sure to launch her body clear of those volcanic rocks situated directly below the splash.

Feet first is the only way to survive this, amiga. Keep the knees locked. Leg muscles need to be clenched rigid. Heels pointed sharply down. Dropping that kind of distance, you'll completely crush your genitalia if your feet are spread even slightly on impact.

Chenoa gritted her teeth at the thought.

It gets worse, Chief. You'll need to hit the water perpendicular to the surface. Don't look down when you land. If you do, the water will smack your face hard enough to break your nose and knock you out. Keep your hands locked to your sides, too. They might wrench sideways against the water on impact. You could dislocate both of your shoulders and drown.

Winterhawk watched the log dip sharply over the edge and began to plummet, mist from the falls rising like spirits from the jagged basin below.

It was ride or die time.

Just as the log dipped to a full ninety-degrees over the Looking Glass Falls, Winterhawk let go of her grip. She exploded from her kneeling position; pushed out with her legs. Then, she was airborne. Still secured to her belt, the sling's dogbane cordage flapped noisily behind her as she fell.

The log tumbled straight down the waterfall. It crashed hard against the rocks and cracked into pieces.

Now beyond the reach of those rocks and falling directly over the deep pool, Winterhawk pointed her feet down. She kept her spine absolutely straight; hands locked together, and elbows and shoulders rigid.

Her impact with the water drove the air immediately from her lungs. Once fully submerged, she felt her limbs going limp; rigidity replaced with elasticity. Chenoa felt blackness enveloping her as she sunk deeper into the pool, water driving its way up through her nostrils.

You need to kick before you drown.

KICK!

With one final, last-ditch effort, she kicked hard. Chenoa felt herself being propelled through the water. Her lungs started to burn as she brought her head up, seeking the surface.

But her shoulder collided hard against sand and rocks. She had somehow gotten turned around in the water; had kicked down instead of up.

Panic gripped her as blackness splotched her vision.

There was a hard tugging coming from behind her. Remarkably, she felt her body being pulled up and backwards through the water. Her lungs had been fully depleted, and she felt herself reflexively gulping underwater for air.

Water rushed into her mouth; senses blackening as she spiraled into total unconsciousness.

CHAPTER 21

"Woe is mine."

Akando Winterhawk turned sharply from his view of the Malheur River. He wore the type of smile that looked like it had never met his face before. Joviality was a luxury tax he'd never bothered to pay.

The valley below the Baxter Mines was thickly clogged with black smoke from the multiple *Sulaco* explosions and the detonation of the *Lathos*.

It was Briggs who spoke first. He was the type of man who always did. "Fuck, man."

Akando cast a weary glance at him. "What's on your mind, Briggs? If you'll please excuse the exaggeration."

Ivers snorted loudly and kicked a smoldering dirigible plank as his frustration boiled over. He had a dried crescent of Ferro's brain matter dangling from his ratty beard. It jiggled with each raspy intake of breath.

"The front page," Briggs answered, his tobacco-stained teeth gleaming, "is that this bitch beat you like no man ever could. The redskin princess destroyed a blimp, took down over half our men, and then blew up a damn boat!"

"And stole our map," Ivers added, his pockmarked face twitching nervously.

"Burned it," Akando corrected.

"Burned is abso-fucking-right!" Briggs touched the tender flap of skin on his neck where the bullet had grazed it. "What she *did*, Akando, was torch all of our plans right down to the ground. Months, man; months of setting this fucking thing up. Now, everything is gone because of *her*."

"It's unfortunate," Akando admitted.

"Unfortunate." Briggs's grotesquely enlarged Adam's apple seemed to bob in tandem with his thundering heartbeat.

It was true. Chenoa had just burned them—badly.

The ordinance that had taken out the barge had been meant for President Roosevelt. But the truth was that Teddy's assassination had always been a decoy carrot meant to entice these pathetic Army mules. The explosion at the Owyhee Dam was planned to divert attention; a distraction from the main explosion at Elkhorn Peak. The flood was always going to be the main event.

Two years of careful planning was up in smoke now.

Akando bristled internally.

He'd underestimated the daughter of Jolon. He vowed that it wouldn't happen again.

Ivers nervously cleared his throat. "But she's dead now…right? I mean, who could survive something like that?" There was an annoying twinge of desperation in his voice now.

"It's possible."

"Possible?!" Ivers snorted with irritation. "Possible Winterhawk survived, or possible she didn't?"

"Neither outcome matters."

"It doesn't, Akando? It mattered plenty before."

"Soldiers understand when battle objectives change."

"Yeah. Right" Briggs gestured at the burning fragments of the *Sulaco*. "There's a tiny piece of what used to be Misciso down there that understands plenty."

Akando patiently shifted his gaze between Briggs and Ivers. He couldn't blame them for having this reaction. They'd just witnessed Chenoa pull off the most amazing displays of aerial acrobatics and death-defying escapes outside of Barnum & Bailey.

Truth be told, it *was* impressive. Chenoa wasn't at all what he'd been expecting. He had anticipated that her capture would have terrified her into total complacency. That after she'd found out about his deadly plans for blowing up President Roosevelt and drowning the Nez Perce, she would have begged him to spare their lives. He'd even fantasized about the moment she would have been on her knees, tearfully pleading with him to spare her life.

Instead, he had only awakened her rage.

Akando thought back to the question Ivers had asked him. If it was anyone else, he would have conclusively answered that she was dead. It was true that nobody should have been able to survive all of that. But as a warrior, Chenoa had just proven that she was her father's daughter.

And that troubled him a great deal.

Akando glanced up at the sun, seeing that it was past midday. They needed to begin the journey to the Carson Mines because, *if* Chenoa was still alive, she would be making her way to Elkhorn Peak right now. He understood that she would stop at nothing to save her people.

He would make sure she died trying.

But first, he needed to bolster his remaining team. Losing five men hadn't been part of the plan, which made Briggs and Ivers frightened when they needed to be strong.

After all, boom time was waiting for them.

He felt giddy about what he knew was coming.

Chief Joseph never had the backbone to stand up to the Europeans. He had lacked sufficient vision to lead his own people; brokered useless peace deals and honored phantom treaties. When Akando had displayed tactical foresight by bringing a bloody war right to the very doorstep of the white settlers, Joseph had punished him for his bravery. He had been banished forever from the Nez Perce; forsaken by even his own brother.

No home.

No family.

No mercy.

But after tomorrow, the memories of Jolon and Joseph would be sullied forever. The flood survivors would be looking for retribution; they would be crying out for a savior to lead them. That's when Akando would take his rightful place as the *real* Chief Winterhawk. He would lead his people out of squalor and shame, and rebuild them into the fierce warriors of the past.

And this time, there would be nobody left to stand in his way.

Akando laughed at the ease it had taken him to gain the confidence of these weak soldiers before him. It had taken so little to buy their disloyalty. The men had taken the money, and foolishly believed there was more gold to come.

In a way, Chenoa had done him a favor by killing so many of them already. It saved him from having to dispose of more corpses later. Thanks to her misguided antics, he only had to bury the hatchet on three buffoon skulls now.

But for the moment, he needed these men very much alive. Which meant that he somehow needed to regain the tenuous trust of Ivers and Briggs.

Woe is mine, Akando thought bitterly. He looked Briggs and Ivers up and down, a theatrical sneer forming on his lips.

Ivers shifted uncomfortably. "What are you looking at, Akando?"

"Snowmen."

Briggs frowned. "Snowmen?"

"I'm seeing soldiers who've gotten cold feet."

"Not a chance!" Ivers snapped. "It's just that we had a plan."

"Very true."

"And *she* altered it."

"Yes," Akando agreed heartily. "Chenoa derailed our objectives. She also took several of our key operatives permanently out of play. But while a military tactician attempts to think of every conceivable variable during combat, the unexpected can sometimes occur."

"You mean that you misjudged her," Ivers said.

"I underestimated."

"Underestimated." Briggs unleashed a sloppy grin. "I think it's more like somehow, somewhere, someone forgot to mention to us that Chenoa Winterhawk had the mythical ability to kill two stones with one bird. She's got skills that would make a wendigo shit its bed."

"No matter what she might have been before," Akando said carefully, "she is very much dead now."

"I believe that she's alive," Major Quinn interjected

Quinn hadn't spoken a word since Chenoa's escape. Akando was surprised to hear him chime in about this. He arched a quizzical eyebrow. "And how can you be so sure?"

"Qin Liangyu."

"Gesundheit," Briggs snickered.

Akando waved Briggs off with annoyance. "Please explain."

"When Huan was a little girl," Quinn continued, "she used to beg my wife to tell her the story of Qin Liangyu at bedtime. Li ended up repeating the tale so often that I memorized the damn thing."

"I'm captivated," Akando said. "Let's hear it."

"I can't really do it justice, not in the way Li always did. But then again, you three assholes don't really deserve justice; at least, not the storytelling kind."

Ivers loudly drummed his finger against the butt of his holstered Colt. "Big mouths can always be made bigger."

"Now, Ivers," Akando said, "come off the rimrock. Without the map, Major Quinn is now our only way to find that underground river. So, let's play nice."

Turning to Quinn, Akando clasped both hands together in an apologetic gesture. "Please continue, Major."

Quinn nodded. "Qin Liangyu was famous in China for fighting off the Qing invaders at the end of the Ming Dynasty, and crushing numerous other rebellions while—"

"Horse hockey!" Briggs threw up his hands in frustration. "This guy doesn't know the smell of dung from the taste of honey. If Quinn thinks our Nez Perce lightskirt is anything like this celestial Ming-a-ling, then he's really off his mental reservation."

Quinn grinned at him. "After killing all their warriors, Qin sent the Head General's severed testicles back to the Qing Emperor in a vase. She had attached a note: 'He wasn't man enough.' "

Ivers clapped mockingly. "Great story. Would you mind telling us what it means?"

"After Chenoa Winterhawk cuts off your balls," Quinn answered, "you'll have to crawl up the asshole of a chicken if you ever want to get laid again."

Ivers and Briggs exchanged looks of utter astonishment.

Akando shook his head. "I need to remind you of something very important, Major Quinn. The map you brought us as a bargaining tool for the life of your daughter? That's the only reason you're still breathing right now."

"You must be suffering from selective amnesia," Quinn said. "Chenoa burned the map, remember? I don't have it."

"Then you'd better damn well imagine it," Akando growled. Spinning around, he bore his gaze into Briggs and Ivers. "Enough talk! Let's saddle up. There's a lot of hard miles to cover before we have to kill a lot of soft people."

CHAPTER 22

Elkhorn Peak
Blue Mountain Range
Eastern Oregon, 1905

When First Sergeant Shane McNichols grinned, it looked like a cadaver had just sprung back to life on the mortician's table. It was the way his waxy skin stretched taut over his high cheekbones, almost as if invisible rubber bands were being pushed to their very limits somewhere inside his skull. The slapdash greyish tone of his flesh certainly didn't help offset things. It had the appearance of being spread on by a drunk with a broken spackle and a bad attitude.

The high-pitched cackling laughter emitting from McNichols could barely be heard above the coughing engine of the Harley-Davidson Model 1. He was hunched high over the handlebars, head dipped low as he skidded the motorcycle precariously across a crooked trail of volcanic rocks.

"Do you see it?!" McNichols yelled excitedly into the air, the wind whipping his words behind him with the velocity of a flag flapping in a Nebraska tornado.

"See what?!" First Sergeant Bryce Troost was following close behind McNichols as they navigated the terrain at the base of the Blue Mountains.

Both men were "sappers" within the Army Corps of Engineers, a term given to combat engineers trained in the art of specialized terrain warfare.

They got the sap part right, Troost thought bitterly.

He sure as hell hadn't graduated with honors from West Point just to end up at the ass-end of the Pacific Northwest sharing latrines with higher learning rejects who couldn't even spell MIT.

"You gotta open those damn peepers!" McNichols shouted at him again. The easily excitable First Sargeant pulled hard on his motorcycle, whipping it around a sharp bend in the trail and shooting down a rough incline.

Although he had better success with navigating his own Model 1 across the uneven terrain than McNichols, Troost considered the whole trip wrought with peril because of the very machines themselves.

What might be a sedentary excursion on horseback turned into a wide-awake nightmare when taking that same trip on these motorcycles.

But McNichols had, of course, insisted on taking them.

Built in 1903, the Harley-Davidson Model 1 had been fitted with a single-cylinder engine that featured a 405cc displacement, capable of reaching 50 miles-per-hour. The suspension system, however, could still be best described as extremely primitive.

Which was also an apt description for McNichols himself, Troost thought. *The man was a certified genius when it came to irrigations and excavations, but getting an opportunity to play with toys always turned him into an infantile cretin.*

While a combat engineer can be any enlisted rank from Private Pay Grade E-2 to Master First Sergeant Pay Grade E-8, the soldiers needed to first hold a Military Occupational Specialty. For McNichols and Troost, their MOS happened to be Irrigational Regiment.

In saloon settings where females were within earshot, McNichols liked to explain their duties more simplistically: "We're damn good with dams!"

Their most recent success was the construction of the Owyhee Dam in eastern Oregon. The entire build had been the first he'd ever encountered in the pacific northwest without violence. There had been some angry pushback from the local indigenous population being relocated, but Troost couldn't blame their animosity one bit.

He knew that some of those tribes—particularly the Nez Perce—had been forcefully relocated multiple times over the last 50 years. To make things worse, these tribes had been made promises in exchange for their peaceful cooperation. The trouble was, not a single one of those government promises (like electricity) had been kept for any of the tribes.

It was a horrible thing to see happen to these people; especially all over again. He'd even met a Nez Perce elder once, whose tales of loss haunted him. But Troost wasn't a politician. He was just a standard issue soldier who knew how to follow orders. And most recently, those orders had entailed setting up a small base camp near the Wenaha River.

He and McNichols were to meet a small group travelling to the region by dirigible. One of them was in possession of a valuable map showing the location of a large water source inside the Carson Mines. But neither the map or the dirigible had ever arrived.

Earlier in the day, after waiting hours for the group, McNichols had suggested going to Elkhorn Peak themselves. "We can leave a fire going in the camp," he had explained. "It'll scare off any animals that'll come sniffing around for food. It's only 20-miles to the mine. If we take the Harleys, we'll be there and back before dusk."

After that comment, Troost had glanced with uncertainty over at the pair of motorcycles. He was still finding it hard to get used to them.

Harley-Davidson had entered into a production deal with U.S. Army in 1904 to supply vehicles abroad. It was Brigadier General Alexander Mackenzie of the Army Corps of Engineers who'd ensured that combat engineers had access to several while building dams in Oregon and Washington.

"And what about the dirigible?" Troost had asked.

"If they're still enroute, they can find our camp easy enough."

"I don't know..."

"Come on, Bryce! Essayon! Essayon!"

That was the infamous U.S. Army Engineer motto. Essayon was French for, "Let us try!" It was a call to adventure that McNichols knew that he wouldn't be able back away from; at least, not with the complete package of his manhood still intact.

Let us try, indeed.

Sneaky bastard.

Hours later, Troost now found himself *trying* to maintain control of the motorcycle as he hurtled behind his partner along the unforgiving terrain. He knew that Elkhorn Peak was close; he'd seen it pushing upwards from the forest line several miles back. But after several twists and turns through the dense woods, he had lost sight of it all over again.

What was beginning to concern him was the roundtrip distance from the camp to the Carson Mines. It would be dusk soon, and the woods were absolutely unforgiving once nightfall landed. Aside from their heavy jackets and sidearms, neither one of them were prepared for those kinds of conditions.

Then, there was the matter of the Harleys themselves. The motors used a vacuum-operated overhead intake valves and mechanically actuated side exhausts, but it was a battery supplying juice to the ignition. To even start the cycles was a formidable task because of—

"Look, Bryce; lookie-lookie-lou!"

The cry from McNichols got Troost's immediate attention. He snapped his head up from over the curve of the handlebars. The bikes had just powered over a sharp rise. The full expanse of Elkhorn Peak stretched out before them.

A few ghostly remnants of the Carson Mining Company lay strewn around near base of the peak. Abandoned buildings, hydraulic pit elevator, and a placer water cannon attached to a steam boiler and large storage tank.

The yawning entrance of the mine itself was pitch-black, with a long stretch of rusty minecar tracks running down its gullet. Both men steered their motorcycles towards it. Disembarking in tandem, they set the bikes carefully down on their sides. Neither man took their eyes off of the mouth of the mine as they walked slowly towards it.

Troost suddenly felt an odd sensation. His skin prickled with gooseflesh, as if a cold wind had just caressed his arms. He looked to the trees surrounding the area. None of the branches were moving.

There was no wind. And yet—

"I felt something, too." McNichols stood right beside him, but his voice sounded impossibly distant. It was as if the words themselves had tried to remain hidden; like they hadn't wanted to really be spoken.

"What is it, Shane?"

McNichols answered with a confused head shake. His eyes roamed across the rocky crevices that pockmarked the area around the front entrance of the mine.

"Something's been watching us," McNichols whispered ominously. His hand drifted towards his gun belt; fingers tented on the stock of his weapon.

Troost took an involuntary step back, eyes scanning the area. The sun had already sunken considerably in the sky. The western edges of the Blue Mountains appeared to be softly cradling it. Soon enough, the sun would disappear behind the mountain range. "It's almost dusk. I think we'd better get back before—"

"There is...*something*," McNichols interrupted. His waxen features glistened with a fresh sheen of sweat. His eyes were slightly bulged out of their sockets now, looking like overripe grapes ready to turn brown in the heat.

"It's just animals," Troost said. "This whole place's been abandoned for years. Who knows what's made its home up in those mines by now?"

"Right." McNichols slowly nodded. "Who knows?"

"We're just spooking ourselves," Troost said. He wanted to sound convincing, but the slight tremble in his voice betrayed those intentions. "Let's act like the Great Shepherd and get the flock out of here."

The wind was really starting up now. It was coming in from the east. Troost could feel it tussling gently with his hair; heard the faint whispering of it in the nearby branches.

It also brought with it an unusual smell. It was a primal, pungent odor. Troost scrunched his nose as he inhaled it. It was an overwhelmingly animalistic scent. "What is that—?"

McNichols darted forward. "I see something in there, Bryce!" He moved fast towards the mine entrance.

Troost squinted. He could make out something in there, too. Just inside the mouth of the mine. It looked like something trying to press itself against the shadows of the cavern walls.

Troost took off running after his partner. "Shane! Wait!"

McNichols ignored him, pulling out his sidearm. He ran into the mine entrance with reckless abandon as the inky blackness swallowed him up.

Yanking his own firearm free, Troost followed after him.

What he saw placed just inside the mouth of the mine stopped him cold in his tracks right beside his partner.

McNichols lowered his gun. "What the hell is going on here, Bryce?"

Troost shook his head in confusion. "Dunno."

They were both staring at a massive A-car. In the largest mining operations, the A-car was used to transport the biggest of loads. It was a one-ton dump car used to move broken rock and ore from out of the mines. But seeing it still sitting on the tracks after all these years wasn't what had bothered them.

It was what had been placed inside the A-car that was so troubling.

There were two 50-lb barrels stashed inside of it. Each barrel had been marked as being the property of the U.S. Army. There was one word painted on each of them: NTO.

"NTO," McNichols muttered with astonishment..

Nitrotriazolone was a highly explosive material that had only recently been discovered and utilized by the military. NTO was extremely sensitive to heat, friction, and impact. Combat engineers considered it the most dangerous and volatile substance on earth.

What were two canisters of it doing *here*?

"Something ain't right," Troost said.

"No," McNichols fully agreed. "Whatever somebody is planning to do here, they're going to do it with a bang. There's enough NTO in those canisters to put a hole in the world."

Troost stepped closer to the A-car. He moved around to the rear of the car so he could get a closer look at things. Glancing around, his brow was furrowed with concern as he noticed something else.

A third 50-lb barrel of NTO had been set on the ground. It had been placed away from the cart, and was resting just inside the mine entrance. Casting his gaze further down the cavern wall, he saw an older-model 200-lb oak mine cart sitting off the rails. Its wheels had been stripped for parts long ago. Just beyond that was total blackness of the mine itself. In the eerie stillness, he thought he could hear the faint sound of rushing waters.

Troost's stomach clenched.

What kind of unauthorized operation had they just stumbled upon? The Carson Mines had been closed for decades. The rumor of this miner's map showing the possible location of an underground river was intriguing to say the least. The possibility of an undiscovered water source here was fraught with potential for the arid farmlands directly to the east of here. It was no wonder the Army Corps of Engineers had placed such a high premium on investigating its validity. Tapping into a river here would be a huge victory for the Land Reclamation Act.

But you wouldn't want to use NTO anywhere near an underground river, particularly one buried deep within a mine. It was too powerful and unpredictable. The slightest miscalculation could potentially unleash an uncontrollable river and flood the wrong valley.

Troost remembered where the Nez Perce tribe had relocated within ten miles of Elkhorn Peak. They were now living on the banks of the Wenaha River, which wouldn't be able to handle a bifurcation event if it was braided with this underground river. If that were to happen, the damage to the land would be catastrophic; the massive loss of life inconceivable.

The animalistic stench had returned. It filled the air with a pungent odor so thick that he nearly gagged. "What do you think that awful smell is?" Troost asked disgustedly. "Something die in here, or what?"

He was greeted with silence. Turning, Troost stepped back around the A-car.

The mine entrance was empty. He was alone. McNichols was gone.

"Shane? Where the hell are you?"

He saw blood splattered all across the floor. It had pooled beside the cart. Freshly spilled, it dripped methodically off the tracks like tap water from a leaky faucet.

Troost frantically unholstered his weapon, heart hammering. "Shane!"

A flash of movement. Far right edge of the mine. A massive creature, thickly matted with fur and cords of rippling muscle. It dragged the prone body of McNichols out of the mine with astonishing speed.

Troost blinked at the image of what he thought he had just seen. It was impossible, but that creature had been standing upright. He could have sworn that it had also been walking.

NO.

The shadows and his overactive imagination were playing some kind of morbid trick. The size of the animal he saw could only have been a grizzly. That bear must have made its den right here; it had been waiting for them.

That would explain the pungent smell, and the feeling of being watched.

He looked again at all the blood on the ground. His partner was severely injured; possibly even dead. If he was still alive, he had to help him.

"Shane!"

Troost took off running. He careened out of the mine at top speed, banking hard to the right. He had his gun arm stretched out in front of him, eyes dancing fearfully in all directions as he ran.

There was no sign of the bear, but plenty of signs of blood.

Troost kept running, following the trail of blood. It led him towards the southwest corner of the abandoned mining camp. He raced passed the placer mining water cannon, bolting sharply around the steam boiler.

The massive hydraulic pit elevator loomed just ahead. The blood trail ended right at its edge.

Troost slid to a stop along the precipice of the fifty-foot-deep basin stretched out behind him. It was empty now, but at one time it had been filled with enough water to continually power the steam engines that ran the boiler and the placer hose cannon.

Directly in front of him, the hydraulic elevator loomed upwards two stories off the ground. Troost swung his gun around, frantically searching for signs of—.

Sudden movement from above.

He looked up with shock.

It was McNichols coming straight down at him.

But not his whole body, it was only—

His decapitated head.

Troost wasn't fast enough to react before the head smashed onto his upturned face. He felt his own nose break with the impact; heard the distinct crunching of bone as McNichols's head balanced perfectly on his upturned face.

Troost dropped his gun in shock, His hands swatted the severed head from off his face and threw it to the ground.

"What the FUCK?!" Troost screamed. He was disorientated; brain spinning with confusion. His broken nose throbbed with immense pain.

His gun! He needed to get his weapon before—

McNichols's headless body suddenly fell at his feet with a wallop, landing directly over his dropped gun. Then, an earth-shaking growl reverberated through the abandoned camp.

Troost snapped his head up towards the terrifying sound, whimpering as a wide-awake nightmare filled his entire vision.

What he saw looking down at him wasn't a bear.

Troost recognized it from the legends he'd long heard. Whispers from Indians about a terrifying myth about the Wen'ey'ti, an ancient mountain creature who roamed the woods and devoured human flesh.

Troost lost control of his bladder, feeling the warmth spreading across his pants.

High above him, the Wen'ey'ti had straddled the side of the two-story pit elevator like a massive gargoyle. Its crimson eyes were focused downwards; maw stretched open to expose rows of jagged teeth. Large globs of parotid secretory dripped steadily out of its mouth.

The monster was salivating.

Troost staggered backwards, spinning his body around. He caught a glimpse of the motorcycles laying on the ground thirty feet away. If he got to the Harley, not even this creature would be fast enough to catch him. It was his only chance.

Troost exploded into a sprint, arms pumping wildly.

He glanced once with panic behind him, but the monster was still perched on the top of the elevator shaft. It was eyeing him with curious indifference.

Troost was closing in fast on the motorcycles. He was only a few strides away. He was close enough to detect faint fumes from the Harley's exhaust. Just another few steps and—

A massive shadow appeared on the outcropping of the mountainside that he had been running parallel with. Troost saw a quick flash of fur before the shape launched itself high into the air.

The ground shook as a second Wen'ey'ti landed directly behind him,

Troost screamed as he felt himself being lifted upwards by the creature. He heard a vicious snapping, then felt a multitude of crunches as dozens of his bones were instantly pulverized.

He had the odd sensation of being folded; excruciating pain being blanketed by absolute numbness. His body had just been folded in half; spinal column broken.

Troost was spun around like a plate on the monster's claws. He screamed as he watched the creature pull the lower half of his body into its mouth. The Wen'ey'ti savagely bit deeply down into his groin area, head yanking ferociously backwards; loops of intestines were impaled on its teeth.

Troost mercifully died as the monster began to ravenously slurp the fluid-filled sac inside of his spleen.

CHAPTER 23

Coldness. Darkness. Wetness.

Chenoa was trapped inside a raging storm cloud. Her body was shackled to lightning, and her heart chained to thunder. She'd grown wings and had soared to an impossible altitude before dark clouds had imprisoned her. Savage winds battered her body. The stinging rain was blinding; the pain intensified until it felt like a needle pricking relentlessly against her fluttering eyelid.

The storm cloud began tightening around her as she flew blindly in circles.

There's always a way through; always a way out. People die because the path ends, and they believe there's no way forward. Warriors understand that when the path does end, that's when you stand your ground and fight. Are you listening, Chief?! FIGHT!

A slit suddenly opened up within the ominous cloud, emitting a sliver of sunlight into the blackness. Still flying, Chenoa banked sharply and soared through the opening. She immediately felt the rejuvenating warmth of the sun. She could feel the sunlight moving down her face.

But something was wrong.

The light felt hot, sticky...and bloody.

Winterhawk's eyes snapped open with a start.

She gasped loudly.

The crawdad perched on her cheek felt the movement, momentarily stopping its skittish journey across her face. It held her right eyelid in one pincer, the skin stretched dangerously taut. It had already dug into the edge of an eyebrow, a rivulet of blood dripping down from the gouged flesh.

She was sprawled out on her back, jagged stones pressed up against her body. One of her legs was in the water, while the other was stretched out on the sandy embankment. She couldn't feel any broken bones, but her entire body ached fiercely.

The crawdad pulled hard against the eyelid. It was about to gorge on her eyes.

Chenoa slammed both fists together, satisfied with the crunching noise the crawdad made between her hands. The pincer slowly opened as the creature died, releasing her eyelid like a reluctant child returning a pre-dinner cookie after a scolding.

She angrily flung the crustacean aside. It bounced unceremoniously across a bed of rocks before sinking into the Wenaha River. She turned her neck, seeing the Looking Glass Falls in the distance behind her.

Chenoa frowned.

She must have drifted down the river for a short while after blacking out, but how had she gotten out of the water? The last thing she remembered was becoming disorientated after the fall, then hitting her head on the floor of the river before—

Being yanked backwards beneath the water.

Chenoa slowly sat up, the muscles in her body screaming with revolt. Glancing down, she noticed that the Shepherd's sling fastened to her belt had been pulled unusually taught. It stretched out to its full two feet of length as if it had been caught on something.

Glancing around, she saw that it had.

The log she had ridden over the waterfall had landed on the rocks and splintered into two halves. One piece had remained lodged beneath the falls, while the other had been shot further down the river like a cannonball.

The trailing end of the Shepherd's sling had caught one of the wood knots on that half, effectively pulling her out of the water as it passed her. Then, the log had been stopped by a bend in the riverbed. It had slammed into the embankment with considerable force and flipped onto the shore, dragging her unconscious body to safety.

The Shepherd's sling had miraculously saved her life again.

People have had it wrong for centuries, Chief. You can forget all about rabbit's feet and four-leaf clovers. It's slingshots that'll bring you luck...unless you happen to be a Philistine warrior, of course,

Winterhawk climbed unsteadily to her feet. The river had completely drenched her clothes. She shivered with the cold as she disengaged the sling from the trunk. This time, she secured it around her wrist.

She looked around in an attempt to get her bearings. The sun had already sunk below the trees, which meant dusk was fast approaching.

Turning to the east, she could also see Elkhorn Peak jutting into the sky fifteen miles off in the distance. She knew that Akando and his group of traitors would already be navigating Qualen Pass, and would reach the mines by noon tomorrow. If she pushed forward now, she could make it there before dawn.

But Winterhawk needed to find a way to get warm. With as wet and cold as she was, she wouldn't last an hour after the sun went down. Hypothermia would take her down quicker than a bullet.

She faintly smelled something.

Smoke.

Turning, she scanned the horizon until she saw it. Three miles away. The white wisps of smoke coming from the northwest. It was a campfire. Chenoa recalled that McNichols and Troost had set up a base camp several miles from the Wenaha River. This had to be them.

Wrapping her arms around herself for warmth, Winterhawk began walking purposefully in the direction of the smoke.

CHAPTER 24

Night had descended by the time Chenoa reached the campfire.

While she had badly misjudged how quickly she'd be able to navigate her way through the forest after enduring the punishment she'd put her body through today, what she wasn't mistaken about was the campfire itself.

It was the base camp for the combat engineers.

After stealthily surveying the area from behind a lightning-toppled tree, Winterhawk had ascertained that Troost and McNichols were not around. She figured that they had probably gone out searching for the *Lathos*.

Convinced that there wasn't an immediate threat, Winterhawk entered the base camp. She began looking around.

A massive tent had been erected along the southern perimeter. There was a supply wagon and a tethered horse on the northern side. Her stomach jabbed with hunger pains as she noticed a pot of stew suspended from an iron rack above the fire.

Ignoring her growling stomach, she decided to approach the horse first.

Chenoa could see that the animal was well taken care of. The buckets of water and grain left out for him had barely been touched. The horse eyed her with a calm suspicion, but allowed her to gently stroke his nose.

"Where did those men go off to? Can you tell me?" Unfortunately for her, the horse decided to play coy. He didn't answer.

Leaving the horse, Winterhawk made her way to the tent. Inside there was blankets, geological equipment, and cases of rations. She gratefully grabbed one of the thickest blankets in the pile. As she turned to leave, something stashed in the back corner of the tent caught her eye. It was a Boss & Co. SxSxS 16-bore triple-barrel shotgun.

It made sense that the combat engineers would have such a heavy-duty weapon with them. Fending off bear and cougar attacks was a job hazard for members of the Army Corps of Engineers stationed in the remote wilderness.

As Chenoa hefted it up, she saw that a sheepskin strap had been attached to the stock for ease of carry. There was also a bandolier of specialized shells on the ground beside it. And next to that, a battery-powered Edison lamp.

She also picked up the bandolier and the headlamp.

This was a good haul.

Winterhawk left the tent and approached the campfire. She set everything carefully down, then moved closer to the simmering pot of stew. The rich aroma of the meat and vegetables was nearly intoxicating.

Grabbing a bowl, she dipped it into the pot and scooped out a generous portion. Taking one of the spoons, she sat down and began devouring the food.

While eating, she wondered again about McNichols and Troost. It was dark now, and they had yet to return. While she had originally assumed they'd gone searching for the *Lathos*, she now thought it was more likely they'd gone ahead to scout out Elkhorn Peak for themselves.

But if that was the case, why hadn't they returned? Had those men also been compromised? Was it possible that Akando had gotten to them, too? They could be hiding out in those woods right now, ready to ambush her the moment she let her guard down.

Setting down the empty bowl, Winterhawk pushed all of those thoughts aside. The meal had been nourishing, but sheer exhaustion was now catching up to her. What she needed was to get warm, and to get a few hours of sleep.

She stood up and made her way around the campfire. She happened to look down, seeing that the flickering firelight had just revealed something she had missed earlier.

Tire tracks.

She bent down and examined them. They were motorcycle tracks. Two pairs of them leading out of the camp in the direction of Elkhorn Peak. She touched the indentations with her fingers. She guessed the tracks were several hours old.

Chenoa slowly stood up. Having motorcycles would certainly explain why they had left their horse behind. And should McNichols or Troost return to the camp later tonight, the noise of those machines would alert her while they were still miles away.

She felt her eyes burning with the need for sleep.

Returning to the campfire, Chenoa carefully spread out the blanket as close to the heat as was safely possible. Placing the shotgun on the ground beside it, she stretched out on the blanket.

She gazed into the flickering flames.

Years ago, her father had warned her about Akando. He'd made her promise that if she ever saw him again, she wouldn't hesitate to kill him. That moment had already passed, but she was getting a second chance soon.

It saddened her to think of the life that Akando had led. He could have followed in the very same footsteps as his brother. He and Jolon could have lived as family heroes instead of dying as tribal enemies.

But that was the underlying power of decisions. There are some things that, once set into motion, cannot be easily undone. Akando had made his bed; he'd burned his bridges. While nothing would ever change that, the reality was that he was her own flesh-and-blood. With her mother and father gone, this hateful and vengeful man was her last remaining family. And now, she was going to have to kill him before he murdered hundreds of innocent people.

His death was necessary.

He'd brought it upon himself.

That didn't make things right. It just...*was*.

That's the way the mop flops, Chief. Choices have consequences in this life; and those same consequences dictate things in the next life, too. Sooner or later, everybody pays what they owe.

She stared deeper into the fire, watching as a pair of flames appeared to be dueling with one another. Even in something as innocuous as a campfire there was a representative of the smoldering duality of this world.

Chenoa felt the wound from the crawdad throbbing on the side of her temple. She touched a finger to it, tracing the pattern of dried blood.

Sonsela had chosen love, but had received death. Hadn't what happened to him also changed the course of her own life? She hadn't chosen that love to die; yet, it had, just the same. On that awful day, grief had singled her out to be its unwilling participant.

She had understood how, but never fully understood why.

Why did it have to happen, amiga? Easy: because of today. *That's the reason behind everything. Things seem inexplicably complicated until you come to terms with the fact that all our trails somehow intersect. The circumstances that appear completely out of our control might very well be those times when the Great Spirit is molding things because of today. You were placed here— exactly here, exactly now—because today you are needed to save your people. What's past has passed, Chief. It couldn't have happened any other way.*

Chenoa wiped tears from her cheeks.

Knowing it was destiny didn't make the pain any easier to endure. Fate didn't take away the fear. Accepting she was chosen didn't remove the crushing loneliness.

Sooner or later, everybody pays what they owe. Her father's words repeated again in her head.

Chenoa didn't remember closing her eyes, but sleep welcomed her like an old friend. It had a kind embrace.

CHAPTER 25

The mind can convince itself of anything. There's an inherent justification to the sort of half-truths that motivate the circumvention of personal guilt. We readily prescribe blame to others, but very rarely to ourselves.

That's because, Akando Winterhawk thought, *we are always the victim in our own stories.*

He also understood that memories work in much the same fashion. We magnify every slight ever made against us, but we have muddy clarity whenever recalling those times when others claim grievances about our own behaviors.

That's why scars have always been the great equalizer. The permanent marks on the body don't offer agendas. They are the impartial witnesses of pain. Scars bear testimony to things endured. They don't need embellishment because their unspoken words cannot be contradicted. Scars bridge the gap between victim and victimhood in a way that nothing else can.

The scars we carry are what truly set us apart.

Akando imperceptibly shifted from his cross-legged position in front of the campfire. He had been staring up at the canopy of stars stretched out across the sky like a jeweled blanket. His thoughts hadn't been on the glories of the cosmos, but rather on the suffering he'd endured countless times under the unblinking gaze of Heaven itself.

The Creator had promised a reward for those who suffer. If that was truly the case, then he'd be expecting an inheritance of riches larger than that of King Solomon.

His scars were incapable of lying. He had them crisscrossed along the flesh of his chest and back; some made from bullets, but most created from steel. He found little comfort knowing he bore scars while those who inflicted them—hundreds of men and women—never walked again.

Death followed closely behind him like an obedient dog.

And he was its master.

Akando brought his gaze down from the stars, focusing instead on the flames dancing drunkenly before him. He wondered if the fires moved so jovially in Hell, whether they performed jigs during torment to keep the demons entertained.

He briefly turned his head; he didn't need to see when he could clearly hear. His own hell on earth were in a deep slumber on the outer edges of the camp. The snorts and snores emanating from Ivers and Briggs ricocheted off one another like poorly timed tennis volleys.

Major Quinn was the only silent one among them.

His bold outburst at Baxter Mines had surprised them. Afterwards, he kept to himself. The man was mulling over possibilities and probabilities, and coming up short with each new scenario that had run through his head. He had obviously resigned himself to the fact that he would lead them to the location of the underground river, or run the risk of forcing his daughter into the role of harlot.

Quinn's considerable girth was now spread out on a blanket, his back to Akando as he slept. It was a symbolic gesture; childish, but effective.

Akando paid the man no heed. He was weak to begin with, even more so that he had allowed Chenoa to take the map from him with such ease. If it had been so valuable to him and to the welfare of his daughter, Quinn should have fought her to the death for it.

Instead, he allowed himself to be battered and scratched.

Pathetic.

Akando couldn't wait to put the man out of his misery.

HOURS EARLIER, THE ragtag group had embarked on their journey through the Qualen Pass on horseback. Aside from their weapons and the barest of provisions, they had travelled light.

While it was only 20 miles from the Baxter Mines to their destination at Elkhorn Peak, he hadn't wanted to navigate the terrain in the darkness. The decision to make camp was made once they had reached the Wenaha River. It had been the first time the ragtag group had actually agreed on anything.

Akando had urged the men to get some rest because of the arduous day ahead. Surprisingly, there hadn't been any pushback about it. The day's grueling events had finally caught up with them.

After building a fire and having dinner, the soldiers had packed themselves in for the night. They'd been fast asleep a few minutes later.

But even when they were awake, men like this were still very much asleep. When these types of soldiers traded their politics for cash, they slumbered on their principles. And when they dreamed, it was only about money.

True ideology was the only real priceless commodity in the world these days. It couldn't be traded, and it couldn't be bought. It had the power to bring nations together, and it had the power to rip families apart.

Especially brothers.

Growing up, Jolon and Akando had never been as close as brothers ought to be. The death of their father should have bound them together; instead, it had created a gulf that seemed to widen with each passing year.

Especially when Jolon agreed to be Chief Joseph's puppet, enlisting in the U.S. Cavalry and betraying the Nez Perce. Elders protested, but Joseph's empty promises smothered their cries.

The majority of the tribe had always acquiesced to his foolish leadership.

When Akando had refused to grovel to the Europeans and had taken the bloody war straight into the very bedrooms of the settlers, there wasn't a single person within the Nez Perce who had rallied around him in support.

Not even his own brother.

Jolon and Chief Joseph punished him severely for his so-called war of attrition. He'd been banished forever from the Nez Perce; his name stricken from the Winterhawk lineage. For over three decades, he had never returned home.

Until now.

A generation within his tribe had passed. Chief Joseph and Jolon were now dead. Ironically, *he* was the one who was still very much alive.

Akando thought again about his plan for tomorrow.

After the flooding, he'd convince the survivors that it had been President Roosevelt and the Army Corps of Engineers who had orchestrated their destruction. That they, and *only* they, had purposefully unleashed the underground river to drown them all like rats. Then, he would become Chief Winterhawk.

Akando briefly wondered if his father's spirit would approve of the flood. The thought quickly flickered, then died. Vengeance was the only path when hatred became its own logic.

He then pictured the survivors, drenched and broken, looking to him to be their savior. He'd stoke their rage, and forge them into becoming warriors that would reclaim their land. *This flood will baptize them*, he thought, *and Joseph's ghost will be forever cast aside.*

Akando was pulled away from his thoughts. He sensed eyes boring into the back of his skull. There was something tangible hanging in the air now; heavy with thought, reeking of urgency. He recognized it for what it was: opportunity.

Akando cocked his head, not turning around. Instead, he kept his gaze focused on the campfire. "I gather you're awake now, Major Quinn."

There was a sharp intake of breath, followed by absolute stillness.

In the outer fringes of the camp, the noisy slumber of Ivers and Briggs sounded off loudly. Akando waved a hand dismissively at them. "I'm in my own Garden of Gethsemane. Those men couldn't stay up and watch with me for even an hour."

"Am I to believe that you had been praying, then?" Quinn scoffed.

The voice coming from behind him was actually much closer than Akando had anticipated. The big man had moved much more stealthily than he would have thought possible.

"My cup of suffering is enduring the stupidity of others," Akando answered. "Take that rock, for instance."

There was a lengthy pause. "What rock?"

Akando sighed with obvious irritation. "The triangular-shaped rock you kept staring at throughout dinner. The one you clumsily pulled close to your blanket with your boot earlier while feigning difficulty standing. The rock that you're holding now."

Quinn's hand trembled before the rock slipped from his hand, thudding softly into the dirt. "You see a lot for a man who sees nothing at all."

Akando swiveled his torso around on the ground until his back was now against the campfire. There was a hint of amusement in his eyes as he stared at his captive.

"What was the plan, Major Quinn? You were going to drive that rock deep into my skull; then, heave my body into the fire. By the time my screams of pain woke those two slumbering imbeciles, you would have commandeered one of the horses and galloped your way to freedom."

"Something like that." Quinn was standing a few feet away. Sweat seemed to be glistening from every pore in his face. He was hesitating, unsure of his next move.

"You wanted to kill me," Akando said.

"I wanted to try."

Akando plucked a branch from the ground, tossing it into the fire. Sparks erupted, casting jagged shadows across Quinn's sweating face. "Hesitation is the greatest weakness," Akando said, his voice low as the flames roared.

"You would certainly know all about that," Quinn said. "Your hesitation with Chenoa today was masked by foolish bravado. You were too busy delivering campaign speeches when you should have been letting your actions be doing the talking. It'll cost you plenty, Akando."

"If listening to you pontificate like a schoolmarm who just bit into a worm-filled apple is the price, then I've already paid it." He gestured to the ground. "Sit."

Frowning, Quinn reluctantly sat back down on his blanket.

Akando tossed him an appreciative glance. "I actually admire you, Major Quinn. You've steadily risen in the ranks of your profession. You have a lovely daughter; you *had* a beautiful wife. Those are all things in this life that one should aspire to. Sadly, people learn too late that life is built only on memories. To harbor regrets in the end, that's the real hell on earth."

"Do you feel regrets, Akando? It's not too late; it never is. Give yourself up. I'll do everything in my power to make sure that you're treated fairly."

"Spoken like a true liar."

"I assure you, the United States government would—"

"Hang me. You know it, and I know it. Must I remind you, that this same government of yours has already threatened to deport your own half-breed daughter? Your people care very much about themselves, but very little of those who might be shaded differently."

"The entire Civil War contradicts that statement."

"Yet, the genocide against my own people affirms it."

"Are you referring to the same tribe that you're now planning on murdering? Is drowning innocent people how you make restitutions for their past treatment?"

"I have my reasons," Akando answered coldly.

"So did Lucifer."

"The Devil sought to dethrone God. My ambitions aren't nearly as grandiose. I'm going to destroy legacies—both of Chief Joseph and of my own brother—before leading the Nez Perce into a bloody rebellion against those who have taken everything from us."

"That's madness."

"The people in Noah's age undoubtedly felt the same way when they first cast their eyes upon the Ark. But it was a holy flood that cleansed the earth, and it will be a flood that offers rebirth to my people. After it's all over, I'll be there to lead them out of the wilderness and to the Promised Land of my choosing."

"You claim to fight for your people," Quinn said, "yet you'd drown all of them for your own personal glory."

"When the Creator points the way, His hand also clears the path."

Quinn smiled thinly. "My late wife once told me that the Chinese have an old proverb: A clay figure fears the rain the way a liar fears the truth."

Akando narrowed his eyes. "There's also an old saying among my people: Those who lie down with dogs, stand up with fleas."

"Touché," Quinn muttered.

Akando thought back to his encounters with Alvinston.

The old man had certainly been many things. He'd been a teenage Confederate soldier during the Great Rebellion. After the Civil War ended, he had joined the Knights of the Golden Circle and continued the war effort against the North. Alvinston had even secretly buried the monies he'd been skimming before his capture.

In fact, everything he had confessed to Akando at Fort Alcatraz that night he'd died had been the truth.

Everything except one small detail.

It turned out that the amount of loot he had stolen was equivalent to the power of the Knights of the Golden Circle themselves: exaggerated. After Akando had dug it up, he hadn't unearthed several million dollars; just a fraction of that sum. But it was more than enough to begin putting this plan into motion.

Then, he needed to assemble a band of conspirators.

Akando had encountered Briggs first. The man had harbored such a hatred and resentment for the domestic policies of President Roosevelt it acted like a magnet that brought him into contact with other like-minded sordid military characters.

Akando had divvied up Alvinston's loot among them, promising to double it when his mission had been accomplished. The fools had been so greedy that they'd believed his every word. He'd never met a soldier who couldn't be persuaded by the promise of gold.

Until now.

Major Quinn was an idealist and an opportunist, but he wasn't a traitor. That he was also shrewd and clever was a minor annoyance that would soon be rectified by the edge of a knife. The soldier was a patriot who would never take a bribe, but he wasn't beyond bartering for his own life for the sake of his daughter's. And that was going to cost him everything he had.

Akando was pulled away from his thoughts again as he noticed Major Quinn carefully studying him. "I'm going to die tomorrow, aren't I?"

Quinn's eyes momentarily drifted. He recalled Li's final moments. Her cough had rattled as she handed him the map, its edges worn from her father's hands. "This is Huan's future," she'd had whispered, her eyes fierce despite the sickness.

Akando was staring at him. "We all die someday, don't we?"

"You're going to kill me after I show you where the river is." Quinn rubbed a hand across his mouth, wiping spittle from his lips. "Tonight, right here and right now, I need you to understand something. I'm not going to cry for mercy down in that mine, and I'm not going to beg. I'm going to do exactly what you want because you are going to do exactly what *I* want."

"I am?"

"Yes." Quinn steeled his eyes, leaning closer. "My wife gave me her father's map while she was on her deathbed. Li made me promise that it would be leveraged for Huan's safety. My wife passed that burden on to me, and now I'm giving it to you."

"And it's not even my birthday."

"You get what you want; I get what I want. That's the price of my obedience. I'm laying down my life for her."

Akando nodded. "You lead us through the mine tomorrow—no tricks—and I give you my word that I'll never lay a finger on Huan."

Quinn motioned at the sleeping soldiers. "And what about these two pieces of human debris? What can you guarantee me about them?"

Akando grinned. "They'll be too preoccupied with *other* matters to ever think of your daughter again."

Quinn stared at him for a long moment. "You know, this is the first time I have ever believed you."

"A leader never makes a promise that he can't keep. Tomorrow, my promises will be heard for generations, and for generations yet to come."

"Promises," Quinn repeated. "Well, I think Chenoa made a few of her own. Today, she promised to come back for me. And you know what? I believe she will. But I also think that she made another promise today."

Akando narrowed his eyes. "And what would that be?"

"I think she promised her father that she'd be the only Winterhawk left alive after this was all over."

"Woe is mine." Akando threw his head back and laughed. "I think I'll keep you alive tomorrow just so you can see how mistaken you are. You can watch me braid her flesh after I carve it off her body. And if Chenoa does call upon Jolon, it will only be to curse him because she was ever born."

Quinn remained silent. He watched the shadows of the flicking campfire dancing across Akando's massive body. He had never once prayed for God to send anyone to Hell, but he did so now.

There are some people who behave so unconscionably in this life that they maneuver themselves far out of the reach of redemption. They escape justice by slithering beneath the discarded rocks of their own morality.

He prayed that when Chenoa Winterhawk kicked over Akando's rock, she'd stomp the living shit out of what she found cowering beneath it.

PART THREE
THE EPOCH OF THE WEYEKIN

CHAPTER 26

Elkhorn Peak
Blue Mountain Range
Eastern Oregon

Chenoa Winterhawk stood at the southwest corner of Elkhorn Peak. Deep frown lines were etched onto her face with such perfect exactitude that it was as if a sculptor had used a chisel to create it. Her stare was transfixed on a carved-out section of rock looming hundreds of feet above her.

She shook her head with mild disbelief.

Nothing was ever easy.

What are you pulling a sad face for, Pocahontas? It's only a three-hundred-foot solo climb...give or take a concussion or two.

This particular area on the southwestern edge of Elkhorn Peak was what she had seen earlier on Quinn's map. It was a secret entrance into the mines. Because Akando and his men would be coming in through the mouth of the mine in the northeast, *this* was going to be her element of surprise.

Miners called them 'gophers.' In reality, these small tunnels were safety measures. Gopher tunnels had been constructed above main mine arteries as a means to offset catastrophes. They were used as emergency exits in the case of landslides or flooding; or additional ventilation that kept toxic gas from becoming trapped inside the tunnels.

Hearing a nervous neighing, Chenoa pulled her eyes away from the rock face. The horse she'd ridden from the engineer camp was standing a few feet away, staring intently at her.

"What is it?'" Chenoa asked. 'I said you could go—get out!"

But the horse stayed, nervously shaking out his mane. Something was definitely spooking him.

After sleeping until dawn, Chenoa had decided to saddle up the horse and ride it to Elkhorn Peak. She had been mildly surprised that neither McNichols or Troost had returned throughout the night. Something must have gone seriously wrong. She couldn't imagine what might have happened to them.

Akando and his goon squad would be coming from the northern section of Qualen Pass, so she made sure she kept well to the south. She was still counting on the element of surprise when it came time to confront them.

Akando had proven to be a clever tactician. He had displayed a methodical patience over the years, planning his every move of revenge down to the most finite of details. Once he had set things in motion, he wouldn't allow anything to stand in his way.

But now Chenoa wondered if she might have misjudged his strategy somehow. His men had indicated the explosives needed to flood the mine had already been delivered. Plus, Akando still had Major Quinn as a hostage to guide him to exactly the right location in the mine.

But there still might be a variable at play here.

If Akando truly believed that she had somehow survived the boat explosion on the Malheur River, he might have already altered the mission. Given that she had crippled his plans of assassinating President Roosevelt, he could have decided that taking her out first had become their highest priority.

Winterhawk turned her head, intently scanning the tree line. She thought that it was possible that he could be hiding out there right now, waiting for the perfect moment for an ambush.

But Chenoa shook her head at the thought. It wasn't very probable. Akando hadn't seen the map, so there wasn't any way he had learned about the gopher tunnel beforehand. And even if Major Quinn himself knew about it, he wasn't going to go around blabbing to those other soldiers about its possible existence.

Whatever had been spooking the horse wasn't Akando. It had to be something else. But what, exactly?

Chenoa thought once again about the strange disappearance of the two army engineers. They had left behind all of their equipment and provisions at the camp, but had taken those motorcycles. She'd assumed they'd gone to have a better look at the abandoned ruins of the Carson Mines; why hadn't they returned? Had she misjudged them? Were they dead, or had they betrayed her? The thought gnawed at her, but she pushed it aside—she had to trust her instincts now.

Something had stopped those soldiers. Right now, she didn't have time to find out what that might have been.

"Get going!" Chenoa clapped her hands loudly. "Go!"

The horse reared back, startled. He stared at her for a long moment before bolting, running towards the forest at a fierce gallop. Even after she lost sight of him through the trees, she could hear his hooves thundering over the underbrush.

Then, everything was silent again.

Turning away from the forest, she glanced up at Elkhorn Peak. She focused her gaze at the gopher exit that would be acting as her entrance into the mines.

It would be a three-hundred-foot free climb. The face of the peak was pockmarked with deep crevices and lengthy sections of walled rock. If a climb of that distance had been predicated by surface familiarity and the correct gear, it would have normally someone with her experience around an hour. But given all of the unknown variables she was currently facing, Chenoa estimated it would take her at least 90 minutes or more to reach the tunnel.

She inhaled deeply.

Calm heart, calm mind.

Winterhawk tightened the sheepskin strap that was fastened to the shotgun, making sure both it and the bandolier were both angled tightly across her back.

Chenoa briefly touched a hand to the locket that still dangled over her heart. It was dented into a crescent shape from the impact of the bullet. It might have been badly damaged, but it was like her now: a survivor.

And it was time do it all over again.

She walked to the base of the mountain. Her fingers dug into the first crevice, muscles straining as she pulled herself up. Loose rocks skittered below, a reminder of the drop.

Chenoa began the grueling ascent.

CHAPTER 27

Higgins Haven
Blue Mountain Range
Eastern Oregon,

Agent Travers didn't realize his mouth was open until he felt the slimy concoction of Red Man chewing tobacco and warm saliva dripping down his face. The residual glob of the Pinkerton Tobacco dangled just beneath his bottom lip, momentarily hugging the uneven contours of his dark beard before slithering its way off his chin.

Hearing the chew spit tap against his left boot like a polluted raindrop, he absently wiped the back of his hand across his mouth to clean off any leftover residual of the Red Man.

He found that there wasn't any.

Travers realized that was because his mouth was empty. He'd somehow swallowed the remaining chewing tobacco that had been tucked into the side pocket of his cheek. It had slid down the gullet without him even being conscious of it; now, it was mixing with the venison and beans he'd wolfed down just a few hours earlier.

He felt his stomach clench at the thought.

A gust of wind tickled the front of his teeth, reminding him that his mouth was apparently still open. Astonishment took on a life of its own, apparently. Muscle memory became second nature when the mind was faced with a—

"Nightmare."

Travers turned, glancing over at the man who had squatted down beside the bloody corpse of Colonel Higgins. "Correction: a *fucking* nightmare," Agent Michaels said. He was nearly two decades older than his partner, with a distinctively gravelly voice tinged with equal amounts of grief and bluster.

Travers nodded in solidarity. "What do you think happened here, Michaels?"

"What happened? Well...*everything*."

"Everything."

As he said it, Travers felt a twinge of fear race behind the back of his eyes. That's where he always felt it. The epicenter of anxiety for him was never the butterflies fluttering in his stomach, but the wasps flying around his brain. And when he got scared, those pesky wasps sure liked to sting; they liked to sting *hard*.

He felt them do it now, wincing with the pain. He could feel the sharp jabs directly behind his eyes as nervousness flooded his system like a child's mud dam collapsing under the force of a rising river tide.

Recently, the parameters of their job with the Secret Service had gotten considerably wider. And with that, things had become a whole lot more dangerous.

The U.S. Secret Service had been first established by the Department of the Treasury in 1865 to prevent counterfeiting. They assumed full-time responsibility for protecting the president after the assassination of William McKinley. Being surrounded by a constant security detail was something that his successor, Theodore Roosevelt, found greatly annoying.

Truth be told, none of the agents were particularly thrilled with the assignment, either. The secret code name for Roosevelt among them was 'Hunter,' which was apropos because of his love for the sport...and in the way he relished treating secret service agents as nothing more than his prey.

Hunter's unscheduled visit to Higgins Haven was a perfect example.

While it wasn't listed on his official itinerary, nor were any of his plans leaked to the press, President Roosevelt had made it perfectly clear that he planned to stay with Colonel Higgins for an entire week. Teddy felt he was due a vacation after all the political strife and turmoil that he'd endured in getting Newlands Reclamation Act passed into law.

So, after his speech at the Owyhee Dam tomorrow, Roosevelt was going to spend time with an old war buddy. And no matter how much he'd been cautioned about the potential security risk, Hunter had refused to take no for an answer.

Which is exactly why Travers and Michaels were here now. To scope out the area for threats, and to stay at the cabin and guard President Roosevelt for the duration of his stay. They'd both been irritated by an assignment that appeared fraught with nothing but constant boredom.

Of course, that was before they had encountered a murder.

And stumbled upon a massacre.

Travers shook his head.

Yes, this job had certainly become a lot more dangerous.

Agent Michaels slowly stood, knee joints popping loudly like a piece of wet campfire kindling that finally surrendering to the heat. "Higgins was cut to pieces by a shotgun at close range. He wasn't carrying any weapons, either. That means that either the killer took the Colonel's gun after cutting him down, or Higgins didn't feel the need to carry any firearms because—"

"The person who murdered him wasn't a threat," Travers said. "Colonel Higgins must have thought that his killer was a friend."

He motioned towards the abandoned freight wagon and the four barrels of water stashed inside of it. The hollowed-out carcass of a mule lay close to it; its bones nearly picked clean. "You reckon it was Traff? The water hauler that the Colonel told us was delivering supplies?"

"It stands to reason," Michaels said.

Agent Travers instinctively touched the butt of his holstered Colt, eyes nervously flicking towards the tree line. "Then Traff must still be out there. He's waiting to ambush Hunter. He's waiting out there for the chance to kill *us*, too."

Michaels sighed with impatience, but didn't make a move towards his holstered weapons. Travers couldn't help but think that his partner looked rather nonplussed for a man who just discovered that he likely had an assassin's target on his forehead.

"Traff ain't out there," Michaels said.

"No?"

"No." Agent Michaels motioned at the ground in front of him. "Poor bastard never left Higgins Haven alive."

Travers squinted hard. "How do you know that?"

"Because you're standing on what's left of him."

Travers stepped back reflexively with a grunt, eyes darting immediately to the ground. There was nothing but clumps of dirt, faded grass, and several misshapen stones. He focused his attention on one rock in particular. It was plum-colored and flat, looking almost like a torn leather satchel. He noticed thick tendrils snaking out from either side of it, with insects swarming all over it.

Travers gasped with the sudden realization. "Is that a—?!"

"Heart." Agent Michaels bit his lower lip in contemplation. "What's left of it, anyway. Given the onset of rigor mortis, I say it's been cooking out in the elements for at least a day. It's been mostly eaten, too."

"Mostly." Travers swallowed hard.

He bent down closer to the peculiar stone. He could now clearly see that it was a gnawed-on piece of heart ventricle, with ragged chunks of the pulmonary still attached to it.

He stood back up quickly, shaking his head with disgust. "Where is he, then? If this is a piece of Rico Traff heart jerky, where's the rest of him?"

"That," Agent Michaels said, "is an excellent question. And for that, Agent Travers, I have no answer."

"C'mon, Michaels. I can see the steam coming off the back of your head from here. That old brain of yours must be cooking up some wild theory."

Michaels pinched off a smile.

"Well, If I was to guess, I'd wager the hauler's corpse was carried off by whatever it was that took down his mule. There are several prints—large ones—on the west side of the wagon. Biggest damn tracks I've ever seen."

Travers felt his blood go cold. "Grizzlies?"

"Bigger."

"Bigger." Travers stared at him for a long moment. "What the hell is walking around out there that's bigger than a damn grizzly?"

"Beats the shit out of me, amigo. I just work here."

Travers looked over at the splayed corpse of Colonel Higgins. "Why'd they leave him, then? Why leave fresh meat behind?"

Michaels slowly ran a hand under his stubbled chin. "Maybe buckshot interferes with their digestion. In any case, those things are long gone."

Travers felt the stinging behind his eyes slowly ebbing as he gained more control over his fear. "You're sure?"

Michaels nodded resolutely, gesturing towards the west side of the forest. "Underbrush badly trampled; tree limbs broken all around. Whatever came through this way, they also *left* that way."

Travers turned and looked at the wooded area behind the wagon. The two horses they had ridden to Higgins Haven on were tethered to the thick branches of a nearby fallen tree. Standing close to the mule carcass, they certainly didn't seem to be spooked, or even a little bit agitated. The horses almost look bored; which certainly wouldn't be the case if they had smelled predators lurking nearby.

Looking closer into the woods behind the horses, Travers could now make out the damaged underbrush leading into the forest, the haphazard pathway littered with dozens of cracked tree limbs. It looked just the way Michaels said it did. Like some very large animals had decided to carve out their own scenic route through the dense woods.

He shifted his gaze higher, staring up at the sight of Elkhorn Peak jutting above the treetops. He figured they were within two miles from it. He didn't realize at first that Higgins Haven had been built so close to the old Carson Mines. But in retrospect, he thought that made sense.

After the mine had been permanently shuttered several years ago, this area of the wilderness had been all but deserted. It was a perfect place to overcharge gung-ho yahoos for a private hunting party.

Turns out it was also the perfect place to get yourself eaten, too.

"You see where that leads?" Agent Michaels asked, interrupting his thoughts. "Those big boys must have marched their hungry asses back to Elkhorn Peak."

Nodding, Travers pulled his gaze away from the mountain. "I did see that, but I seemed to have missed seeing anything else that was out here."

Michaels shrugged with indifference. "Don't be too down on yourself. I was an Army reconnaissance specialist in my previous life; you were obviously just an asshole in yours."

Travers guffawed loudly. "I was overqualified."

Michaels grinned. "I don't doubt it."

"So," Travers said, eyes dancing around the perimeter, "I think it's safe to assume that somebody was planning to seriously fuck with President Roosevelt here."

"Maybe *si* and maybe no."

"Maybe?! We've got a dead colonel, a picked-clean-to-the-bone mule, an abandoned water wagon, dinosaur tracks, and a leftover piece of Traff's heart baking in the sun like Indian frybread."

"I'm actually impressed that you remembered all of that without even consulting your notes. Maybe you *do* have a future with the Secret Service, after all."

"And for those of us with really short attention spans," Travers continued with irritation, "I'll remind you that all of this happened just days before President Roosevelt was *secretly* planning on staying here."

Michaels nodded his head in agreement. "It does all seem rather too fanciful to be just a coincidence."

"Higgins Haven has been compromised."

"I like that word: 'compromised.' You must have started reading the dictionary again."

Travers sighed. "The question is: what do we do now?"

"That's not the question."

"No? Then what is?"

With a grin, Michaels motioned with his head towards the cluster of dense woods behind the cabin. "Are you afraid of heights?"

THE TREE STAND had been fastened forty-five feet off the ground. The hunter's platform was securely nestled against the massive trunk of one of the tallest Douglas Fir trees that flanked Higgins Haven. Built as a way to elevate the hunter and provide a better vantage point, this particular stand was large enough to accommodate two people at any given time.

And it had been something *else* that Travers hadn't noticed when they had first come upon the cabin.

Michaels appeared nonplussed about his continual oversights, but Travers was wondering how much of a mission liability his partner was now thinking that he was.

"Hell of a view, ain't it?" Michaels had asked a few minutes earlier. The man had barely broken a sweat scaling the long rope ladder up to the platform, and his lungs weren't heaving from the exertion.

The same thing couldn't be said of Travers.

He felt like he'd just taken a swim in the Malheur River while being fully clothed, with sweat stains turning his white shirt into a stylish shade of dishwater grey. After he'd finally ascended the ladder and pulled his body onto the platform, his lungs had begun to sputter like an underfed motor of a donkey steam engine

And to make matters worse, the stinging pain behind his eyes had returned again in full force. That was something he knew that needed to be ignored. His focus should only be on external factors, not the internal forces that had created the distraction.

But it was like trying to ignore hunger pains.

It was much easier said than done.

Before scaling up to the platform, the Secret Service agents had retrieved field binoculars stashed in the saddle bags on their horses. Michaels was already peering through his own, head turning as he scanned the forest.

"If you're looking for trees," Travers huffed, "I reckon you'll find a few." With sweaty fingers gripping tightly onto his own pair, he brought the binoculars up to his face and peered into it.

The tree stand was perfectly situated. It provided an impressively spectacular 360-degree view of the area. He skimmed quickly over the tree line before focusing his attention on Elkhorn Peak. With the binoculars and the positioning of the hunter's platform, he was afforded an unobstructed view of the mouth of the old Carson Mines.

He felt his heart suddenly race.

With his own binoculars also focused on Elkhorn Peak, Agent Michaels loudly clucked his tongue. "Interesting."

He'd just seen it, too.

Four men were walking towards the entrance of the mine. Three of them were wearing Army uniforms. The fourth man, a gigantic Indian who was dressed like a civilian, was casually bringing up the rear.

Travers focused his binoculars on the man leading the group. Rotund and moving slow, the man turned as he walked, listening to something one of the soldiers behind him had just said.

As he turned, Travers could now clearly see the insignia rank on the front of his uniform. He let out a sharp gasp.

"That man walking out in front of the group," Travers said, "it looks like he's a—"

"Hostage."

Travers frowned. "What? No, I was going to say that he's an Army major."

"He's that, too."

Hostage...

Travers studied the two soldiers walking behind him more carefully. The major was unarmed, but the others weren't. He also saw that they were wearing Army Corp of Engineers uniforms.

Travers shook his head with confusion. The Carson Mines had been closed for over a decade. Why were these soldiers going there now? Was it somehow all connected to Hunter's visit to the cabin?

Both men prodded the major roughly with their weapons, propelling him towards the entrance of the mines. He could see them laughing as the major stumbled over some rocks, his uncoordinated girth coming dangerously close to kissing the ground.

Recovering his balance, the major squeezed both fists in anger and kept on walking. He was obviously a man who wasn't in control of the situation.

Travers lowered his binoculars and stared hard at his partner. "How did you know that man was a hostage, Michaels?"

"Because of Akando."

"Who?"

"The Goliath taking up the rear."

Travers quickly returned his gaze back to the binoculars, now focusing his attention on the Indian striding behind the group of soldiers. The man was absolutely massive, looking to be at least a foot taller than anyone Travers had ever seen before. Aside from a wicked-looking double blade sheathed to his waist, the Indian wasn't carrying any weapons. It looked like he really didn't need any.

This man was somebody who was definitely in charge.

"Akando?" Travers asked.

"Tussled with him a few times up in Idaho during my Army reconnaissance days. After some civilian bloodshed, the Army took down his entire band of Sheepeaters."

"But not him?"

"Akando evaded capture before he could be hung for his crimes. Last I heard, he had been nabbed and sent down to Fort Alcatraz."

"Crimes? What did he do?"

Michaels lowered his binoculars. "Akando Winterhawk is a killer."

Travers felt the pressure behind his eyes building again. He thought about the massacre they had stumbled upon. Somebody had murdered Colonel Higgins on the eve of President Roosevelt's visit. And now, a known killer and his willing military associates was taking an Army hostage into the Carson Mines for reasons unknown.

Travers took another look at Elkhorn Peak before centering his gaze back on his partner. "What do we do now?"

Michaels grinned. "We're going to save the day."

CHAPTER 28

Elkhorn Peak
Blue Mountain Range
Eastern Oregon

There was a patchwork of blood splattered on the ground.

Standing just inside the entrance of the Carson Mine, Major Quinn squinted down at the floor with a deep frown. He even wondered for a moment, if he might be imagining it. That perhaps it was a vision that was indicative of the blood that would symbolically be on his hands after what would happen today.

He was the one who had made the deal with Army Corps of Engineers: trading his wife's map for his daughter's amnesty. But just like he no longer had Li, he now no longer had the map.

Winterhawk had taken it from him and destroyed it. It had been a calculated maneuver on her part in order to delay Akando's destructive plans; buying her enough time to somehow stop him.

Chenoa had proven herself to be a remarkably clever and resilient adversary against Akando and his Army conspirators. And in the midst of the fight, she had promised to come back for him. Quinn believed that she would.

But the hard truth was that even if Winterhawk had survived the battle on the river, if she somehow made her way here, she would be facing overwhelming odds.

And more than likely, certain death.

It was the same guarantee of death that Akando had also promised him.

There was no getting around that now. He had no delusions about making it out of the Carson Mines alive. He knew that these traitorous soldiers would cut him down the second he delivered them to the underground water source.

His death was all but guaranteed now, but he understood that his sacrifice meant life for Huan. Akando had promised that his daughter would not be harmed if Quinn took him to where the river was buried beneath the tunnels.

Then, it would be more than Quinn's blood that would be shed.

After Akando ignited the explosives, the blast would disrupt the underground aquifers. The rising water would consume the mine in minutes. The mountain would not be able to contain it, so the water would be released into the valley. It would bring death and destruction to the people who now occupied it.

Hundreds of innocents would be murdered by Akando Winterhawk's hand, and because of Quinn's unwitting help.

He was an unremarkable soldier, a failure as a father, and now a mass murderer.

The thought revolted him.

He gazed harder at the blood. It wasn't symbolic, and he wasn't imagining it out of misplaced guilt.

He tapped one of the streaks gently with a boot, saw how the blood clung tightly to it. It was sticky, and still relatively fresh.

Where had it come from?

Some animal attack? Or something much worse?

He frowned hard, eyes darting quickly around the entrance to the mine. He saw nothing out of place. Nothing except the four of them, of course.

"Woe is mine," Akando said. He'd obviously just noticed the blood. The large man stepped forward, dipping his shoulders so his head wouldn't scrape against the ceiling of the mine. He kept one hand on the hilt of the razorback, eyes taking in everything.

"Blood?" Ivers asked. He bent down close to the tracks, examining the unusual splatter patterns that spread across the soil and rocks.

"Could be from our little princess," Briggs said. "Maybe her Aunt Flo came a-knocking." He snorted with raucous laughter, but his eyes betrayed his anxiety. He kept glancing over his shoulder, staring outside the mine for potential danger.

He was a man very much afraid of something.

Akando followed his gaze as well as his train of thought. "Chenoa isn't out there," he said disapprovingly, "and she hasn't been in here, either."

"Somebody sure has." Ivers stood up. Even though he hadn't touched the blood, he wiped his sweaty hands on the front of his pants. "And fairly recently, too."

"Check the equipment," Akando said sharply.

"Right." Ivers stepped quickly through the mine. He moved passed Quinn, heading directly towards the parked one-ton dump car that had been used to move the ore and broken rocks. He peered into the car, temporarily blocking Quinn's view. "Shit is all here, Akando. Two cases of boom juice, clock timer, dynamite sticks, and the helmets."

"Good," Akando said.

As Ivers scuttled away, Quinn saw two large barrels stacked inside the car. They were marked as U.S. Army property, each one labeled as being NTO.

"Nitrotriazolone," Quinn gasped.

"No need to get all fancy," Briggs said. "Boom juice is a lot easier to pronounce."

Quinn's mind reeled at the thought. Nitrotriazolone was a highly explosive material. He had seen the Army Corps of Engineers use just a small amount of NTO to reroute an entire riverway by destroying a wall of gigantic boulders.

"You're totally insane, Akando. Igniting NTO down there will—"

"Ensure that the job gets done, Major Quinn." Akando had envisioned the flood washing away Jolon's legacy as his people now rallied under his banner. This mine was his crucible.

Quinn noticed a third barrel of NTO on the ground just inside the mine entrance. His mind reeled at the prospect of all three barrels detonating inside the mine. "You'll bring down the entire mountain!"

"You've got your own problems," Akando said. "Keep your focus on where it needs to be. Remember for whom you're doing all of this for."

Quinn remembered.

THREE DAYS AGO, he'd said a tearful goodbye to Huan. They had been walking together in the garden path behind their cottage in Hood River. His daughter had listened quietly as he had told her about her grandfather's map, and his plan to use it to trade for her freedom.

"Freedom," Huan repeated. "Momma told me that death was going to be her only freedom from the sickness."

"There is freedom in death," Quinn had said, "just as there is freedom in life."

"I only know the death kind, Poppa."

Her answer had broken his heart. Huan had just lost her mother, and now her father was embarking on a mission that would put his own life in jeopardy.

Huan carefully studied his face. "Will this mission be dangerous?"

"No," he lied.

She gently bit her bottom lip. It was an imitation of one of her mother's patented mannerisms. Whenever Li did it, it meant that she didn't believe a word he'd just said. Apparently, he couldn't fool Huan, either.

"I won't see her until *after* you come back."

Quinn furrowed his brow in temporary confusion. He opened his mouth to ask Huan what she meant, but stopped short when she saw her distant gaze cast over his shoulder.

And then he understood.

The cemetery.

Li was buried on the hillside that overlooked the valley. It was located a mile from their home, giving both of them ample opportunity to frequently visit the gravesite.

He knew his wife was always close to them both now; as close as the nearest memory. But that was something that offered his daughter minimal comfort, if any. She was now without her mother. That meant that the days in which he was gone were incredibly isolating for her.

Quinn offered her his warmest smile. "That's fine, Huan."

She pulled her gaze away from the cemetery, eyes now transfixed on the grandness of the Columbia River to the north. It ran directly parallel to Hood River. It was nature's great dividing line between Oregon and Washington State.

"You're taking grandpa's map to help these soldiers find a river?"

"That's right."

"It's hidden inside a mountain?"

"Underneath one, Huan. Years ago, your grandfather and some other miners discovered it. But after they found it, they decided to keep it a secret."

"Why did they do that, Poppa?"

Quinn had thought briefly about the Snake River Massacre. His father-in-law had been in one of the mining camps that had been attacked. He'd escaped with the map, but thirty-four other Chinese workers from the Carson Mines had been murdered.

He reached down and brushed some wind-whipped hair strands from out of his daughter's face, gently tucking them behind her ear. "Grandpa had his reasons, sweetheart."

Huan stared at him for a long moment. "Because grandpa was Chinese. They hated him for that, so they wouldn't have believed him about finding the river inside the mountain."

Her eyes flashed with anger; mouth twisted open in a frustrated grimace. Her bottom teeth were briefly exposed. He noticed that she had the same familiar, perfectly crooked formation of her mother's.

Seeing that made his heart ache in a way that was nearly painful.

"But they'll believe *you*, won't they?" Huan continued. "They'll listen to you about the river because you look like them, and not *him*. They'll believe you because you aren't Chinese."

It was true, but Quinn had decided to lie. "That isn't true."

There was something else in his daughter's eyes now. The anger was still there, but deep sadness had begun simmering just behind it. "They say all Chinks are liars."

Quinn jolted noticeably at her use of that revolting word. It was somehow even more disgustingly vulgar coming out her mouth than it was from everyone else he'd heard say it over the years.

He took a calming breath. "And exactly who are 'they,' Huan?"

"Kids at school," she said. "Friends."

"Friends," he echoed.

Quinn had felt that same level of betrayal within his own circle after he had married Li. Even his own family had shunned him; then, when Huan had been born, the military had started to do the same.

When the Chinese Exclusion Act became Oregon law, he'd been put on official notice by the Army. In the strictest of language, he'd been officially informed that his marriage to a Chinese immigrant had potentially compromised his standing within the military. As for Huan, the unofficial word from some of the brass was that a mixed-race child was something that could not be overlooked for much longer.

Li's death hadn't lessened the racial scrutiny; it had only allowed the light of injustice to shine all that much brighter on his daughter. Huan had now become their focus, with the threat of making good on her deportation from America getting closer to reality with every new anti-Chinese headline.

The Chinese Exclusion Act's cruelty had haunted Li right up until her death, and now Huan was threatened to face it alone. He had vowed to shield her from it, no matter the price. The map had been the answer. While it hadn't seemed very valuable to anyone in years past, it had now become very important indeed.

Tapping into a large water source would help fulfill President Roosevelt's promise to bring irrigation to the desolate farmlands and mines in the region. And with that map, he had brokered a secret deal with the Army Corps of Engineers: the location of the underground river in exchange for lifetime amnesty for Huan.

He just prayed that this mission wouldn't cost him her father, too. She had already lost far too much. He couldn't fathom what would happen to her if somehow he never made it back.

His daughter was looking at him now. Her brow was furrowed with concern, almost as if she had been reading his mind. "Poppa?"

"Yes?" He braced himself for the question.

"Was it hard for you and momma?"

"Hard in what way, honey?"

"With her being Chinese, and you not being Chinese." She studied his face for a moment before continuing. "I'm the only one who is at my school. Anyway, Ricky Butler, a boy in my class, says that after momma died, that makes me the only Chinese person left in this whole town. Only, that's not the word he likes to use. Ricky Butler likes to call me a half-breed chi—"

Quinn held up a hand to silence her. "You don't need to repeat it again, Huan. You never have to say that word; not *ever*. A word like that is like a ghost, and it will haunt you forever if you aren't careful."

"Ghosts are scary."

Quinn nodded. "Yes, they are. And people like this Ricky Butler, they count on fear to make you feel less than what you are. That's what words like that really do, Huan. They try and make you into someone you're not on the outside by hurting the person you are on the inside."

He thought grimly of some of the men whom he served alongside. After finding out about his marriage to Li, several soldiers had begun whispering something behind his own back. It was a name that was an affront to every moral fiber in his being.

They had begun calling him a traitor.

Names can define you just every bit as much as they can break you. Fools think otherwise; or perhaps only those fools who have mastered the art of lying to themselves.

He closed his fists with quiet anger.

He was going to do whatever it took to secure Huan's freedom from all of this. He'd promised it to Li on her deathbed. He'd promised it to himself, too.

"Poppa?"

"Yes?" Quinn focused his attention on his daughter, watching as a solitary tear slowly crept down the contour of her left cheek. Feeling it, Huan bravely brushed it aside.

"When I look in the mirror, I don't see a half-breed."

"No?" Quinn's voice audibly cracked with emotion. "What do you see?"

"Two halves. When I look at myself in the mirror, I see you and I see momma."

Quinn reached out and pulled her close. He hugged her as tight as he could, pressing her head against his chest. He could feel her body begin to wrack with sobs, the tears flowing freely now.

"All of this will be over soon, Huan."

"Remember, Poppa...you promised. Remember? You promised to come back to me."

Quinn remembered.

AKANDO WAS STANDING beside him now. His massive captor had just stepped into the patchwork of blood, something that Quinn thought was most appropriate.

The men had all put on their Edison battery lamps. The helmets were ill-fitting, hanging lopsided across their heads like a metallic cowlick. But they worked, fully illuminating the mine entrance and chasing away the shadows that had been guarding the tunnel.

"Whenever you're ready, Major Quinn."

Quinn nodded grimly. He placed his hands on the brake release lever on the A-car. The twin barrels loomed large in his vision.

Briggs coughed loudly. "No offense to Captain Tubby here, but I still don't understand why we need this grass-bellied traitor, anyhow. He ain't leading us to some pie eating contest, is he?"

"I should certainly hope not," Akando answered.

Quinn felt his cheeks flush with anger. If he had to give his life down in those mines, he prayed that he could somehow take down Briggs before he died.

"Seriously," Ivers said, gesturing towards the mouth of the tunnel, "unless the Chinks are running us all on some wild goose chase with this, how hard could it be to find a river in there? We don't need some stupid map, and we don't need an even dumber guide. All we need to do is to keep walking until we hear the sound of the damn water."

Akando clucked his tongue loudly in disapproval. "That the Creator must enjoy making idiots is the only possible explanation for the likes of you two."

Briggs narrowed his eyes. "That ain't much of an answer, Akando."

"The reason we wanted that map before," Akando sighed, "and the reason we need Major Quinn now, is that sometimes the treasures we seek are hidden in plain sight."

Ivers shook his head with frustration. "Explain that."

Akando rested a hand on the Razorback sheathed on his hip. His fingers drummed restlessly against the hilt. "It's not where the river is that's important, but where it *isn't*."

Briggs and Iver glanced briefly at each other. Their faces wore masks of confusion, but they mercifully kept any further questions out of their mouths. Each man had their own motivations for silence at this point.

Briggs dreamed of nothing but gold to offset the nightmare of debts that kept piling up. While Ivers, haunted by past moral failures, clung to Akando's promises as if they were lifegiving manna from heaven.

Looking away from the soldiers, Quinn thought of Akando's cryptic answer to them.

The map of the Carson Mines that Li's father had in his possession actually showed nothing more than what could be misconstrued as rough charcoal sketches. The mine itself was massive, with a half-dozen interlocking tunnels, but the location of the underground river wasn't found in any of them.

Akando was absolutely correct.

The water everyone so desperately wanted was hidden in plain sight.

He could suddenly feel Akando's heated stare. Quinn knew that the time for talk was over. He depressed the brake lever on the mine car and, with a grunt of exertion, began to slowly push it forward into tunnel.

He forced a mental picture of the map into his head. Thinking hard, he began formulating the quickest route through the mines. He understood that Huan's future would depend on the exactness of his recollections; his ability to take them to the right location.

He thought once again about those sketches on the map.

Quinn remembered.

CHAPTER 29

The *hueco* had just saved her life.

While the word itself is translated as hollow, early mountaineers from South America had first referred to these distinctive insert handholds as *huecos*. Created on mountainsides by weather and time, these deep hallows of gouged rock could fit your entire hand; sometimes even your entire body.

And Chenoa had just located one while dangling 250-feet in the air.

Her left hand had been jammed tightly into a crimp crevice, fingers trying to desperately support her body weight. Her right arm flailed. She felt her fingers slipping. Just as her strength had just about given out, she'd seen a *hueco* less than a foot above her.

She lunged upwards, jamming her right hand into the hollow in the same instance that the grip with her left arm completely gave out. She found another new handhold, but now her feet dangled precariously above the ground.

She wouldn't be able to hold on like this much longer.

People don't rise to the occasion; they rely on their training. Climbers know that it's what has come before that will see you through whatever comes next.

Winterhawk's mind raced.

What had come before?!

The rock crimp!

She remembered that the crevice she had just been holding onto moments before contained enough space for her feet. Chenoa quickly jabbed her heels down into the small crimp in the rock, using her powerful leg muscles to pull herself as flat as possible against the mountain.

The maneuver effectively took the weight off of her arms, allowing her to remain perfectly balanced against the mountainside. The momentary respite would allow enough strength to return so she could generate power towards the next hold.

Realizing once again how close she had been to falling, she took a long moment to steady her thoughts.

While solo climbing heightened the risks of climbing exponentially, she guessed that she had been scaling the mountainside for close to an hour already. The late morning sun was already baking the clothes on her back. She could feel the barrel of the shotgun getting warmer each time it connected with the bare skin of her neck. Sweat beads continually stung her eyes; threatening to blind her vision for the next handhold.

She desperately wanted to wipe the pooling sweat from her face, but she didn't want to risk making her fingers slippery. Up here, once your grip was gone, it was gone for good.

But even given all of that, the majority of the peak ascent had been fairly smooth. That was, until a few minutes ago. That's when she'd encountered the crimp. That had seemed to signal that the time for easy maneuvers was over.

Calm heart, calm mind. You're over a two-thirds of the way to that tunnel already. On the mountain, it's always altitude over attitude. Keep moving, amiga.

Taking a deep breath, Winterhawk looked above her to see what was coming next.

It was a slab.

She narrowed her eyes with frustration.

A slab was a type of large rock that was positioned at an angle, jutting out horizontally from the cliffside. In her experience, successful slab climbing was contingent on precision handwork, good body position, and precise balance.

And it was never predicated on it being above arm's reach.

It was a good three feet above. Too far to reach from this position. There was only one thing she could possibly attempt.

Her stomach lurched with a sudden jolt of fear at the thought.

In order to reach the overhanging slab above her head, she would have to literally leave the wall that she was now desperately clinging to and jump.

It was a leap of faith maneuver.

The dynamic climbing motion needed to be perfectly timed with that brief second when her body weight wasn't being pulled downward by gravity. To do this effectively, she would need to grab hold of the slab at the very apex of upward motion after her body left contact with the cliffside.

If she misjudged by even a fraction of an inch, she would tumble to the rocky floor.

That's not gonna happen, Winterhawk thought resolutely.

Chenoa sunk into a deep crouching position over the crimp. With a sudden explosion of momentum, she launched her body upwards. Both hands simultaneously disconnected from the *hueco* as she was momentarily airborne, arms outstretched above her.

For a terrifying moment it appeared that she hadn't gained enough altitude;

But her fingers miraculously cleared the slab, allowing her to grab tightly onto the ledge with both hands. She dangled over space for a full second, legs kicking.

Throwing her elbows sideways and placing immense pressure on her deltoids, Winterhawk pressed down against the slab with the palms of her hands. She began to pull her body up until she was finally able to swing her legs up over the ledge.

Chenoa kneeled carefully on the slab, muscles aching with exertion. She pressed both palms against the cliffside for stability as she controlled her breathing.

You really ride with angels, Pocahontas. Death had just come a-knockin', but you had hung a sign on the front door: "Fear doesn't live here anymore."

After a long moment, she looked up. Her heart leaped with sudden exultation. She could see the tunnel just ten feet above her head.

The gopher entrance was now in reach.

Chenoa slowly pulled herself to a standing position, noticing a second slab outcropping jutted out above her. She was relieved to see that this one was well within arm's reach.

Planting both feet firmly onto the slab beneath her, she grabbed tightly onto the rock outcropping. Pushing upwards with her calves, she pulled her upper body up and over the second slab.

Exhausted from the effort, Winterhawk rolled over on the rock until she was flat on her back. She squeezed her eyes shut, breathing heavy. The blazing sun bore down, warming her face through closed eyelids.

Her hands ached from the climb. Each joint in her fingers felt inflamed; throbbing. The bruise on her chest from the deflected bullet pulsated like it had its own heartbeat. The exposed burn wound on her shoulder after falling from the *Lathos* ached tremendously. Her stomach grumbled from hunger; her throat scratched from thirst. The urge to curl up and fall sleep was overwhelming.

Her body had reached its own pinnacle of endurance. She was almost ready to completely shut down.

Almost...

Chenoa had a sudden flash of memory. She'd been six. The night her father had returned home from the war. His final mission with the U.S. Cavalry was over. He'd stumbled out of the woods; bloodied. Tears on his face had been reflected by the campfires. He'd locked eyes with Chenoa.

"You came home, Poppa!" Chenoa had screamed out with joy.

Her father said something next that she didn't understand then; but now, she understood it completely.

"Love never travels far," Jolon said, crushing her into a tight embrace. "It doesn't have to."

Love follows. Love shadows. Love whispers. Love comforts. Love promises. Love embraces. Love remembers. Even in all its various guises and permutations, through our assorted bruises and abundant pain, love never travels so far away that we can never find it again. While it might be forgotten by some, and despised by others, love never relents until it finds us all over again. But we have to choose to *want* that. Love is real, but so is pain. That's the reality of this cold and broken world.

Her mother and father were gone—Sonsela, too—but that didn't mean the search for love had to be gone, too.

Akando had embraced hate. That was the natural inclination of man; it was the easiest choice. His definition of love, if that's what it could ever truly be called, was only for himself. He had chosen his own actions decades ago, and he had chosen them now. It was those very choices that had twisted him into becoming a monster among men.

Chenoa was going to kill him, but it wouldn't be out of hate. It was because she understood that's what she needed to do after everything else had been taken away. It's what she had to do in order to protect the people she loved, both the living and the dead.

Love is also a chameleon, Chief. It hides in the everyday and in the unexpected. There are seasons when you might think it's gone forever, but it never travels far. Not really.

Her father was right about that.

But there was one more thing about love: it protects.

And that's what precisely what she was going to do now. She was going to protect her people, and she was going to protect the honor of her father.

Before, her body had almost shut down.

But almost was before; now is now.

And she realized that love could also be one final thing: brave.

And as if proving that to herself, Winterhawk stood resolutely on the slab, legs were steady as she climbed onto the ledge.

The backdoor tunnel into the Carson Mines faced her now. Blackness seeped out of it like an exposed cavity. It looked like a tunnel, but it was actually more of a release valve.

When several mines had dangerously flooded after accidentally striking underground rivers and streams, workers had begun tunneling these holes—dubbed gophers by the crews—as a way to allow rising water to find its way out of a mountain without drowning everyone trapped inside.

This gopher was now her way inside the Carson Mines.

Taking a deep, controlling breath, Chenoa unslung the Edison lamp from her waist. She fastened it atop her head, fingers switching on the battery. It immediately popped to life.

She shifted the weight of the Boss shotgun on her back so it rode slightly higher. Its stability provided her the smallest of comforts. She knew that death might be facing her, but she also understood that there was also the chance that she'd survive.

Her father had endured much greater odds than this, and he had lived.

And so would she.

Ducking down, she took several steps into the entrance. She carefully moved her head around, getting a sense of the terrain. Looking left, then looking right.

She involuntarily gasped; heart hammering with a sudden dose of fear. The light from her helmet had illuminated something unexpectedly horrifying.

Chenoa was now standing face-to-face with a monster.

CHAPTER 30

The Wen'ey'ti stared at her.

It didn't blink. It didn't breathe. It didn't even move.

Winterhawk took in the full sight of the monster with stunned disbelief, her back pressed tightly up against the far wall of the gopher tunnel.

Her shoulders began to lightly tremble, her hands unclenched. After a moment, she began to laugh.

The Wen'ey'ti didn't respond to her odd display of joviality; it couldn't even if it had wanted to. But judging solely by the fierce expression etched upon his face, the creature most definitely wanted to.

The monster was alive only inside the lines of the impressively detailed and imaginative parietal artwork that had been elaborately drawn onto one section of the cavern wall.

Chenoa was momentarily taken aback by the artistry.

While parietal paintings and engravings found on cave walls were typically associated with prehistoric cultures like the Altamira or the Lascaux, forms of traditional rock art were found in various indigenous groups all across North America.

These works had even inspired other ethnic communities, like the Chinese miners who had painstakingly adorned this particular gopher tunnel.

Using materials they had at hand—charcoal from their fires, ochre clay from the riverbed, and a makeshift brush made of pine needles—the miners had obviously spent a good deal of time painting this wall.

She stepped closer. She tipped her head slightly forward, bathing the cavern with the Edison lamp so she could study the design more carefully.

The artwork depicted a towering, humanoid figure, its body covered in flowing, hair-like strokes. The monstrous face showed an open jaw with razor-sharp teeth and glowing eyes painted in white clay. The large figure stood among stylized trees that were highly reminiscent of Chinese landscape paintings, but with jagged peaks evoking Oregon's mountains. To tie it to their mining life, the Chinese workers had etched simple geometric stencil shapes resembling pickaxes and gold pans below the ferocious creature.

It was a perfect blending of labor and myth.

It greatly resembled similar drawings that she had seen from the Arapaho and Shoshone nations. Those indigenous cultures believed there was a different species of the fabled forest Nu'numic that prowled hungrily among the tallest peaks and deepest mountain caves, with those drawings acting as their proof.

She had grown up with Nez Perce tales from elders. They spoke of the ancient forest Nu'numic and mountain-dwelling Wen'ey'ti. These were giant and terrifying man-eaters from the ancient of days.

How had her father once described them?

"There are monsters in this world, Chenoa. Real ones. They behave purely on instinct, driven by hunger and self-preservation. I know because I've seen some of them up close."

"Monsters," she had echoed.

At the time, she had thought he was talking about the evil men he had encountered throughout his life; in a way, she figured he probably was. But now she realized he'd also been speaking about something else, too.

Legends.

Chenoa thought once again about the unusual scar on the back of his left leg. The one that had resembled a massive claw mark. The wound that he had refused to talk about. Whatever violent encounter had caused it, the experience had left her father waking up from nightmares until the very end of his life.

That's because dreams remind us in the night of those very things we are so desperate to forget during the day. Only sometimes those memories refuse to be forgotten. Sooner or later, amiga, they come out like fissures of steam being vented from cracks in the earth. The heart tattles on what the mind has promised the soul to forget.

She stared harder at the parietal painting.

The Wen'ey'ti the miners had captured on the cavern wall looked savage and hungry. It also looked like something even more concerning: very real.

The landscape of the artwork indicated that the creature had been seen somewhere in the wilderness, with the inclusion of the pickaxes indicating that the Wen'ey'ti had also been right here.

The miners must have seen the monster inside the Carson Mines.

A sudden blast of wind shot down the gopher tunnel. The cold air caressed the sweat on her face, flipping away the hair that had matted wetly against her forehead.

She turned her head sharply, peering down at the end of the tunnel as the battery lamp stabbed into the darkness.

She saw that the tunnel ended with a sharp L-shape. The top rungs of a ladder poked above the ground, leading down to the next sublevel of the mine. The presence of the wind indicated that another entryway must be close to the gopher tunnel.

Chenoa frowned.

She hadn't seen that indicated on the map before she'd torched it. Just the main entrance, and the additional gopher tunnel. She wondered what else she might have missed.

Another gust of wind pressed against her face. It brought something else this time. Her nose crinkled as she inhaled something very animalistic and pungent, the unusual smell blanketed by a wafting aroma of rotted flesh.

She could feel the glowing eyes made of white clay boring into her from the parietal painting beside her.

Knock, knock, Chief.

Winterhawk quickly reached towards the sheepskin ammo sling on her back, sliding out a trio of shells. Cracking the stock of the 16-bore shotgun, she rapidly fed the shells into the Boss while never taking her eyes off the end of the tunnel.

She could feel the weight of everything pressing down on her.

The Creator had orchestrated all the events that had happened before in order to bring her to where she was now. The threads of her life were now completely intertwined with the majesty of Elkhorn Peak.

Behind her, the sunlight streaming from the entrance of the gopher hole was a reminder that retreat down the mountain face was impossible. She knew the climb should have killed her; attempting to go back down certainly would.

That meant that the only way through was to keep moving forward. Down the ladder and to whatever was next.

Right here, and right now, Chenoa understood that death was the only certainty.

If Akando wasn't already here, he would be soon enough. He would have those traitorous soldiers, Briggs and Ivers, salivating at the chance to finally take her down.

Or worse.

Winterhawk thought briefly of Major Quinn, and of his daughter, Huan. Here was a career military man dealing with not only the death of his wife, but the unimaginable anguish of seeing his daughter forced out of the country because of her mixed heritage. The Chinese Exclusion Act had pushed him to make an extreme choice, one that might well end up costing him everything.

Chenoa understood his desperation.

Her own father had chosen to serve in the U.S. Cavalry during the Civil War. In attempting to negotiate a truce with the United States for his people, Chief Joseph had offered to send ten of his greatest warriors to fight for the Union in the Great Conflict. Her father had been one of those ten. He'd also been the only one of them to make it back home alive.

And now, her father was dead as the treaty that Chief Joseph had made with the government all those many years ago. The Nez Perce had been relocated by the Wenaha River, just a few miles from Elkhorn Peak. If Akando released the underground river, the potential flooding would be deadly. Hundreds of her people would drown, and the survivors would never recover from the loss of life and property.

No.

She had to stop Akando.

Chenoa thumbed back the twin hammers on the Boss.

Pushing forward, Winterhawk made her way down to the end of the gopher tunnel. She dipped her head, using the lamp to illuminate the area just beyond the iron ladder. She saw the ground below, judged that it was a twenty-foot climb down the rungs to the bottom.

She paused for a long moment, watching and listening.

The pungent smell was much stronger by the ladder, making her wonder what exactly she'd be descending down to.

There was only one way to find out. And fast.

Slinging the Boss back over shoulder, Chenoa grabbed onto the edges of the ladder. She spread her feet outside of the rails and rapidly slid down it.

Her boots touched the ground seconds later. She immediately sunk into a crouch, whipping the shotgun around as her helmet light tracked quickly across the area.

She inhaled sharply. Her eyes went wide with shocked realization.

Chenoa was now staring at something she thought was an impossibility. She felt waves of fear ripple through her insides.

Welcome to the lair of legends, Chief.

CHAPTER 31

Chenoa knew that she was standing in a large sub-chamber of the mine, but it felt like she had just been dropped inside a massive skeleton. Enormous piles of bones were scattered all around her; most came from various animals, but others were distinctly human.

The stench of rotted flesh was overpowering.

She realized immediately that the Wen'ey'ti had made their lair here.

Above her, pockets of light punched through the ceiling from a pair of jagged holes. At one time those holes had been made by miners who had carved their way through the rock for additional ventilation. Now, they resembled something like cave entrances dug into the ceiling.

She noticed deep claw marks gouged all around the ventilation holes. The creatures had widened them to allow for alternate ways in and out of the mine. That meant they weren't just ruthless, but also cunning and intelligent creatures.

Does that shock you, Pocahontas? Because it really shouldn't. The Wen'ey'ti haven't survived millenniums by practicing accidental cleverness. Just like the Nu'numic, they've had to constantly adapt to their surroundings. That's how legends don't end up becoming myths.

She frowned.

Her father always spoke his wisdom to her from a place of personal experience. But he had never once shared stories about having any encounters with the Nu'numic. Of course, she'd always had her suspicions about it, just the same. Just because something sounds incredible doesn't necessarily mean it's impossible.

That's the thing about life, amiga. When you come right down to it, only the most unbelievable parts are ever true.

She shook her head at the thought.

Growing up as a child within the Nez Perce, stories about the monstrous Nu'numic had been nearly as prevalent as tales of the earliest Nimiipuu people who had first settled their tribe in the Pacific Northwest. In point of fact, they both seemed as ubiquitous to her culture as the cemi'tk berries were to fry bread.

The legends she heard in hushed whispers over campfires was of the Nu'numic being giant protectors of the forest. The massive creatures had supposedly been roaming the woods for centuries, savagely defending their homes against the steady encroachment of mankind.

Mountain tribes had similar stories about the Wen'ey'ti, a similar species of creature that made their homes in caves...

And mines.

Elders said the Wen'ey'ti guarded their sacred caves, punishing intruders with claws and teeth. The paintings here confirmed it. The miners must have been witnesses. As incredible as it was, those men had *seen* the monsters.

Had the creatures lived in the Carson Mines for decades?

Centuries ago, the Yupik and Inupiaq nations settled along Alaska's northern coastlines. They told stories of the Ancient Ones—massive bipedal creatures that migrated from the far east before the Big Flood separated the land masses. Those flood waters had eventually receded, but the Ancient Ones had remained.

She thought that those creatures must have evolved during the migration, becoming different species over the years as they staked territorial claims across different landscapes and different altitudes.

You know, Chief, you really shouldn't be concerning yourself right now with all the unnecessary why's and the how's. Seeing that bone currency stacked around you should make you question only one thing: where *are they?*

Chenoa gripped the shotgun tighter, head slowly swiveling as she took in more of her surroundings. Sunlight was reflecting off the hundreds of bones strewn around the sub-chamber. It effectively chased off all the shadows, offering illumination in every corner of the monster's lair, including the sharp dip of the tunnel leading down to the east side of the mine.

She sensed she was alone—for now.

But when those monsters returned to their lair—

An agonizing scream suddenly reverberated through the sub-chamber. It was an echo, coming from somewhere deep inside the mines.

It sounded off again; this time much louder.

The scream belonged to a man.

She now recognized the voice.

It was Major Quinn.

Chenoa felt a hot flash of anger course through her. Akando must be torturing Quinn because he hadn't taken them to the correct location of the river. Or maybe Quinn had, and Akando was hurting him, anyway.

Casting away all thoughts of the Wen'ey'ti, she charged forward through the sub-chamber and towards the dip in the tunnel just ahead of her.

It was time to show Akando what true Winterhawk courage looked like.

CHAPTER 32

The barrel of Nitrotriazolone placed just inside the entrance of the Carson Mines looked like some kind of wide-awake nightmare. Agent Travers gently tapped it with the tip of one boot, listening carefully as the dangerous liquid sloshed gently inside.

The 50-pound barrel was full.

"I'll be damned," Travers hissed.

Agent Michaels glanced over at him from his perch on the mine tracks. "Probably." He then shrugged with rehearsed indifference. "Occupational hazard."

Travers absently slurped a glob of Red Man from off his lower lip. His cheeks twitched with barely controlled anxiety. The colony of stress wasps nesting behind his eyes had already begun to take flight. Any moment now, he knew that he would feel their painful jabs in his brain.

When the Secret Service agents had arrived at Elkhorn Peak moments ago, they hadn't known what they might encounter. But one thing was for certain, neither one of them would have guessed that NTO would have been a selection on their carnival Beano boards.

Travers took a calming breath. It didn't help.

Michaels took notice. "Are you sure that you're okay, Travers?"

"Uh-huh."

"I'm not convinced."

"Believe it. Momma taught me never to tell lies."

"Too bad you didn't listen to her," Michaels said. He glanced over at the two discarded Harley-Davidson Model 1 motorcycles that sat just outside of the mouth of the mine.

Travers followed his gaze. "That's some pretty expensive hardware to leave unprotected out in the elements like that."

"Those are standard-issue motorcycles for the Army Corps of Engineers." Michaels stated it like it was an answer to a question that hadn't yet been asked. "Seen lots of them out in the field in my time. The thing is, I've never seen any operating out in this kind of wilderness."

Travers thought of the giant Indian they'd seen earlier through the binoculars. He surprised himself by easily pulling the name from memory. "Maybe those bikes belong to Akando Winterhawk. He probably brought them here."

Michaels shook his head. "We would have seen him with the motorcycles. All those boys brought with them were bad attitudes and a hostage."

Travers needed to think for a moment.

He absently swished his tongue around, carefully depositing a clump of Red Man from one side of his cheek to the other. The chewing tobacco felt hot in his mouth. The overly sweet taste always reminded him of raisins and chocolate. Those were two frequent delicacies in his home when growing up. His mom would often bake cookies with those ingredients, and you never knew which was which until after you bit into one and—

"Do you need a wilderness guide?" Michaels asked.

Travers blinked in confusion. "I'm sorry—a what?"

"I asked if you need a guide," Michaels answered, "because you seemed lost there for a moment."

"Yes. No. Sorry." Travers nervously cleared his throat as he quickly thought of something to say. "I was just thinking about…uh, what you said about those motorcycles belonging to soldiers from the Army Corps of Engineers."

"Yeah? What about them?"

"For starters, *where* the hell are they?"

Agent Michaels stared at him for a long moment. "Dead, *obviously.*"

Travers felt the stress wasps begin to sting the back of his eyes; his head immediately throbbed with sharp pain. The day's horrific events rolled like a boulder down a mountain of absurdity. Each revelation gained speed, threatening to crush him.

He honestly didn't know how much more of this he could possibly take.

Travers recalled his first mission, and how he botched an arrest of a lunatic gunman. His nerves that day had nearly cost lives. Now, those same nerves threatened to destroy his very own.

"Dead," Travers echoed quietly. The inflection in his voice was as lifeless as the very word he just uttered. He brought a hand down towards his gun belt, allowing his fingers to stroke the stock of his holstered Colt .45.

It did little to comfort him.

Agent Michaels rested his hands on his hips. His own .45 was secured in a well-worn shoulder holster. He looked like a man who'd already forgotten how many times he'd already had to use it.

"In case you didn't know, "Michaels said, "the reason I'm perched on these mine tracks is because I don't want to be soiling my best boots with that sticky blood."

"Blood? Where?"

"Over there."

"Over there." Travers sighed with weary resignation. He dropped his gaze to the mine floor, eyes tracking across the mud and the rocks...and the blood. There was a crisscross splatter several feet away from the barrel of Nitrotriazolone. He also saw that several different pairs of boot prints had already trampled across it.

Michaels followed his gaze. "Those tracks are from Akando and his posse earlier. Their boots sunk into that blood like it was mud. Fresh blood would spread out in patterns after being disturbed, not clumps."

Travers nodded. "This blood wasn't fresh, then. Probably leaked out from those Army boys with the motorcycles."

"Yup."

Travers looked around the entrance of the mine. "No bodies, either. Just like that water hauler back at Higgins Haven. Whatever ate that mule and left those weird footprints back at the cabin must have played hide-and-seek with these bodies here at the mine."

Agent Michaels appeared to be genuinely impressed. "I reckon that's right."

"We need to get more men down here." Travers cast an anxious glance into the dark cavern of the mine. "Those *things* probably live in there."

"Probably. But Akando Winterhawk is in there somewhere, too...and that's a whole helluva lot worse."

"Worse?" Travers stared at him for a long moment. "Worse for us? Or for that hostage?"

"Does it matter?"

Travers looked once again at the barrel of NTO, wondering once again how protecting President Roosevelt had led him here to—

A man's scream tore through the air. Both agents jerked their body towards the sound. It had emanated from somewhere deep inside the Carson Mine.

Travers immediately pulled his Colt from its holster, fanning the weapon towards the mine entrance. He felt the cold air coming from the cavern gently swiping at the sweat blanketing his face.

Silence settled over them once again.

Then, there was a second scream. This one sounded like it was a mixture of agony and mournfulness. Travers didn't know which one of those was worse.

Agent Michaels pulled out his handgun. "Let's move!" Leaping off the tracks, he began to sprint into the dark entrance of the mine.

With the wasps stinging mercilessly inside his head, Travers followed close behind him.

CHAPTER 33

The Carson Mines clawed into the very heart of Elkhorn Peak until it had become nothing more than a jagged scar on the Blue Mountain Range. For decades, the mine had lay abandoned, its interworking tunnels silent except for the occasional whisper of ghosts in the wind.

Its labyrinth stretched nearly a mile through granite and basalt, a testament to the miners who had toiled long and died quick within its darkened depths.

The Carson Mines had three levels—stacked at 100, 500, and 900 feet below the main adit—that plunged down into the mountain's core. Each was a maze of drifts and crosscuts, their foundational timbers now nearly rotted away over the years. The jagged cavern walls glinted with quartz, which flickered off shattered glass residue from discarded carbide lamps, lying like bits of forgotten fool's gold.

On the 500-foot level sprawled the pit chamber: a cavernous void in the floor that had been dug 25-feet wide. At its heart gaped an open stope, a large pit that miner's often referred to as "the tomb." It was here where broken tools and useless chunks of granite were dumped during excavation. It was a mining garbage heap that had once been 50-feet deep; now, the tomb was barely ten.

A steam crane, its 15-foot arm frozen in rust, was perched on a ledge above the tomb, its cables dangling down into the stope like 10-foot metallic spectral vines.

A 6-foot-wide ventilation raise—known as the chimney—had been built directly above the tomb. It soared straight up to the surface of Elkhorn

Peak, where its timbered shaft exhaled the cold air that hushed the mountain's secrets.

But further down, the Carson Mines held an even deeper mystery.

On the 900-foot level, a hidden cavern cradled a secret underground river. Its deep current snaked through the darkness with a low, relentless murmur. It was concealed by a false floor; the water beneath it pulsed and slithered like a snake's cold vein.

The water lived and breathed as if it had a mind. The river gurgled loudly as if in constant anticipation. The familiar cadence of its heartbeat had become the roaring flow reverberating inside the cavern. It was as if the underground river had been waiting years for someone to return and set it free.

And soon, it finally would be.

THE EDISON LAMP flickered atop his head, casting jagged shadows across the cavern walls as Major Quinn carefully parked the cumbersome A-car. He depressed the brake handle on the car, watching as it moved another foot along the rusted tracks before coming to a stop.

The two 50-pound barrels stacked inside the A-car briefly jostled against each other. If they collided with too much force, the resulting detonation would vaporize everyone inside the cavern in an instant.

Quinn's heart thudded as he watched the barrels finally come to a quiet rest.

Huan's face—her mother's crooked smile mirrored in it—anchored his resolve. Sweating profusely, he took a stabilizing breath.

The map flickered once again in his mind, then skittered away into the forgotten recesses of his subconscious. The imagery of it was gone, but he really no longer needed it. They were now standing exactly where they should be.

Quinn had remembered.

The Edison lamp strapped to his forehead flickered as he took several measured breathes. Glancing up, he noted that fissures had cracked along some sections of the cavern's ceiling over time. These jagged holes were evidence of long-abandoned mining blasts and temperamental moments of geological rage.

The unevenly spaced tears in the ceiling allowed for swaths of daylight to slice into the darkness below like spectral knives. When they began their descent, haphazard beams of daylight illuminated things their head lamps missed.

As they had trudged silently through the interlocking tunnelways, they'd seen rusted pickaxes and shovels, as well as discarded bone piles—elk, deer, and human—festering in shadowy areas.

Those cracked skulls gleaming like cursed relics beneath the light had been disturbing enough, but seeing the basalt walls nearest the bones deeply scored by unusual large claw marks had been even worse.

Upon this fearsome discovery, Akando had stood for a long moment, studying the marks with great intensity.

"What's a bear doing all the way down here?" Briggs had kicked one of the human skulls as if it added punctuation to his question.

Ivers had shrugged off the sight of the bone piles like it had been a heavy garment weighting him down. "If we find one, you be sure and ask him."

"I think this mine holds many secrets that we don't yet understand," Akando had said. He had turned away from the wall just then, eyes blazing. "Isn't that right, Major Quinn?"

Quinn hadn't said a word in return, and *that* had been a very loud response.

THE FOUR MEN were now on the 900-foot level of the Carson Mines. They were standing almost directly beneath the chimney vent that had been dug through each level of the mine. Accessible by ladders, those vents reached all the way up to the very top of Elkhorn Peak.

To Quinn, they looked like pathways to freedom. He briefly glanced at the ladder; saw the faintest glimmer of natural light streaming down from the surface.

If he could somehow make his escape, that's the direction he would go. He could never hope to outrun them, but maybe he could—

"Why have you stopped here?" Akando asked with mild irritation. "I don't see the river, Major."

Turning around, Quinn nodded. "You're very perceptive."

Ivers menacingly placed a hand on the butt of his holstered revolver. "Maybe you have too much fat between your ears, Major Quinn. You might not have heard it, but Akando just asked you something."

"I heard him."

"You did?"

"Uh-huh."

"Then why didn't you answer him?"

"Because the question was rhetorical."

Ivers's left eyelid twitched. "Rhetorical."

"Akando loves hearing himself talk. In fact, you should really try asking *him* a question."

Ivers squinted with dull suspicion. "What kind of a question?"

"The third barrel of nitrotriazolone."

"So?" Briggs asked. "What about it?"

"Ask Akando why he left the barrel up there at the mouth of the mine."

Ivers and Briggs exchanged confused glances. They had both seen the third barrel, but hadn't given it much thought—until now.

"I was sort of wondering about that," Briggs remarked.

"I honestly wasn't before," Ivers said, "but I certainly am now."

Akando stared hard at the two soldiers. "Curiosity killed the cat, but satisfaction brought it back."

Quinn shook his head. "Nothing's coming back, not after today. When this is all over, the truth of what really happened will be buried forever inside here."

Quinn began to feel more emboldened. Rage had replaced the fear that had wound its way through his body ever since he'd set foot off the *Lathos*. He knew that he was a dead man. But if he could somehow convince Ivers and Briggs that they were too, that might provide him with an opportunity to somehow escape.

His entire military career had been nothing but a series of calculated risks. And now, it was time to make to make a big one.

Quinn shifted his gaze to the soldiers.

"Akando asked you to betray your country in exchange for some nonexistent gold. You sold your very souls for a lie. He's going to kill me down here, and then he's going to kill the both of you. If the river doesn't do the job for him, then that third barrel of NTO will. Whether it's by water or by fire, Akando is going to turn the Carson Mines into a tomb for each of us."

A long and foreboding silence hung in the air.

Ivers and Briggs now wore looks of concern. They were obviously mulling over what he had just told them.

Men without scruples weren't ever swayed by matters of the truth unless lies had been attached to their blood money. Deep down, both of these soldiers must have harbored those doubts about Akando. It was greed that had plugged their noses from smelling his bullshit.

If Briggs and Ivers turned on Akando, there was still a chance of walking out of here. Quinn felt a flash of hope fire up in his stomach at the thought.

The heavy silence was suddenly broken by Akando's deep laughter.

"Don't pay any attention to Major Quinn, gentlemen." Akando's lips curled into a tight grimace. "He doesn't have a leg to stand on."

Moving with a sudden agility that seemed impossible for a man of his size, Akando unsheathed the deadly Razorback. He thrust his massive arm forward, sinking the double-bladed weapon deep into the meaty flesh of Quinn's left thigh.

Quinn immediately emitted a high-pitch scream.

Twisting his hand, Akando flicked his wrist downwards. The Razorback sliced cleanly across the patella, scraping against bone before completely severing ligaments and tendons.

"Stop!" Quinn cried out loudly in pain, falling heavily onto the cavern floor. He clutched his leg and writhed in agony. "Please...STOP!"

"Stop?" Akando loomed over him, the Razorback knife dripping Quinn's own blood onto his face. "I haven't even started..."

"You can't kill him!" Briggs's voice was hitched with momentary panic. "Not until he tells us about the river."

"We didn't come all this way for nothing," Ivers growled. "Make him tell us!"

Akando grinned. "He's going to tell us where the river is." He lowered the Razorback, scraping the double blades slowly across Quinn's crotch. "Because if he doesn't, the punishment will be just *nuts*."

Quinn shook his head with horror. "No...!"

"Then show us where the river is! NOW!"

Grunting with pain, Quinn slowly dragged himself toward a nearby granite slab. Its polished surface blended almost seamlessly with the cavern floor. His fingers began probing frantically around the seams.

"It's here," Quinn rasped. His voice was cracked with agony. His Edison lamp caught the edges of carved design of a dragon's claw. He pried forcefully at it. With a distinct click, the slab suddenly shifted under his touch. It slid several feet across the ground on a mechanized pully that had been expertly camouflaged against the cavern floor.

The men stared with incredulity at the ingenuity of the Chinese miners.

Then, Briggs stomped madly forward. His Adam's apple bobbed like a vulture's crop, his Parker shotgun slung over his shoulder. He kicked the slab aside to reveal a ten-foot diameter hole. Inside of the hole rushed a torrent of tar-black water; it frothed like a caged beast, mist spraying upwards against his face.

Angered, Ivers also stepped closer. His Edison lamp further illuminated the jagged hole and the churning current that had been beneath their feet this entire time. "Why did they go to all this trouble of hiding it like this?"

Akando kept his eyes fixated on Quinn. "Because they knew the river was more valuable than what they were pulling out of the rocks. They thought they could someday negotiate business terms with that leverage. Then, the Snake River Massacre occurred. The Chinese who weren't arrested or killed fled further west in fear. The father of Quinn's wife had been one of them. Before he died, he made sure those secrets were scribbled on that mining map."

Briggs spun around, levelling the shotgun. "Then, I guess we don't need you around anymore, Major!" He stepped closer, moving the shotgun barrel inches from Quinn's face. "You've now become as useless as a pussy on a pickaxe!"

"Enough!" Akando snapped. He roughly grabbed onto Briggs' arm, shoving the shotgun down. "There's a second river down here, you idiot!"

Stunned, Briggs stared at him. "A second...*what*?"

"Another river? Down *here*? What the hell are you talking about?!" Ivers asked.

Even though he was consumed with pain, Quinn found his mind racing back to the map. As unbelievable as it might be, there *was* another river flowing deep inside Elkhorn. His father-in-law had been the one to actually discover it, and now its location was cleverly hidden inside the mine.

He recalled what Akando had said earlier, when the group of them had been standing at the mouth of the mine. He'd mentioned that where the river wasn't was even more important than where it was. That's because it wasn't at all where you would expect to find it.

And he had just led these murderers right to it.

The memory of Huan filled his vision.

Quinn temporarily pushed aside the tremendous knee pain, and focused only on her. His original plan was to trade his daughter' amnesty to the Army Corps of Engineers for the location of the river. Now, he was giving his own life to a madman so she would be spared unimaginable suffering. It was a trade he would give willingly, and without regrets.

What his conscious could not justify was realizing how many Nez Perce would be killed in the flood. The very river that Li's father coveted right up until the day of his own death would now bring wanton destruction onto a group of innocent people.

Had he just doomed the Nez Perce for Huan's safety?

Quinn hadn't spent very much time in his life petitioning the Lord, but he began praying profusely now. He squeezed his eyes shut, listening to the frothing water emanating from the open hole on the cavern floor. This prayer wasn't about him; wasn't about his survival. With how the blood flowed from the savage gash on his thigh, he knew he was far beyond saving.

No, his prayer was about Chenoa. He prayed that she was still alive, he prayed that she was already here, and he prayed that she would be able to save her people.

"Please, God," he whispered aloud.

"God isn't here, but the Devil always has time to listen."

Quinn's eyes fluttered open. Akando had squatted down beside him, and was leaning close. "It's the Devil that wants to hear your confession now. He wants you to tell him all about that second river. There's another water vein—one that's much bigger—hidden somewhere down here. Now, where is it, Quinn?"

"It's close." Small blood bubbles had begun to form between his lips. "Written on the map: 'It lies behind the eyes.' It's right behind you, Akando."

Frowning, Akando swiveled his body around. He slowly stood up, his lamp sweeping across the cavern walls.

He suddenly stopped, focusing his light on one section of the cavern.

Ivers emitted sharp a gasp when he finally saw it.

Briggs had just seen it, too. "What's with all this caveman shit?"

The massive Wen'ey'ti carving staring back at them did not answer.

CHAPTER 34

"This isn't caveman shit," Akando growled.

One entire section of the mine wall had been covered with parietal paintings and engravings. A legion of monsters stared down at the men from the cavern walls. Their charcoal forms snarled, white-clay eyes glinting like embers. Ferocious Chinese dragons coiled around pickaxes, scattered throughout the carvings. The elaborately detailed Wen'ey'ti and Nu'numic paintings dominated over them.

Ivers shook his head at the sight. "What the hell are we looking at, Akando?"

"The Wen'ey'ti and the Nu'numic."

"Gesundheit," Briggs muttered.

"They're called the Ancient Ones," Akando elaborated. "The Nez Perce elders spoke of them when I was a boy. They're creatures of myth; watchers of the forest bound to the mountains and the rivers."

"Watchers of what?" Ivers asked.

"Us."

"Us," Ivers echoed.

"Mankind," Akando elaborated. "The Nu'numic protect the forests, while the Wen'ey'ti guard the mountains. Tribes all over this continent have similar stories, tales of Sasquatches and Ape Men roaming through the woods."

"Protectors?" Briggs snorted loudly. "Then where were they while all you brownies were being wiped out by Mr. Whitey? If you ask me, these guardians have done a pretty shit job."

Akando grinned. "Nobody asked you, Briggs."

The two men locked hard stares.

Ivers stepped between the two of them, squinting closer at the series of Wen'ey'ti and Nu'numic paintings stretching down the wall. He took note of their hands, seeing the claws curled as if ready to leap at him right off the wall.

"What I don't understand is why would those Chinese miners waste their time drawing Indian monsters? Don't they have myths and mystical beings of their own?"

"These miners had been drawing what they had seen," Akando answered.

"Horseshit!" Briggs slammed his fist into the face of one of the parietal paintings. "If want to jerk off to these fairy tales, then go right ahead and spray your baby batter all over these caveman drawings. I don't want to listen to another word about monsters. All I want to hear is where that second river is, and when you're going to give me the rest of my goddamn money."

Akando allowed the smallest of smiles to flicker across the crook of his mouth. "I want you to remember something very important about that money, Briggs."

"Yeah? And what's that, boss?"

"That gold will only make you rich...for life."

Briggs swallowed hard, his large Adam's apple twitching like a salmon caught in a bear's paw. He tightly clutched his Parker shotgun, eyes flashing angrily. "Major Quinn better be all wrong about this, amigo. Fat boy thinks you plan on making this mine our tomb instead of our payoff. Well, don't even *think* about doing that. You might have an awfully big set of balls, Akando, but I've got an awfully big mouth. If you fuck us over, I'll tear off your balls with my teeth and feed them to you like hairy wads of Spruce gum. Do we have a mutual understanding?"

The mine was filled with a long, heavy silence, broken only by the river's sloshing beneath their feet.

Staring up at the two men, Quinn felt his heart hammering. He shifted uncomfortably in a pool of his own blood, feeling its sticky warmth soaking the back of his uniform. He clutched the gash in his leg with both hands; the throbbing of his knee was becoming unbearable. And yet, he couldn't take his eyes off of Briggs and Akando.

The tension between the two men had far exceeded the breaking point.

It seemed now that they were hurtling towards Armageddon.

Ivers understood that, too. His eyes had grown as wide as saucers, and his hand was nervously resting on the grip of his Colt.

It felt dangerous now to even breathe.

Akando was the only one among any of them who wore a mask of calmness. He appeared like a man who was still in complete and total control.

The massive portrait of the Wen'ey'ti directly behind Briggs appeared to have glinting eyes, its white-clay stare pulsating against the swath of battery light. Akando fixated his gaze directly on it.

Briggs shifted nervously on the heels of his boots, keeping the shotgun level.

What happened next, happened fast.

"Enough talk!" Akando roared. He lunged forward with frightening speed, the Razorback spinning around in his hands. The blades connected with the barrel of the Parker, wrenching it out of Briggs' hand. As the shotgun clattered uselessly to the ground, Akando kept charging forward. He brought the Razorback up and across his chest.

Briggs tried to grab onto his hands and somehow stop him, but he was too slow. He watched helplessly as the vicious double-bladed Razorback was thrust forward, whistling directly past his face.

And impacted against the wall behind him.

Briggs staggered sideways in stunned surprise, glancing back over his shoulder at Akando. "What—?"

"Quinn said that the location of the second river is 'behind the eyes' on the map." Akando strode purposely up to the large Wen'ey'ti carving. Both blades of the Razorback were impaled directly between its glaring white-clay eyes.

Grabbing onto the handle, Akando pried forcefully against the granite with the Razorback like it was a crowbar. The panel ground opened with a loud screech that sounded like some kind of dying beast.

Dust swirled in the fractured light, revealing a six-foot wide hole that had been dug behind the head of the painted creature.

Incredibly, there was a roar of water thundering from within the walls. It was a geological corkscrew vein, its large flow dwarfing the river running beneath the false floor. Together, both of them unleashed would produce a churning maelstrom that would completely swallow Elkhorn Peak in one big gulp.

"There it is," Akando growled, head lamp catching the second vein's frothing imagery. "This is the *real* killer, Briggs."

"Real killer?" Briggs frowned with confusion. "I thought the flood was—"

"This isn't just a flood, Briggs!" Ivers ranted. His voice was manic, cracking like brittle bone. This was obviously exciting him. "It's aquafication—confluences, you see! These two rivers down here, they're going to become some damn apocalypse! After the detonation, the confluence will surge these waters like a thousand locomotives. The flood will bury the entire eastern valley, and every living soul caught its path will be swept away."

Akando nodded with satisfaction. "It's time to drown history itself. My people will see that it was Chief Joseph who brought the Creator's wrath down upon the Nez Perce. For any survivors, this flood will be their baptism. They'll rise up from the waters and discover that the real Chief Winterhawk is waiting to lead them."

"Maniacs." Quinn shifted backwards on the floor, painfully moving to a sitting position against the wall. "You're nothing but a bunch of sadistic maniacs."

Ivers held up a scolding finger. "Correction: rich maniacs."

"Damn straight." Briggs shouldered the Parker. "Now, let's blow this shithole."

Grinning, Akando sheathed the Razorback and moved over to the A-cart. He gingerly picked up the first barrel, hefting it like it had all the weight of a pinecone.

He set the NTO down next to the open slab on the floor; next, he grabbed the second barrel and positioned it beneath the opening on the wall.

Briggs and Ivers pulled two brass clock timers from the cart. Each of them was fastened with Bickford blasting cap fuses and attached to a triple bundle of dynamite sticks. They set the timers for 30 minutes and placed the bundles down beside each of the barrels.

"We've got 30 minutes to get the hell out of here," Briggs warned.

Ivers motioned nervously at Quinn. "Whatever you're planning on doing with him, you'd better do it now—and quickly."

With his back still pressed up against the wall, Quinn stared up at Akando. His face was wracked with pain, and he felt weak from loss of blood. He knew that he would probably pass out any moment now. It would probably be more merciful in the end if he did.

"What are you going to do now?" Quinn asked.

Akando slowly unsheathed the Razorback. "Kill you."

"My daughter…"

"She won't be harmed, Major Quinn. You fulfilled your end of the bargain, and I will fulfill the end of mine."

"This plan isn't going to work." Quinn's shoulders began to shake. He felt alarmingly cold. He realized that shock was starting to seep into his system. He hoped that it would soon numb the terrible pain.

"I'm going to tell you a story now." Akando squatted down carefully beside him. "This happened in Oregon, around 1866. The Silver Vein Mine in Baker City." He kept his voice low. He was relishing the memory like a wolf savoring fresh carrion. "Miners there hit a large water vein. They thought it was just a trickle at first before a larger stream joined in. Soon, it became a massive problem. Water flooded the shafts in minutes, and half the town drowned by dusk. Bloated bodies were found in the Snake River for days after. There was nothing left behind after that but wreckage and ruin."

"Sounds just like your life, Akando," Quinn muttered.

Ignoring him, Akando gestured at the corkscrew vein behind the wall. "This one here is bigger than Baker City. After the explosions, these rivers will turn the Elkhorn flood into a legend. And just think, you'll be down here to watch it all happen."

"At least I won't be alone." Quinn shot a glance at Ivers and Briggs. "Ask him about the third barrel of NTO he left at the mouth of the mine. Please!"

Akando shook his head with mild irritation. He reached down and grabbed Quinn by the shoulders, roughly lifting him up off the floor. Quinn let out a shrill cry of pain as his injured leg took some of the brunt of his weight. He teetered sideways, nearly falling, but Akando held him up against the wall with one outstretched arm. His other arm was holding the Razorback over his head.

"I would ask if you had any final words," Akando said with a grin, "but with my luck—"

He stopped in mid-sentence. There was something different about Quinn's expression. He was now intently focused on the chimney vent directly above them. The pain in his features had been replaced by something else: hope.

And that could only mean one thing.

"Chenoa Winterhawk!" Akando boomed loudly into Quinn's face. "I'm so glad you could join us again!"

Beside him, Ivers and Briggs had already raised their weapons.

Akando spun around and looked up.

Chenoa was inside the chimney vent, dangling from a ladder 20-feet above them. She had a Boss shotgun aimed down at them.

The two soldiers quickly sighted their target.

"Take her down!" Akando hissed.

Briggs and Ivers fired without hesitation.

Then, the entire cavern was filled with nothing but gunfire.

CHAPTER 35

...barrel of nitrotriazolone at the mouth of the mine...”

Chenoa Winterhawk halted her ladder descent as Quinn's voice echoed from the cavern below. It was raw and panicked, and his words carried the desperation of a man staring death in the face.

She knew that meant his time was nearly gone.

Her time was slipping too.

She had to move much faster.

Chenoa thought back to several minutes earlier.

She'd raced from the Wen'ey'ti's bone-strewn lair, its stench still clinging to her as she found the first chimney vent at the end of the gopher tunnel. The ladder she discovered there would undoubtedly be her only shot at the element of surprise.

The Chinese map was etched in her memory. It showed three levels—surface, pit chamber, and a 900-foot cavern—with the main tunnels too risky for stealth. The chimney vents, with their six-foot-wide shafts with ladders, offered her the only real element of surprise.

Now, clinging to one of those same splintered wooden ladders, Chenoa resumed the descent from the gopher tunnel toward the second level. The triple-barrel Boss shotgun slung across her back was now a familiar anchor.

The Edison lamp cast jagged shadows across the narrow chimney vent as she climbed, illuminating endless mineral tracks that appeared to snake into nothing but blackness. The mine's stale air stung her lungs, with each rung creaking under her boots as her muscles burned from the 200-foot climb.

She glanced at the steam crane looming beside the pit chamber. Its 15-foot rusted arm held dangling cables, like metallic fishing lines over a tomb of discarded pickaxes and jagged rocks.

The map had marked another ladder opposite the crane that supposedly led down to the 900-foot level. The Chinese miners had circled that particular area on the map, so she knew that's where Quinn was going.

Winterhawk's boots scraped for traction as she reached the second level, heart hammering. A new sound stopped her cold—the distinct roar of two separate rivers thundering from below.

She suddenly understood what she was hearing.

"Two rivers?!" she hissed.

Thinking back, she realized that the map's faint double lines scribbled on the bottom level had already confirmed it. President Roosevelt's Land Reclamation Act coveted these waters for dams, but to the Nez Perce, they signaled annihilation if Akando unleashed them.

She moved rapidly to the next ladder. Whatever happened next, those rungs led to her destiny.

That's a tad bit dramatic, ain't it, Chief? Ladders go one of two ways: up or down. It's the same as life. Pick your path, or it'll pick it for you.

Her father's voice rumbled in her mind. His words always served as both a memory from years gone by, as well as being as present as her very next breath. She couldn't possibly explain how and why it started to happen; nor did she really want to. All she ever understood is that her father had promised to always be with her; even after death.

Fresh screams from Major Quinn drove her forward.

Midway down the chimney vent, she glanced down. Horror instantly seized her. Quinn was slumped against the cavern wall, blood pooling beneath his leg. Briggs and Ivers stood nearby, weapons glinting. Akando loomed over him, the Razorback's blades gleaming.

It looked like Quinn's murder was only seconds away now.

She had to do something!

Chenoa's shoulders strained as she reached behind her back for the Boss. Beneath her, the ladder creaked loudly under her shifting weight.

Hearing the noise, Quinn's eyes flicked upward, locking onto her. A faint smile touched his lips. He had entrusted his life to her care, and her failure to protect him was like a knife in her gut.

He was going to die all because of her.

Akando caught Quinn's glance, and knew immediately what was behind it.

"Chenoa Winterhawk!" he boomed, his voice echoing like a war drum in the tight shaft. "I'm so glad you could join us again!" He tossed Quinn to the ground like a broken doll.

Briggs and Ivers had already raised their weapons, lamp lights pinning Winterhawk to the ladder like an insect.

Akando narrowed his eyes suspiciously when he saw her.

She stared down at him with pure venom. She held out her open right hand from the side, palm down. She then turned her hand quickly outward, bringing her palm back up.

It was a Plains Sign Language gesture that the Nez Perce had used for centuries. All warriors had learned it for silent battlefield communication. Akando knew exactly what it meant.

She had just told him that Death was coming.

"Take her down!" Akando screamed with rage.

Chenoa quickly twisted her body around so she was facing forward, hooking her feet firmly behind the rung directly beneath her. Releasing her grip on the ladder, she let her body fall forward.

Briggs and Ivers fired their weapons.

Splinters of wood showered into the air as the bullets impacted where her body had been a split second earlier.

She was now completely vertical, hanging precariously from one of the ladder rungs by her feet. The Boss was now in both hands as she aimed the weapon down at Akando.

Death can be a real gift, Chief. It's time for this bastard to open his present now.

Chenoa pulled the trigger.

CHAPTER 36

The shotgun blast was enormous as the barrel flash illuminated the cavern like a lightning strike.

Akando had flung himself sideways as she fired, but the three-inch shotgun shells gouged into his left thigh, ripping a fist-sized hole out of his flesh. He screamed with pain, collapsing onto the rock floor.

Briggs and Ivers had both reflexively stepped backwards when Chenoa had fired at Akando; now, they were swinging their weapons back up.

Winterhawk shifted the triple-barrel over towards them, taking aim.

A deafening crack echoed—not gunfire, but the ladder snapping where the bullets fired from Briggs and Ivers had chewed through the splintered wood.

Chenoa's stomach lurched as the upper section broke free, swinging down inside the chimney vent. She dropped the Boss, hands flailing for purchase.

Careening downwards, the ladder slammed against the rocky wall, jamming into a crude L-shape. The sudden impact jolted her. Her feet slipped out from the rung where she'd hooked them. Arms pinwheeling, she barely caught the horizontal ladder section, her fingers digging into the splintered wood.

Her shoulders screamed with effort as her body now dangled 80 feet above the cavern floor.

The Boss was falling, spinning end-over-end as Akando snatched it out of mid-air.

Seeing his opportunity, Briggs leveled his Parker at Chenoa's dangling body. "Time to pluck the feathers of our sitting duck—"

"No!" Akando raged, using the Boss as a crutch to stand. "The bitch is mine! Do you understand?! She. Is. MINE!"

Briggs jerked back, lowering the rifle, exchanging an apprehensive glance with Ivers. "Things have gotten off the rails here. You're hurt bad, boss."

"I'll be fine," Akando snarled, "after I squash our blubbering outhouse bug over here."

From his slumped position against the cavern wall, Major Quinn moaned, his voice a broken whisper. "Chenoa..." Blood seeped from his mouth, his chest heaving with shallow, ragged breaths.

Hearing her name, Winterhawk looked down. She met Quinn's frightened stare. "I'm sorry," she whispered.

Quinn coughed up blood. It dribbled out of both corners of his mouth in frothy clumps. He didn't bother to wipe it off. Instead, he took a deep breath. "Huan," he said weakly.

Huan.

Winterhawk felt the weight of that word like it was fastened to an anchor around her heart. She'd dragged Quinn into this—his map, annotated by those Chinese miners, had led him right to his own slaughter.

Her heart clenched, guilt crashing over her like the hidden rivers below.

She locked emotional stares with Quinn.

"Huan." She repeated her name as if it was some kind of unspoken promise between them. Because that's exactly what it was.

Major Quinn's shoulders began to shudder as tears spilled down his face.

"Touching!" Akando growled. He hobbled his way over to Quinn and grabbed a clump of his hair. "On your feet, soldier boy!"

Akando lifted Quinn up off the floor with relative ease, slamming his body roughly up against the cavern wall. He unsheathed the Razorback, pressing its blades against Quinn's throat.

"You're a dead man now," Major Quinn said. "Even after all of your posturing and all of your planning, you're going to end up dying down here. Only it won't be from the flooding or the explosions."

"No?"

"No." His eyes flicked upwards towards Chenoa. "It's going to be because of *her*." Quinn began to laugh, the noise building deep from inside his chest as—

Akando squeezed the Razorback's handles. The blades sliced clean through Quinn's neck, severing his head with a sickening crunch. Blood fountained, painting the cavern wall like a red sheet. His eyelids fluttered with momentary confusion as his head rolled down his shoulder and fell to the ground.

"He never did have a head for this job," Akando muttered, sidestepping the geyser of blood. He savagely tossed Quinn's twitching corpse aside, wiping the blades clean on his pant legs.

Now, Chenoa would be next. Akando's soul burned to crush her and erase Jolon's legacy with her death.

Ivers glanced nervously at the timer ticking beside the NTO, the roar of the exposed river beneath it nearly deafening. "Do whatever you have to do, Akando, but do it fast. We don't have much time."

Hanging from the ladder, Chenoa followed Ivers' gaze. She saw the dynamite and the ticking timer. There were now 25 minutes until everything down here was blown to smithereens. The explosion would unleash a flood, drowning the Nez Perce valley.

Then what are you hanging around here for, Chief? You heard the man, and you know the drill. It's too late to save Major Quinn, but it's not too late to avenge him. And since you very well can't avenge him if you're dead, it's high time that you pulled yourself out of this mess.

Pull.

PULL!

Grunting, she clawed the jagged wall, and pulled herself up onto the swaying ladder. It threatened to fall apart on her at any moment.

Near the unbroken ladder section leading to the pit level, a rusted cable from the steam crane dangled less than five feet away. She would need to swing to reach the pit level safely.

Once there, she prayed that she would be able to find some type of weapon. She'd need to find something because Akando and those two soldiers would be coming after her next with everything they've got.

Winterhawk scrambled to her feet, the ladder swaying dangerously. Her shadow glided beneath her. The noonday sun beaming through the vent above cast it.

Then, her shadow vanished.

It was as if something had just blocked out the light.

A pungent, animalistic odor filled her nostrils.

Heart hammering, she quickly looked up.

Perched on the pit level's ledge, the massive Wen'ey'ti stared hungrily down at her, its savage mouth opened wide to reveal layers of sharp teeth.

Roaring, the monster leaped off the ledge and dropped into the chasm.

CHAPTER 37

Akando sneered as he watched Chenoa claw her way along the jagged chimney wall and haul herself onto the swaying ladder. With his bloodied leg trembling and eyes burning with rage, he hefted up the shotgun and took careful aim.

He suddenly froze, finger resting on the trigger. He had just caught a flicker of something moving on the pit level ledge right above Chenoa. He couldn't make it out in the fractured light.

It moved rapidly through the shadows, monstrous, and very much alive.

He felt a twinge of panic as—

Two new voices shattered the cavern's tension.

"Akando Winterhawk!"

"Drop those guns!"

Akando, Ivers, and Briggs whirled around in astonishment, their weapons raised.

Travers and Michaels were now standing just inside the main tunnel. After they had entered, they'd tracked Akando's distinctive boot prints to the very heart of the mine. Now, the Secret Service agents pointed their firearms at the men.

Agent Michaels chortled. "I guess what we have here is a Mexican Standoff."

Akando's eyes lit up with recognition. "Michaels, you miserable bastard. Have you crawled on your belly all the way over here from Idaho?"

Michaels' jaw clenched, his Winchester locked on Akando. "You slipped my noose once, but you won't do it again." The gravel in his throat was thick with loathing. "Drop the shotgun, or I'll drop you."

Agent Travers shifted his Colt .45 between Briggs and Ivers. He swished a glob of Red Man between his teeth, but its sweet burn offered him little comfort. "Where's that Army major you dragged in here?"

"Quinn? He's the one with the missing head by those barrels of jackrabbit juice back there," Briggs answered.

"Jackrabbit juice," Michaels said. "You've got bombs down here?"

Ivers nodded. "In 20 minutes, this mine will flood worse than a toddler's nappies after a chili feed."

Travers shook his head, disbelief warring with fear. "Flood? You're mad."

"I'm mad, alright," Akando said. His laugh sounded like a guttural war drum echoing off the cavern walls. "The NTO will crack open Carson Mines' rivers, and flood the valley. Then I'll lead my Nez Perce warriors to burn farms and gut families. It'll be an eye for an eye, and a genocide for a genocide. I'll make Roosevelt choke on his own blood before I'm done."

Travers's voice was tight with tension. "Making war against the president? That ain't gonna happen, Winterhawk."

Akando clucked his tongue with disapproval. "I don't know how you found me, but you really should've hung me back in Idaho. Because now, it's you who is going to die."

Michaels' voice was a deadly growl. "I'll bury you first, you son of a bitch."

The cavern crackled with the anticipation of violence. Each man was waiting to see who was going to make the first move. Fingers twitched on the triggers, waiting for the spark from hell that would ignite the encroaching firefight.

Briggs' nose suddenly wrinkled. There was a pungent, animalistic stink choking the air.

There was also something else: sounds.

Faint claw scrapes; guttural growls.

Briggs looked in the direction of the noise. His eyes darted to the tunnel walls, taking in the parietal paintings of snarling creatures and outstretched claws.

Unbelievably, one of them started to move. He blinked with astonishment.

The shape standing against the cavern wall was made from flesh, not stone. The second Wen'ey'ti had stealthily approached from the opposite end of the tunnel as the men had become distracted.

It had piercing eyes, claws flexing like blades.

"Sweet mercy—!"

Briggs' scream was choked out as the creature twitched, teeth hungrily snapping as it pounced.

CHAPTER 38

The Wen'ey'ti dropped off the pit level ledge. Above Chenoa, it became a monstrous blur of jagged teeth and fur as it fell

It would be on top of her in three seconds.

Chenoa knew that her only hope was to reach the rusted steel cable from the steam crane. It was dangling over the edge of the vent, more than five feet away. She would need to jump to reach it.

The legends are real, she thought with disbelief. Those tribal tales of the Wen'ey'ti, born from nightmares and myths, were really just flesh and fury.

The most unbelievable thing here isn't that this legendary monster actually exists; it's that fighting them has now become a family trait. I don't know about you, Pocahontas, but I'd have rather inherited a knack for doing undergarment needlepoint with my toes than throwing hands with these man-eating fur engines.

The creature's foul stench now completely flooded the chimney vent, its claws slashing through the air as it prepared to rip her to pieces.

Chenoa reacted on pure instinct, sprinting forward. Her boots momentarily slipped on the swaying ladder's half-rotted rungs, threatening to topple her down to the cavern floor.

Then, with a loud double-crack, the ladder splintered beneath her.

Taking one final step, Winterhawk leaped upwards, arms outstretched.

The creature fell directly beside her, close enough for her to feel its filthy fur brushing the side of her face. The Wen'ey'ti was momentarily confused, expecting its prey to remain stationary, not move toward the ledge.

The monster twisted its massive shoulders in midair, its claws ripping through her uniform as their bodies grazed each other. The wound instantly drew a hot gush of blood that burned like fire against her ribs.

Winterhawk's raw fingers snagged the dangling cable, her body swinging wildly through the air. Directly beneath her, the horizontal section of the ladder fully exploded under the beast's weight as it crashed through it.

The Wen'ey'ti had both arms outstretched, its claws raking the chimney wall with a screech, slowing its descent as it continued falling down to the mine floor.

Chenoa clung tightly to the cable, swinging fast toward the beckoning arm of the steam crane, its rusted bolts anchored to the pit level's platform.

She kicked forcefully with both legs and released her grip on the cable, landing hard.

Cracked rock, discarded pickaxes, splintered ore carts, frayed ropes, and jagged heaps of quartz and iron ore lay strewn around her.

Clutching her blood-soaked side, she scanned frantically for any weapon that she could use. But there was nothing; nothing but broken tools.

Chenoa heard frantic shouting coming from below. It was distinctly more than three voices; the party had grown to five.

She frowned. Who the hell else was down there?

Terrified screams ripped up from the cavern floor, followed by a symphony of gunfire.

CHAPTER 39

The cavern had erupted into total chaos.

Just as the second Wen'ey'ti had revealed itself to Briggs by the painted walls, the first monster had finished its descent from the pit level and hit the cavern floor with a bone-rattling thud.

The five men were temporarily frozen by the sudden appearance of the monsters, fear and shock etched all across their faces.

"What in the actual hell?" Ivers shouted.

The Wen'ey'ti's matted fur bristled as it lunged, massive paws shaking the ground with each thunderous step.

The creature seized Ivers, its talons sinking deep into his shoulders, piercing layers of muscle and bone. Ivers' shriek pierced the cavern as the Wen'ey'ti's talons tore through his body, the metallic scent of blood flooding the air as his flesh peeled like rawhide.

With a roar, the creature hurled him straight into the cavern wall. The impact snapped his spine with a wet crunch. Ivers' body crumpled, blood fountaining, eyes frozen in horror.

Akando, Briggs, Travers, and Michaels unloaded their weapons on the monster in unison. Shale dust rained from the cavern ceiling, the walls trembling with each gunshot, as if the mine itself had recoiled from the Wen'ey'ti's wrath.

Multiple shots tore into the second Wen'ey'ti's hide, bullets ripping muscle, the cacophony of deadly rounds shredding the creature's flank. The barrage of gunfire flung it backward, spinning the monster against the edge of the exposed slab. It frantically tried to find purchase with its claws before plummeting down into the roaring river below. Wounded but alive, the monster vanished into the churning foam and was swept away into the very heart of the mine.

Enraged, the other Wen'ey'ti in the tunnel lunged toward its nearest target: Agent Michaels.

"Get back!" Agent Travers yelled, throwing himself between Michaels and the creature. He fired his Colt, bullets slamming into the Wen'ey'ti's chest. The monster roared, undeterred by the shots.

The monster seized Travers and hurled him towards a jagged basalt spike protruding from the cavern wall. The spike pierced his chest with a wet crunch, impaling him in mid-air, his body spasming.

With a mixture of blood and tobacco trickling from one side of his mouth, Travers sunk his chin against his chest. "Failed... Roosevelt," he sighed.

His gun clattered against the floor in tandem with his final heartbeat.

The Wen'ey'ti snarled, its gaze sweeping once again over the men, as it turned on Briggs.

Reacting quickly, Briggs unloaded with the Parker. The blast punched a hole into the monster's upper chest. Reacting with anger, the Wen'ey'ti swung its arm around. The massive blow connected with Briggs's shoulder, knocking the weapon from his hands and spinning him sideways.

The monster fastened its maw onto the back of Briggs's neck; powerful teeth crunched through bone and sinew. Briggs emitted a high-pitch scream, convulsing in horror as the creature latched onto him like a lion taking down a gazelle.

Akando and Michaels both fanned out in opposite directions, firing upon the creature.

The Wen'ey'ti howled from the impact of the bullets. With a guttural snarl, it darted forward. Seeking safety, it began to scale the chimney chute. With Briggs's twitching body still clenched between its massive jaws, the monster dug its hands and feet into the jagged walls and began to climb rapidly.

The Boss was now completely spent of its ammunition, and Akando dropped the weapon. Ignoring the pain in his leg, he spun around towards the new threat.

Always the soldier, Agent Michaels was already moving towards Akando. The horror of the Wen'ey'ti attacks had done nothing to derail his hatred. "I'm looking at a dead man now!" Michaels was lightning fast with the Colt, firing it a split second.

But he was still too slow.

Sensing the movement, Akando had already flung his body sideways. The slug slammed harmlessly into the cavern wall, ricocheting wildly. Hitting the ground hard with his shoulder, Akando somersaulted forward.

Michaels tracked him with the Colt, attempting to fire again, but Akando had gotten too close. He lashed out with his good leg, connecting with Michaels's left knee with a sickening crunch.

Agent Michaels yelled out in utter agony, falling sideways, gun spinning out of his grasp.

The moment Michaels hit the ground, Akando rolled on top of him. "If your eyes cause you to sin, pluck them out!" Akando jammed both thumbs into his sockets, grinding down with incredible force until both eyeballs burst wetly.

Michaels screamed, blood streaming from the ruined sockets, clawing blindly into the air.

Rolling off of him, Akando glanced at the nearby timer: 12 minutes left until detonation. His wounded leg throbbing with pain, he climbed to his feet.

Incredibly, Agent Michaels staggered up beside him. Sightless, he launched a desperate kick. It landed on Akando's wound, fresh blood spurting from the gouged flesh on his thigh.

Akando roared with furious anger. Bending down, he grabbed onto one of Michaels's flailing arms and lifted him completely off the floor. Spinning fast, he slammed his face into the rock wall's parietal paintings. Blood fountained as Michaels's skull totally cracked apart. Now lifeless, his body dropped hard to the ground.

On the wall, his face had left a gory imprint beside the ancient creatures.

Akando's eyes flicked to the ticking timer, his plan teetering but his hatred for Chenoa burning brighter than before. He staggered over to the chimney ladder and looked up. There was an entire section of the ladder missing, but with his immense height, he would be able to navigate his way across it with relative ease.

Besides, he still had some unfinished business running around up there.

"Chenoa!"

She appeared suddenly, staring down at him with venom from the pit level's ledge, 100 feet above.

"How does it feel knowing you're about to die?" Akando asked.

Chenoa flashed a crazed grin. "I'll make sure and ask you that right before I kill you!"

Snarling, Akando grabbed the ladder and began to climb.

His wounded leg was dragging but his rage was unyielding.

CHAPTER 40

Moments ago, the entire cavern floor had sounded like a slaughterhouse. The air reeked of blood and gunpowder, while the walls trembled with the echoes of gunfire and the guttural roars of the Wen'ey'ti.

When the shooting had started, Chenoa had been crouched near the pit level's edge, staring down at the carnage below. The chimney was too narrow to offer an expansive view of what was happening, but she had heard everything.

Five voices had echoed below: Akando's sharp commands, Briggs' gravelly curses, Ivers' panicked yelps, and two strangers barking in clipped military tones, until all she could make out was terrified screams and the crunch of bone.

Either the monsters would soon be clawing their way back up here, or the monsters of men would be. She guessed that the timer on those two barrels of nitrotriazolone would now be closing in on a ten-minute countdown.

She couldn't climb down there and attempt to disarm the dynamite amidst all the carnage and chaos, but there had to be another way to stop the flooding.

And as much as she prayed that Akando would somehow end up as jerky for the Wen'ey'ti, she had to assume that he would escape the slaughter and hunt her down. After all, his survival rate was so far the same as hers: 100%.

Now, she was back on the hunt for suitable weapons.

Chenoa's side burned, blood seeping through her fingers as she pressed her hand against the gash. Her shepherd's sling hung from her wrist, useless against the threat she knew was coming. Then, her fingers brushed up against the bandolier of shells she was still wearing. She yanked it off her body and tossed the bandolier to the ground. Without the shotgun, those shells would do her absolutely no good now.

She continued to look around the area. The pit level was a wasteland of broken tools: splintered ore carts, frayed ropes, and heaps of iron ore.

Her eyes suddenly caught two pickaxe heads half-buried in quartz shards, their long wooden handles long since broken.

She scrambled over and grabbed them. She hefted both pickaxes, pleased by their weight. Balanced in her hands, they looked like twin tomahawks.

Chenoa maneuvered her feet into a fighting stance, swinging the pickaxe heads purposefully. They whistled a dangerous tune.

The Nez Perce trained their warriors for tomahawk combat using the Okichitaw system, which was based on the Plains Cree warrior methods that had been integrated into the migrating western tribes. Her father had overseen her training on it personally, and she was confident that—

A cacophony of new sounds echoed behind her.

Winterhawk whirled around, poised to strike at her attacker. Seeing what it was, she slowly lowered the weapons.

The Wen'ey'ti scaled the chimney with terrifying speed, its foul stench choking the air as its talons gouged deep scars into the rock. While it was navigating up the walls, the beast also carried Briggs between its teeth like some kind of hunting trophy.

The creature must be taking him somewhere to feed.

Sensing her, the Wen'ey'ti stopped climbing. It stared at her from its grip on the wall, letting loose a deep warning growl.

"Winterhawk!" Briggs' voice broke with terror. 'End it, Winterhawk! Don't let it eat me!'"

She felt for the sling on her wrist. Her hand briefly hovered over a quartz shard that lay on the ground. She could use it like a stone. One precise hit with it from the sling and Briggs would be put out of his suffering.

But she pulled her hand back.

His eyes pleaded for mercy, but Chenoa's blood boiled. She was remembering Briggs' betrayal of Quinn; mercy wasn't an option for a traitor.

"There's worse things than death," she said, "but nothing's worse than *this*." Her voice was like ice shards. "Here comes the pain, asshole!"

Grunting, the Wen'ey'ti climbed higher, vanishing from sight as it scaled the rock walls. Briggs' high-pitched screams continued to echo loudly through the mines. After a moment, they became incredible wails of agony.

"Chenoa!"

Winterhawk turned towards the direction of the voice. It was Akando, calling out to her from the mine floor. She raced to the ledge and carefully peered over.

Akando was grabbing onto the ladder, staring up at her with hatred. He was bleeding profusely from the shotgun blast; unarmed except for the sheathed Razorback.

"How does it feel knowing you're about to die?"

"I'll make sure and ask you that right before I kill you!"

Grunting with pain, he began to climb.

Chenoa moved quickly away from the edge, tightly gripping the twin pickaxes.

Are you ready for the main event, Chenoa? This is a battle unlike anything you've ever experienced. Akando doesn't want you to suffer, he just wants you to die—badly. He wants to take everything he's ever hated about his life out on you now. Do you understand the power of that kind of hate? It's nearly superhuman, and it absolutely refuses to die.

Chenoa swallowed hard.

She did understand hate; she felt it every bit as much as she'd experienced it. But she understood something else, too. Hate would only get you so far, and no further. Because hate is cannibalistic; when it can't get what it desires, it'll begin to eat you from the inside out. It will consume everything about you until even the heart and soul have been chewed to pieces.

Hate is also a conduit, Chenoa. Not just for ignorance or for fear, but also for revenge. To Akando, your death isn't about you, or the Nez Perce, or even Chief Joseph—it's all about your father. Spilling your blood means also spilling mine. Getting revenge on me is all he's ever wanted..

That enraged Chenoa even more. Her father was already gone; death had taken him into the embrace of the Creator. But Chief Winterhawk's legacy and his memory were still alive. That's what she was protecting, and that's what she was fighting for.

Akando would never be able to take those things from her.

We all live and we all die. But like the grasses and the trees, we find ourselves renewed from the very soil of the grave by our own seeds. Our sons and daughters, they witness the fruits that we were never able to harvest. Those things have been planted in hope, Chenoa. We make these sacrifices not for just us, but for those whom we will never know.

Chenoa thought of Major Quinn and his daughter, Huan.

Her father said that hate could act as a conduit, but so could hope. It could bring restoration to the hurting, and bring back to life what was once thought to be dead.

The air became electrified as Akando's silhouette emerged from the dust below, his survival a grim testament to his relentless hatred. He climbed off the ladder and rolled his body over the ledge and onto the pit level.

He slowly got to his feet. "It's time to meet your destiny, Chenoa."

His massive body was drenched with sweat; face clenched from the exertion of the climb. His leg was bleeding profusely from the shotgun blast, forcing him to limp as he stepped towards her.

His eyes darted to her hands, noticing the weapons she was holding. Something like a smile touched his lips. He looked pleased about the fight that was about to happen.

Akando unsheathed the Razorback and held it up, engaging the twin blades. "No matter what you might think, I'm *not* going to enjoy this."

Chenoa held up both pickaxes. "But I will."

Akando grinned. "I want your blood, Chenoa."

"Then come and get it!"

There's one more thing that hope does, amiga. Can you tell me what that is?

Her eyes flashed like steel.

Yeah...

Hope dies last.

CHAPTER 41

Chenoa was balanced in an Okichitaw fighting stance, tightly gripping the two pickaxe heads. Ignoring the burning pain in her side from the claw wounds, she spun the repurposed tools like tomahawks.

Standing ten feet away from her, Akando deftly tossed the Razorback between both hands as if he was a swordfighter.

He glanced at the crude weapons in her hands. "Pickaxes," he smirked.

Chenoa motioned towards the Razorback's twin blades. "Scissors."

Ignoring her, Akando tilted his head. "Do you hear that, Chenoa?" He pretended to listen with exaggerated intensity. "Do you hear those timers ticking their way down to doomsday? In eight minutes, the fires will cry out and those rivers will rise. Then, they will consume everything that gets in their way."

"I'm not going to let that happen."

"Then it's time to join your father!"

Akando suddenly charged at her, the Razorback slashing upwards in a brutal arc.

Chenoa darted sideways, agile as a bobcat. She swung with the right pickaxe, its rusted edge carving a gash across Akando's forearm.

He roared, undeterred, swinging the Razorback at her head.

Chenoa ducked beneath the blades, her boots skidding on the damp shale, loose pebbles scattering into the mine's shadowed crevices. She countered hard with the left pickaxe. It sliced directly into his bleeding shotgun wound.

Akando bellowed out with pain and dropped the Razorback. It clattered to the ground as he took a lumbering step forward; off-balance and stumbling.

Chenoa moved directly behind him, bringing up both arms, aiming for his upper back as she drove the pickaxes down—

It was all wrong.

She had sensed it too late.

Although wounded, Akando's stumble had been carefully orchestrated. He had stepped forward just enough to regain solid footing. He had wanted to draw her in closer, to present himself as an easy target.

And instead, she had just made herself one.

With his back turned, he pivoted on his good leg, the mine's uneven floor crunching beneath him as the pickaxes sliced the air where he had been standing a split-second before.

Chenoa staggered forward with the force of the missed swing.

Still in motion, Akando had one arm pulled back. His entire body swung around as he slammed his fist against the right side of her face.

Chenoa's nose crunched wetly, a blinding pain searing through her skull as blood gushed, the cavern spinning in a haze of black and red.

Akando sneered, his voice dripping with contempt. "You're no Nez Perce warrior!"

Chenoa swung blindly at his voice with the pickaxe in her right hand, but he managed to easily sidestep it. "You're just like Chief Joseph: weak!"

Akando walloped a fist against her left deltoid. A sickening crack echoed as the humerus popped out of the glenoid socket, dislocating the shoulder. Pure agony lanced through her body, forcing her to drop the pickaxe from her left hand.

But she still had the one on the right.

Chenoa staggered, her vision blurring, but forced her trembling legs to hold, swinging the pickaxe in a desperate arc.

Akando raised an arm and blocked the intended blow. His other hand clamped down onto her dislocated shoulder, squeezing mercilessly.

Chenoa screamed with pain and collapsed to her knees. The second pickaxe clattered uselessly against the floor as the intense pain fully consumed her.

"And now, you'll soon be just like your father: dead!"

Akando lashed out with his boot, kicking her hard in the stomach. The savage blow knocked her flat onto her back. And then, she lay still.

Her entire world had become nothing but a swirling cauldron of blackness intermixed with the coppery taste of blood. The intense throbbing agony of her fresh injuries was the only thing keeping her from slipping into unconsciousness. She knew she needed to get up and fight, but her body seemed incapable of doing anything but bleeding.

Staring up, Chenoa saw patches of sunshine poking through the chimney chute far above her. She felt hot tears spilling down her cheeks as her body throbbed with unbearable pain. Hate had driven her to fight, but hope—her father's hope—felt like a fading ember.

Defeated, her fingers brushed against the locket around her neck. "I'm sorry...Poppa," she whispered.

But his voice had turned silent. There was no answer.

"Pathetic," Akando chuckled. He limped over to the Razorback and picked it up from off the ground. "Even now, Chenoa, you call out to him like a baby." He walked closer, squatting down directly behind her. "I want to hear you scream Jolon's name as you die."

He grabbed a handful of her hair and viciously pulled it back until she was looking into his eyes. "It's been nice *not* knowing you, daughter of Jolon." He pressed the Razorback's blades against her scalp, his grin widening as blood trickled down her forehead.

Chenoa suddenly realized that Akando was going to scalp her. Her body buckled helplessly on the floor; her hands batted futilely against him. But she was far too weak, and he was much too strong.

Akando clucked a tongue with sympathy. "There's nobody in this world who can possibly save you now."

A new voice echoed through the mine with the force of a cannon blast.

"You're right about that, amigo."

Chenoa felt her heart leap at the sound.

A sage-scented gust swirled with a faint hum before coalescing into blue light that pulsed like a heartbeat. Then, the silhouette of a Weyekin warrior stepped out of that light and onto the floor. The figure was ceremonially dressed in breechcloths and a deerskin war vest.

The warrior's face was covered by the entire skin of a wolf's head that had been adorned with bear's claws and hawk feathers: the traditional burial attire of a Nez Perce warrior.

Chenoa recognized the garb because it was what she had dressed her father in before burying him three years ago. Tears streamed down her face.

The Weyekin pulled off the wolf's head, letting it drop to the ground.

"Jolon?!" Akando was in absolute shock. The Razorback trembled in his hands, his eyes wide with terror and disbelief.

Chief Jolon Winterhawk stood before them. He was holding onto a familiar-looking 12-inch Girandoni gunstock war club that had been specially modified by fitting the underside with razor-sharp whale bone.

He gestured down at Chenoa with it. "My daughter won't die screaming my name...but *you* will, Akando."

Akando stepped carefully away from Chenoa's prone body. His eyes flicked down to the war club. "Father's weapon?"

Jolon shrugged. "I've always been a sucker for poetic justice."

Groaning with agony, Chenoa clawed her way to a sitting position. Her face was battered nearly beyond recognition, left shoulder hunched forward, blood oozing from the claw marks on her ribs. "I... had this...Poppa." Her voice was a cracked whisper through bloodied lips. "No problem."

Jolon stared at her for a long moment. "Yeah. I can see that."

"The legends of the returning Weyekin warriors are true," Akando said with incredulity. "But my brother, it's time to create another legend now. Only this time, it'll be about you: the man who died twice."

"Funny you should say that," Jolon said, hefting the war club. "The Creator allowed me to come back here to kill you. But since He works in mysterious ways, He didn't say how. I guess He left that up to me. Wanna see what I've come up with?"

"Woe is mine," Akando grinned. "It's time to put you out of my misery."

Chenoa sensed the chamber thrum with otherworldly anticipation as the two brothers began circling each other.

She heard the faint ticking of the explosive timer from the bottom level ticking down to its final five minutes.

In the next instant, everything was drowned out by the ferocious clashing of weapons as she witnessed the wrath of legends.

CHAPTER 42

Malheur Indian Reservation
Change of Worlds Longhouse
Eastern Oregon
1902

"I played hide-and-seek with death better than most," Chief Jolon Winterhawk said wearily. "I should have been killed during the war; hell, I should have been killed *after* it. But when it's time for your book to close, there's no use begging the Creator to keep on writing your story. When the Great Spirit puts His pencil down, you'd best be prepared for the long sleep."

Chenoa shifted closer to his sick bed. Her fingers trembling as she adjusted the bighorn wool blanket over Jolon's frail form. "You're not always right about everything, *Tota*. You might be very sick today, but you could find healing tomorrow."

Jolon glanced over her shoulder at the shaman staring grimly down at him. "It seems the shaman here doesn't share your optimism."

The Nez Perce medicine man, who'd tended to Jolon since childhood, turned away, his shoulders shaking with unspoken grief. His moccasins scuffed the earthen floor as he fled the longhouse, hiding his tears.

Chenoa watched the shaman leave with great sadness.

The longhouse felt larger than its 150 feet, its vastness amplified by the weight of impending loss. Originally, the Nez Perce lived in villages made of earth houses. The tribe made these homes by digging underground rooms, building a wooden frame, and then covering it with tule mats and cedar bark.

Longhouses were of the same basic design, but they weren't meant to be dwelling places. They were built for community gatherings, food storage for the entire village, worship centers, and places for the sick and the dying to live out their final days.

Chenoa had already seen her *Pik'e* take her last breath inside the Change of the Worlds longhouse a year ago.

And now, she would lose her father, just as she'd lost her mother.

Her father had gotten very sick, very fast. Though no doctor had confirmed it, Chief Winterhawk was clearly afflicted with *lood doo na'ziihii*: the sore that does not heal.

"I would ask about a penny for your thoughts," Jolon said, "but I'm afraid you'd give me change."

Chenoa smiled warmly. "My thoughts are secondary to your comfort."

"If only I could have gotten your mother to embrace that motto."

They both laughed loudly at that together. The sound was indicative of the warmth of shared memories; seasons of life where there was always sunshine to be found amidst the worst of storms. She thought that's what the family dynamic truly was: lightness.

But soon, her entire world would turn into black again. She felt the smile pulling away from her lips as the laughter they shared vanished into yet another memory. She wondered if it would the last moment of amusement that they would be sharing together. She figured that it probably was.

Looking up at her, her father grew visibly saddened when he saw her smile dissipating. He was resting comfortably on a bed layered with buffalo hide mats. Tucked beneath a thick chocolate brown blanket made from the wool of bighorn sheep, he snaked one hand out from beneath it and gently reached out for her. "What is it, Chenoa?"

Her eyes welling up with tears, Chenoa grasped his hand tightly. She tried not to take notice how frail and weak his grip was now. "Why don't we leave this place and go to La Grande, *Tota*? There's a Lutheran Hospital there, and they might—"

"Cure me?" Jolon shook his head. "We both know that I'm never walking out of here. What came and took your mother away from us last year has decided to return for me."

Chenoa gently squeezed his hand. "What happens now, Poppa? Where do I go from here?"

"If the answer seems impossible, Chenoa, that's because you probably fumbled with the question." Jolon coughed loudly. "People tear things apart in their life just to prove they weren't really whole to begin with. Don't be one of them."

"It isn't always self-sabotage," Chenoa said. "The worst parts of life bring out the worst in people."

"You're talking about death."

"Yes," Chenoa took a deep breath. "Are you prepared for it?"

"No," Jolon answered truthfully. "Any man who answers otherwise is a few sandwiches short in his picnic basket. Death is its own regret, Chenoa. It doesn't need any help from us. What we leave behind is the hope of how this world will remember us."

And hope dies last, Chenoa thought.

"How do I get through this, father?" Chenoa asked tearfully.

"That reminds me of an old joke my father used to tell Akando and me when we were still boys. Each time we would complain about the difficulty of having to do something that felt impossible to us, our father would always repeat the same joke." A faint, familiar smile broke across Jolon's face, as it always did when he recalled the happiest memories. "How do you eat a bison? One bite at a time."

Letting go of her hand, Jolon reached up and gingerly wiped the tears off of her cheeks. "Dealing with grief is just like that. You eat through it one bite at a time, one memory at a time, and one day at a time. You can never eat it all up; not really. But if you manage those emotions one bite at a time, you'll make sure the grief never eats *you* up, instead."

"Can I ask you something important, Poppa?"

"Go ahead." Jolon gestured at the bed. "I'm a captive audience."

"Tell me about the Happy Hunting Grounds."

Her father looked surprised. "You speak of ancient things."

"I only inquire about the truth."

Before the Nez Perce were widely converted to Christianity by the arrival of Protestant missionaries, the earliest tribal members believed that souls would journey to the Happy Hunting Ground after death. Like so many of her generation, Chenoa had grown up believing in the Presbyterian faith, but some traditional spiritual practices of her ancestors still persisted.

"That was a spiritual realm connected to earthly hunting grounds," Jolon answered carefully. "The Happy Hunting Grounds is our Heaven. It's a source of eternal sustenance and life."

"Do you believe that Heaven exists?"

"Yes."

"Why?"

"Because of all that I've seen, and because of all that I haven't."

"Like *Weyekins*?"

Her father's eyes twinkled. "So, you *do* remember."

She thought back to her sixteenth birthday, when she and her father had scaled the rockface. It was the day that he had shared with her about Akando. It was also when he had first told her about the *Weyekins*.

"You told me that your father believed in the power of the *Weyekins*. You said grandfather thought they could become like guardian angels walking through this world."

"That's right."

Chenoa had grown up hearing stories about the afterlife. In ancient days, the Nez Perce had held onto the belief that sometimes the spirits of deceased warriors could return to protect their loved ones. This power, once manifested, could take either a spiritual or physical form. Had her grandfather actually been one of them?

Jolon was studying her. He knew the unspoken question that she had wanted answered. "My father returned from death as a *Weyekin*. I would have met my own demise without his guidance. I don't know how or why the Creator allowed this to happen, Chenoa...but it *did* happen."

"I believe you, Poppa."

"Good. So also believe this: I love you. And even after death separates us, I will harness that same love to guide you. And should it also be the will of the Creator, I will even return from death to protect you."

Chenoa, crying softly, positioned herself gently beside her father on the bed. "I love you, too, *Tota*." She stroked his hair and gently kissed his cheek. "You look so very tired, Poppa. You need to try and get some sleep now." The longhouse's cedar-scented air became heavy with grief as she tucked the blanket around Jolon's shoulders.

Jolon reached out a hand to touch the familiar locket around her neck. After staring at his daughter, he closed his heavy eyelids and drifted off. After a long moment, Chenoa did the same.

They lay there together until the approach of dawn. When the morning sunlight drifted into the longhouse, Chenoa awoke and opened her eyes.

Chief Jolon Winterhawk never did.

CHAPTER 43

Jolon Winterhawk swung the Girandoni war club down like it was a thunderbolt. It clashed against Akando's Razorback with tremendous force. Sparks flew against his face, flickering like a swarm of lightning bugs.

Akando grunted with the sheer power of the blow, staggering backwards. "You move pretty well for a corpse!" He was bloodied from Chenoa's pickaxe strikes and wounded badly from the shotgun, but he still fought with feral desperation.

"Death isn't what it used to be!" Jolon dove to the floor, rolling beneath the swing of double blades and somersaulting to his feet.

Chenoa clung to a basalt outcrop for balance, helplessly watching the battle. She wanted to join the fight, but her many wounds were far too extensive. All she could do now was watch as the two brothers circled each other near the ledge of the pit.

"You betrayed the Creator!" Jolon said.

Akando spat on the ground, his voice thick with disgust. 'The Great Spirit betrayed me! After this flood is unleashed, the Nez Perce will be reborn! I will be their new leader!"

"Our father would be ashamed if he saw what you have become, Akando."

"You speak lies!"

"Father gave his life for us, and for his people! You took that sacrifice and turned it into something evil!"

"NO!" Enraged, Akando charged forward.

The Girandoni war club met the Razorback in a brutal dance, each ferocious clash shaking the pit's wreckage of twisted crane parts all around them.

"After I strike you down, I'm going to feed Chenoa her own eyes! She will enter into Hell with the blindness of her allegiances!"

Jolon sidestepped a wild lunge as Akando's blades harmlessly grazed his war vest.

"This bedtime story ends here," Jolon growled. He launched himself into the air with lightning speed, swinging his arm down with tremendous force. The war club arced like a crescent moon, its whale-bone edge gleaming beneath the sunlight streaming from the crevice cracks high above. "Sweet dreams, Akando!"

The savage blow began to cleave diagonally through Akando's torso from shoulder to hip. With a yell, Jolon sawed completely through his brother's body until the Girandoni lodged against his hip bone.

The Razorback fell from Akando's hands, clattering against the shale. A guttural scream choked in his throat as his body began splitting completely open, blood spraying upwards in a crimson arc.

Jolon forcefully yanked on the war club, pulling the weapon free.

Akando stared at him with eyes filled with horror. Even through the excruciating pain, he could feel his upper torso sliding in two separate directions. He reached out his arms towards his brother, hands clenching the air. "Jolon..."

Jolon shook his head grimly, stepping away.

Akando let out a high-pitched shriek as his upper half finally tore free, toppling his head and shoulders backwards; then, his lower half crumpled, legs twitching.

Both halves of his body fell over the ledge, vanishing into the pit below.

"He's not half the man he used to be," Jolon muttered. Moving to the ledge, he looked down at the carnage below.

Akando's upper half had landed directly beside the nitrotriazolone barrel by the slab. His arm was outstretched, finger pointing in the direction of the ticking timer.

Jolon's eyes narrowed as he saw the countdown: two minutes until detonation.

"Father!" Chenoa staggered down from the outcrop, and threw herself into her father's arms. "*Tota*," she whispered, tears mixing with blood.

Jolon hugged her fiercely. "You've always been my light, Chenoa." His hand cupped her battered face, gently lifting up her chin. "Now, the Creator calls me home."

"No!" she pleaded, tightly clutching his war vest. "Stay! I need you, father!"

"You've already carried the hope of our people farther than I ever could. Now, I need you to find the strength to carry the Nez Perce even further. The flood's coming, Chenoa. Innocent people are going to die. You have to stop it."

"Stop it? How can I possibly stop it?!"

"The mouth that doesn't speak knows the answer."

"Poppa—really?! Riddles...*now*?!"

Jolon's eyes twinkled. "You sound just like your *Pik'e*."

"Momma?" Chenoa wiped tears from her face. "Is she with you now, too?"

"Yes," Jolon answered. "Where we are now is where you'll also be someday. When the end arrives, the new beginning is more incredible than anything you could possibly imagine."

"Father," Chenoa said, tracing her fingers along the contours of his face, "how is *this* possible?"

"I can't explain it," he answered truthfully. "Like all matters of faith, it just *is*. But I believe the Creator saw an imbalance here, and He allowed me to be the scale that leveled things out. Now, my time guiding you is done."

"I love you so much, Poppa."

"I love you, too, Chenoa. Now, hurry before—"

BOOM!

The twin barrels erupted in a cataclysm of fire that shook the mine to its core. Shrapnel and dust rained down everywhere. The cavern trembled as cracks split open the walls, shale raining as the roar of water surged below.

The shockwave slammed Chenoa to the ground, her broken body skidding across the basalt. Her ears rang and her vision blurred as she reached out for her father.

"Poppa?!"

The silence was deafening.

Chief Winterhawk was gone.

"Goodbye, *Tota.*" She squeezed her eyes shut. "Thank you."

The roar of water surged louder now, a relentless tide flooding the lower tunnels. Those twin rivers were rising fast, and would be completely flooding the pit level within minutes.

She needed to stop it—but how?

"The mouth that doesn't speak knows the answer," her father had said.

Chenoa's heart leapt in her chest as she recalled a snippet of conversation she'd heard earlier while descending the ladder. Major Quinn had mentioned a third barrel of nitrotriazolone placed near the mouth of the mine. She could seal the exit with the NTO, and that would contain the flooding.

Glancing over, she saw the bandolier of shells on the ground. Reaching over, she pulled one free and closed it tightly in her fist.

It wasn't much of a plan, but it was all she had.

Chenoa thought of Huan, Quinn's daughter, and her resolve to save the Nez Perce burned even more urgently.

Chenoa staggered to her feet as the mine continued to shake. Water was now starting to lap at her boots as she began to run towards the exit of the mine.

CHAPTER 44

The Carson Mines groaned around her, dangerous cracks spiderwebbing the basalt walls as the roar of the rising water echoed like a vengeful spirit.

Chenoa's boots pounded the mine tracks as she forced herself to run faster inside the tunnel. Each step was a lance of agony against her battered body, but she pushed the pain away. She was clutching the Boss shotgun shell tightly in her fist, praying that it would be enough to trigger the explosion.

The tunnel darkened considerably as the torchlight from the pit level behind her faded, but a faint glow shimmered just up ahead: the exit.

Winterhawk's breath hitched, legs burning as she sprinted along the rusted tracks. She passed a discarded cedar mine cart that had been shoved against the wall like a forgotten relic, its wheels stripped long ago for repairs.

Just beyond it was a glint of metal: the NTO barrel. It had been placed near the mouth of the mine, just as Quinn had said.

Now, it was time for her to—

A guttural snarl turned her blood into ice.

In the dim light twenty-five feet ahead, the Wen'ey'ti she'd encountered on the chimney ladder was crouched over Briggs' corpse. The monster had dragged its meal to the mine's exit to feed in solitude; claws tearing through flesh, jagged teeth ripping sinew.

Sensing movement, the monster's eyes snapped over to Chenoa. The creature had stopped eating and was now coiled to pounce, muscles rippling under its grotesque fur hide.

Chenoa's heart pounded. She fumbled the Boss shotgun shell into the shepherd's sling fastened around her wrist. Her dislocated shoulder screamed with protest as she brought her arm up and back over her head.

The barrel was twenty-feet away.

In her broken condition, that was an impossible shot. It wasn't the distance itself that was troubling. The challenge was the force needed to sling the shell hard enough to detonate the NTO.

There was only one thing left that she could do.

Chenoa squeezed her eyes closed, and prayed.

Creator, I'm in so much pain. I'm not sure I can do this. I need your help. I'm not asking for my life to be spared; you already sent my father to save me once. No, I'm praying to you about my people. To save them, I need to walk the Ghost Trail of the Locust. I'm asking for the strength to finish this. Great Spirit, I need your help...one last time.

Chenoa snapped her eyes open as sudden adrenaline jolted her body.

The Wen'ey'ti leaped forward, claws outstretched, emitting a roar of primal rage.

Winterhawk released the sling with a yell of agony. The shell streaked like a comet, dipping low, nearly grazing the ground shale—an inch from missing its target—before slamming into the barrel's edge.

The NTO detonated with a thunderous cataclysm of fire.

The massive shockwave flung Chenoa backward, her body tumbling across the tracks like a ragdoll. She slammed against the ground, dust choking her lungs.

Seconds after the blast, the mine's entrance totally collapsed. Basalt and shale crashed down in a deafening roar, completely sealing the tunnel amidst a wall of rubble.

Chenoa's ribs ached from the shockwave, her vision swimming as she staggered to her feet. She peered through the smoky haze. The dead Wen'ey'ti lay buried under the debris, one lifeless leg jutting out from beneath the rocks.

"What a crusher," Chenoa muttered, her voice raw.

A sudden, unearthly bellow shook the earth. It was coming from the tunnel's depths; a living, wrathful force. The underground river, trapped beneath Elkhorn Peak for centuries, erupted into the tunnel like a beast unchained. The river's churning mass, laced with jagged shale and splintered timbers, snarled with ancient hunger.

It had become a seething and ravenous entity.

Chenoa's heart seized with panic. Her eyes quickly darted back to the discarded mine cart. The vehicle's cedar frame, weathered but buoyant, was her only hope against the flood's fury.

She sprinted toward it, boots slipping on the damp shale as the river's surge roared ever closer. The water was now lapping against the tracks at her feet. In the next few steps, it was already up to her knees.

There was a massive roaring sound as a wall of water rose up behind her.

Winterhawk leaped into the cart with a desperate cry, curling into its splintered oak belly. The river current seized the cart, spinning it in helpless circles. The waters slammed against its 200-pound frame as it floated like a cork in a whirlpool.

The river, now seemingly alive, angrily slammed against the sealed mine entrance. The waters recoiled, a tidal pull that dragged the cart backward through the tunnel with tremendous velocity, spinning it wildly amid shale shards and timber fragments.

Chenoa clung desperately to the rim of the cart as the river propelled her back into the very heart of the mine as the seething waters angrily howled like a trapped beast.

CHAPTER 45

Inside the Carson Mines, Chenoa clung to the splintered edge of the cedar mine cart, her broken body battered by the flood's relentless surge. The underground river, a snarling beast unleashed after centuries of confinement, roared through the chimney shaft.

The cart spun like a top, lifted by the water's crushing pressure, rocketing up the 150-foot vertical vent. Moss-slick walls gleamed in the faint sunlight filtering from above as the cart gained speed. Shale shards pinged loudly off its shuddering frame.

Winterhawk pressed herself flat against the sodden wood, her dislocated shoulder screaming with every jolt. She glanced up—the chimney's exit loomed closer, a gaping hole where the river would make its violent escape.

And here she was, just along for the ride.

The flood's roar deafened her as it hurtled with incredible speed up towards the beckoning sunlight.

"How do I get off this thing?!" Chenoa cried out, bracing herself.

With a thunderous surge, the river erupted through the vent. The cart shot skyward, flung out of Elkhorn Peak like a cork shooting from a champagne bottle. For a heart-stopping moment, it hung airborne, then fell back down to earth.

The mine cart landed hard on the 40-degree slope with a shuddering wallop. Winterhawk cried out with pain as her shoulder thudded mercilessly against the walls of the cart with the impact.

Groaning, she reeled from disorientation as the cart lurched forward again.

Fast.

Chenoa's voice trembled. 'What now?'" She gripped tightly onto the edges of the cart and looked out.

After being freed from the mine, the underground rivers had carved a frothing rapid down the mountainside; sweeping scree and boulders in its path. The mine cart now rode this newborn waterway like a log flume, skidding down the rugged slope with ever increasing velocity. Its cedar frame, light yet sturdy, floated defiantly against the flood's crushing force.

At least the way down will be faster than the way up, Chenoa thought grimly.

Chenoa's dislocated shoulder throbbed with each jolt, her battered ribs screaming as she clung to the cart.

Jumping free from the vehicle had crossed her mind, but with her injuries— shoulder, battered ribs—climbing down the peak was a fantasy. The flooded mine offered no retreat now.

She was stuck with riding this madness out to the very end of the line.

Her eyes scanned the edges of the slope. A hundred feet ahead of her, the rapids plunged over a cliff and formed a churning waterfall.

"More waterfalls?!"

But that wasn't the worst of it.

Her breath hitched in her throat when she saw it. Something was rising from the water near the cliff's edge. It began moving rapidly up the slope against the current.

Her eyes widened with astonishment.

It was a second Wen'ey'ti. Its 400-pound bulk loomed massive, brown fur matted with blood from multiple gunshots. Corded muscle rippled beneath its hide; wounded and enraged.

Chenoa hadn't seen this particular one, but she'd heard its savage clash with Akando's soldiers earlier. After being swept into the flood, the Wen'ey'ti must have been carried through the mine's water veins and spat out through a ventilation shaft.

She figured it was probably the mate of the other creature she'd killed.

Now, this Wen'ey'ti stood directly in the cart's barreling path, its rage-fueled eyes focused solely on her.

"Oh, shit..."

The monster leaped, its blood-matted fur rippling as claws slashed through the air toward her.

CHAPTER 46

The Wen'ey'ti crashed onto the cart's rim, its claws gouging the cedar as the vehicle bucked under its 400-pound bulk. The surging rapids spun them wildly within the cart's splintered frame.

The waterfall's edge was now ten feet away, its deafening roar promising oblivion. Chenoa gripped the splintered frame as the cart tilted towards the churning abyss.

The beast lunged at her, jaws snapping.

Chenoa ducked as the Wen'ey'ti's claws raked her scalp, hot blood streaming into her eyes. She scrambled across the sodden floor, fingers brushing an ancient miner's pick wedged between the planks.

Gritting her teeth, she wrenched it free, pain searing her shoulder.

The Wen'ey'ti's rancid breath choked her as it swiped again, splintering the cart's edge. Chenoa rolled aside, the river's spray drenching her as the cart skidded closer to the cliff.

She swung the 2-pound pick, its blunt head smashing against the creature's muzzle. Blood sprayed; the beast howled, rearing back.

The cart lurched, grazing a pine with a splintering crack, shards peppering Chenoa's face.

Five feet away from the drop now.

Seizing the moment, Chenoa stabbed the pick's point deep into the monster's left eye. Black ichor oozed out as it roared, thrashing wildly.

The beast surged forward, teeth glinting, jaws wide.

Chenoa swung again desperately, the pick cracking across its jaw, several teeth snapping off like brittle stone.

She then drove the pick into its shoulder, pinning the creature against the wood. The Wen'ey'ti's agonized roar shook her to the core. The cart's frenzied spin tore the pick free, sending it crashing into the rocks.

Weaponless and trapped, she met the creature's gaze. Its bloodied muzzle twisted, almost smiling—a predator savoring her defeat.

Chenoa spat defiantly, "Come and get it."

The cart tipped skyward as gravity claimed both of them.

Chenoa and the monster plummeted towards the basin before being completely swallowed by the waterfall's mist.

CHAPTER 47

The plummeting cedar mine cart crashed into the basin's icy pool in a chaos of splintered wood and roaring water. The Wen'ey'ti smashed into the water directly beneath the vehicle, its monstrous bulk pinned under the jagged planks as it was driven down to the very bottom of the basin.

Chenoa still clung to the cart as it was fully submerged. While being jolted from the impact, she successfully kicked free of the wreckage. She clawed quickly toward the surface, gasping for air as she broke through. Swimming exhaustedly to the edge of the basin, she slowly dragged herself up onto the basalt shore.

Winterhawk glanced behind her, fully expecting to see the Wen'ey'ti relentlessly coming after her again. But there was nothing but the choppy roar of the waterfall slapping against the basin. She imagined the monster had been pinned beneath the weight of the cart, and had drowned.

The water basin had been bled dry by the Carson Mining Company decades ago, but was now being fully replenished by the waterfall. Soon, it would overflow and a new waterway would be formed as the mine's released rivers forged a way through the wilderness until it reached the Wenaha River in the east.

It would invariably flood huge swaths of the forest before nature accepted its arrival and allowed for a new tributary, but there were no towns or villages directly in its path.

Taking a calming breath, Chenoa took a look at her surroundings.

The remnants of the Carson Mine's greed were still strewn all around the area. The steam elevator loomed high above her like an ominous totem.

Nearby, a 25-foot canvas hose of a water cannon was coiled beside a battered steam engine, its brass nozzle now submerged in the rising waters as the accompanying storage tank was becoming replenished. Long ago, the water hose had been fed from this basin for placer mining. It's enormous power had been harnessed to carve entrances and vents into the mountain.

Chenoa had seen steam-powered water cannons used during the Owyhee Dam's construction. The water pressure from them had been extraordinary, turning the biggest boulders into the smallest pebbles.

Beside the storage tank was the steam engine's dented and decrepit-looking boiler. It bore a cracked pressure gauge that hinted at its latent power. She briefly wondered if the engine would still be operational at this point. She guessed that it would probably throw a mechanical tantrum once it was fired up, but that it would still perform its duties.

Winterhawk squinted as she saw something unusual a little way off in the distance. It was metallic and gleaming in the afternoon sunlight. She blinked in astonishment, unable to believe what she was now looking at: a pair of Harley-Davidson Model 1 motorcycles parked 30 feet away.

During her time as a grizzly guide with President Roosevelt, they had actually encountered these motorcycles while filling up on supplies at the Army's White Salmon Blockhouse in Northern Oregon. Teddy had enthusiastically shown her how to ride one. Afterwards, she had ridden trail loops outside the blockhouse for a solid hour. As with everything she touched, Chenoa had been an awfully quick learner on the bike.

Chenoa remembered seeing motorcycle tracks at the base camp she had slept at the night before. Troost and McNichols must have ridden those bikes here to the Carson Mines by themselves.

But where were they now? She wondered briefly if Akando might have killed them, but then she thought of the piles of bones stacked in the lair she'd encountered.

It was more likely that Troost and McNichols had fallen victim to—

The Wen'ey'ti erupted from the waterfall's mist at the basin's edge. Battered but alive, it had clawed free from the cart's wreckage in the basin. The creature swung its head until its remaining eye fastened hungrily onto her. Its bullet-riddled flank shuddered with uncontrollable rage as the monster unleashed a terrifying roar.

Chenoa's heart hammered with fear.

She couldn't outrun it and without any weapons, there was no chance that she could kill it with her bare hands. But she had to find a way to survive, both for Huan and for herself.

Whatever was going to happen next, she had seconds before the Wen'ey'ti made it out of the water and ripped her to pieces.

Wait...

The water.

Her eyes darted once again to the motorcycles, then to the water hose. The sudden flash of yet another crazy plan flashed through her head.

Her father used to say that if the Creator didn't like crazy people, He probably wouldn't have bothered making so many of them. She took solace knowing that she was in good company.

The Wen'ey'ti flung itself forward, scrambling quickly towards the edge of the basin and began pulling itself out of the water.

The creature was fifty feet from her.

It was time to move!

Winterhawk climbed quickly to her feet, pain knifing her ribs, her dislocated shoulder useless as she lurched toward the engine boiler. Her boots slipped on the wet basalt ash as she approached the machine.

She recalled a wilderness survival tactic that her father had taught her years ago, so she steeled herself for the coming pain. She knew that she needed as much mobility as possible if this plan had even a chance of working.

The monster's roar quickly decided things for her.

Chenoa tilted her body back for momentum before slamming her shoulder against the boiler as hard as she possibly could. The intense, jabbing pain felt like a hot poker searing her tendons. She screamed, but the pain quickly subsided as the shoulder socket was wrenched back into place.

Winterhawk sensed movement in her peripheral vision as the Wen'ey'ti began to charge towards her.

She only had seconds now!

Chenoa moved over to the pump lever valve that was stiff with years of rust. She gripped it with both arms, shoving with all her strength.

The engine sputtered, belching black smoke, then roared to life. The boiler trembled as water was sucked into the intake valve hung inside the basin. The connected canvas hose ballooned with water, jerking up out of the basin like a catfish dancing on the end of a fishing line.

Winterhawk deftly caught the water cannon in midair, spinning around.

The Wen'ey'ti was nearly on top of her now, jaws gaping.

Chenoa twisted the nozzle. Water exploded out of the hose like a rocket blast. The sheer velocity of the water pressure created a massive kickback, nearly ripping the hose from her grasp. But she managed to maintain her grip as the spray impacted against the torso of the charging monster.

It howled with pain as the water punched against its chest, tossing it high into the air and back into the depths of the basin.

Shutting off the valve, Chenoa dropped the hose. Turning, she began sprinting towards the motorcycles. The Harley was her lifeline: speed versus death.

Behind her, the Wen'ey'ti hurtled out of the basin in pursuit.

CHAPTER 48

Chenoa sprinted hard towards the motorcycles as jagged rocks snagged against her boots. Her rib wound continued to bleed, and her newly reset shoulder was throbbing but functional.

Accompanied by a roar of such magnitude that it seemed to shake the entire basin, the Wen'ey'ti charged after her. Its claws scraped against basalt as it picked up speed.

Winterhawk reached the closest Harley. She swung onto the spring-mounted seat and gripped the handlebars. Chenoa furiously pumped the kickstart pedals with her legs until the engine sputtered. It coughed up black smoke, roaring loudly as the belt drive began whining.

A massive shadow suddenly loomed over her.

The Wen'ey'ti lunged, close enough that she could smell its gross breath. Its claws snagged the bike's rear wheel, nearly yanking her off.

With a snarl, Chenoa flung her body forward over the handlebars, popping the bike into a reverse wheelie. As she did this, the rear tire rose up from the ground, spinning free as her weight successfully countered against the creature's pull.

Winterhawk twisted the throttle. The Harley roared as the tire screamed against the creature's face, shredding its fur and flesh for several seconds before a quarter of its skull became partially exposed.

The beast howled in agony, releasing the bike.

Chenoa slammed the rear wheel back down, counter-steering hard and speeding in a wide circle until she was racing back toward the steam engine.

Just ahead, the 25-foot water hose was coiled like a prehistoric python on the ground next to the boiler. Its brass nozzle was still dripping from the earlier blast, the connected tank already replenished by the basin's rising waters. The steam engine's dented boiler hissed loudly, its cracked pressure gauge ticking.

The Wen'ey'ti once again gave chase, face contorted into an animalistic mixture of pain and anger. It was hurt and bleeding and undeterred.

Riding right up to the hose, Chenoa threw her weight hard left. She lay the bike down as it skidded along the basalt, sparks flying from the frame. As it slid past the hose, she grabbed the nozzle as her legs braced against the pedals to balance the skid. With her injured shoulder screaming with protest, she flung her body hard back to the right, jerking the bike back upright with a desperate heave.

Winterhawk spun into a wheelie, tires screeching until she was now facing the charging monster. Tucking the hose tightly under her arm like a knight's lance, she revved the throttle high. The engine roared like a savage war cry.

The Wen'ey'ti barreled forward, unafraid, its massive bulk completely dwarfing her and the bike. In ten seconds, the monster would be close enough to tear her to pieces.

Releasing the throttle, Chenoa sped forward. The Harley's belt drive whined shrilly as she locked her eyes onto the creature.

Five seconds before impact.

Chenoa hopped onto the seat; her boots were planted for balance. She had one hand on the throttle, while the other thrust the hose forward like a medieval joust.

Two seconds...

Letting go of the handlebars, Chenoa twisted the nozzle on the hose and leaped forward, her ribs screaming from the maneuver.

The bike slammed into the Wen'ey'ti with a tremendous crash, metal folding and crumpling around its legs. It jerked its body backwards from the impact, but remained standing.

After a spectacular airborne collision, Chenoa stabbed the hose's nozzle directly into its stomach, impaling it. Because of the force of the impact, the brass sunk deep into its guts as water exploded through the hose.

A high-pressure torrent instantly filled the Wen'ey'ti's body, the incredible velocity powered by the steam engine rupturing its flesh from within.

Chenoa crashed hard onto the basalt near its feet, pain flaring from her shattered cheek as she hit the ground, rolling rapidly away.

The Wen'ey'ti's torso exploded from within, a mass of fur and innards splattering outward. Bone fragments and bloody water splattered in all directions.

The monster convulsed one last time before collapsing to the ground. The creature's single crimson eye dimmed. It was dead at last.

Stretched out on the ground, exhausted but alive, Chenoa wiped copious amounts of stringy viscera from her face. Flinging the goo off her hands, she stared over at the monster's corpse, seeing water still pouring out from its mangled guts.

"I guess he couldn't handle the pressure," she muttered.

Chenoa caught her breath, watching the pool's ripples claim the beast. The basin's water level rose steadily as the underground river poured from Elkhorn Peak. Within moments, the Wen'ey'ti submerged, its torn body dragged into the basin's churning depths.

Soon, it had vanished altogether. All that remained of its terror was scattered chunks of its flesh and fur on the ground. After a while, even those would be gone. The Ancient Ones had returned to myths.

Chenoa's ribs throbbed, her vision blurring as blood loss and pain began to finally take hold of her senses.

Total silence had fallen over the area for a moment, but was now broken by the sound of approaching hoofbeats.

Confused by the noise, Winterhawk made a move to stand.

"Show us those hands!"

"NOW!"

The voices belonged to two men shouting from somewhere behind her.

Chenoa slowly rolled over, squinting.

Twenty feet away, two very large men on horseback were aiming repeater rifles at her. Their faces looked to be etched out of the same iron as their weapons.

The man to her left spat a stream of chewing tobacco, his mustache twitching. "Hands. Where. We. Can. See. Them."

Chenoa shook her head. "I think you can already see my hands just fine," she rasped.

The man sitting on the horse to her right tightened his finger on his weapon's trigger. "Get those hands up before you die from lead poisoning!"

Just then, a third horse galloped into view, coming to a stop beside the two men.

Seeing who the rider was, Chenoa shook her head with a grin. This third man happened to be an old friend.

"Chenoa Winterhawk," President Theodore Roosevelt said from his mount, "still living the quiet life, I see?"

CHAPTER 49

Chenoa pinched off a tough smile like it was week-old bread. "You've always been the king of dramatic entrances, Teddy."

The two other men on horseback exchanged uneasy glances like they'd just been caught passing fixed cards under a poker table.

"Uh, sir?" the first man said. Brow furrowed, his eyes were fixated on the smashed motorcycle lying in a heap on the ground nearby.

Roosevelt motioned at them. "You must forgive my Secret Service detail here. They like to get up on their hind legs whenever they sniff trouble."

"Around you, I reckon they must smell it a whole lot."

"Quite so!" Roosevelt turned on his saddle to face the agents. "Cool those heaters now, boys. Winterhawk is someone to ride the river with. She's above board, gentlemen."

The second agent shifted uncomfortably on his horse. He kept his rifle steady as his eyes kept flicking suspiciously to the gore remnants scattered all over the ground. "Mr. President, I'm not exactly sure about that."

"Contrary to what my stump speeches might otherwise imply," Roosevelt said, "I really don't like repeating myself. Lower those rifles...*now*, if you please."

The men now wore expressions like they'd just found raisins in their chocolate chip cookies. They reluctantly complied, sliding their rifles into waiting saddle holsters.

Nodding, Roosevelt dismounted.

As he walked away from his horse, he made a show of carefully looking around the area. "For a while there, it sounded like the Battle of San Juan

Hill was being fought all over again. Gunfire, explosions, and something that sounded like a grizzly getting his pecker caught in a bear trap."

Chenoa shifted uncomfortably on the ground as her slashed ribs began to painfully throb. "Is that right?"

Roosevelt was now standing over the furry chunks of the Wen'ey'ti. He poked at one the pieces with his boot. "Is that what this was—a grizzly?"

"Biggest damn one I ever saw, Mr. President."

Roosevelt held out an arm to her. Chenoa reached up and grabbed it, allowing herself to slowly be pulled to her feet. Teddy studied her bruised face, then glanced at her wounded side. "Yeah. It must have been."

"You just happened to be in the area catching butterflies?" she asked.

Roosevelt grinned. "Nothing quite so dangerous, Winterhawk. I had planned on spending a week over here hunting with an old friend of mine, Colonel Higgins. In fact, two of my other agents were supposed to be waiting at the cabin for us when we arrived. But we found the cabin empty; sadly, no trace of my friend or those Secret Service agents."

The first man on the horse cleared his throat. "That's when we heard all of the commotion, ma'am."

The second agent nodded in agreement. "We thought somebody had started a damn war."

Not too far from the truth, Chenoa thought grimly.

Roosevelt was carefully studying her. "That explains what I'm doing here, Chenoa, but it doesn't tell me why you are."

Winterhawk took a deep breath. "I was on a mission. There was an ambush. Good people were killed. Some bad people, too."

Nodding, Roosevelt turned to his Secret Service agents. "Chenoa Winterhawk is an Army Indian Scout. Before that, she was my bear hunting guide. Her father, God rest his soul, was a damn good Cavalry soldier and an even greater Nez Perce Chief."

The two men now looked at her with an obvious sense of admiration.

Chenoa felt her throat constrict with emotion. "Thank you, sir."

"I see you're still wearing your father's locket. It's good that you have that connection with something that was his."

"This locket is very special to me."

"Lord knows I understand exactly what you've gone through. Grief can be like cow dung—you step in it and carry it with you. But after you walk with it for a while, you start to forget it's even there. It plays a number on time, too, doesn't it? After you lose someone special, days can feel like years, and sometimes years can feel like days. Hell, I bet it feels like ages now since the last time you even saw your father."

Chenoa touched the locket and smiled. "You'd be surprised, sir."

Roosevelt placed a gentle hand on her good shoulder. "We need to get you to a hospital now; then, I need you to tell me everything that happened here."

"I will tell you everything, but right now, I need to tell you just *one* thing."

"What's that?"

Chenoa motioned at Elkhorn Peak. "There was a soldier who died in there today, Mr. President. His name was Major Quinn." She heard her voice crack with emotion. "He was one of the bravest men I've ever met. He helped me to stop many innocent lives from getting killed...including yours, sir."

Roosevelt nodded solemnly. "It sounds like the United States owes this man a huge debt of gratitude."

"It does," Chenoa said. "And here's what the United States can repay him. You see, Quinn has a young daughter. Her name is Huan. She needs your help. sir."

"Of course. I'd like to hear more about this. But what about you, Chenoa? You've obviously been a hero here today. Is there something I can do for you?"

"Home, Mr. President." Hot tears spilled down her face. "I just want to go home."

Home.

The word felt different today for her than it ever had.

Growing up, she had been taught by Chief Joseph to believe that the Great Spirit sees and hears everything. That in the hereafter, the Creator would provide every man a spirit-home according to his deeds: if he had been good, he would have a good home; if he has been bad, he would have a bad home.

Chenoa guessed that Akando had rejected that theology the moment he'd been banished from his own home with the Nez Perce. But after being struck down by her father, her *Piimx* would face an even worse separation than the one given to him by Chief Joseph. This time, it would be the Great Spirit who would be sending Akando away.

In the end, you pay the bill for the things that you've done.

Her father used to say that you could deceive him about the price, but never about the goods. Sometimes a person didn't know how much their actions were going to cost, but they always knew how much they wanted to buy.

Akando had traded in his entire life for hatred and revenge when he could have sought restoration and reconciliation. He never asked about the price of forgiveness because he was too occupied with buying up wrath.

Her *Piimx* had been born a Winterhawk, but he hadn't died as one. The final blow that had cleaved him in half had been symbolic of his legacy and of his heritage. Akando's legacy had drowned in the very flood he had unleashed.

After striking him dead, her father had remarked that his brother had become half a man. But Chenoa thought those sins ran much deeper. For everything he was and everything he did, she believed that Akando had never been a whole man at all.

Real men fight to protect their homes. Real women do, too.

Chenoa wiped more tears from her cheeks.

President Roosevelt placed a comforting arm around her. He turned towards the agents. "Help me. She'll ride with me to the hospital."

The men quickly dismounted. Each gently taking an arm, they led her to Roosevelt's horse and helped her up onto the saddle.

Roosevelt expertly mounted the horse, sitting directly behind her for support. He wasn't going to let her fall.

"Take the reins, Winterhawk."

Chenoa nodded, but before she did, she took one final look at Elkhorn Peak. She glanced at the waterfall that the underground rivers had created, and marveled at how something so very good could come from something so very bad.

She thought again of her people, thinking of the suffering that the Nez Perce had endured. Was it possible that someday there would be something good to come out of it all for them? The dream that Chief Joseph had died with was to see his people return to their homeland.

It had also been her father's dream.

And now, it was her dream, too.

But it was more than that. It was also a hope for new beginnings, and a hope for brand-new days.

And hope dies last.

EPILOGUE

Upper Valley Cemetery
Hood River, Oregon
1905

The autumn winds whispered respectfully through the pines guarding Hood River's Upper Valley Cemetery. They carried the familiar scent of damp earth and cherished memories.

Kneeling beside a simple gravestone etched with her mother's name, Huan Quinn felt her hair caught in the gentle breeze. She sometimes liked to think of it as her mother's fingers gently caressing her head, the whispering wind acting as a proxy for her calming voice. If she listened hard enough, that voice would be telling her that everything was going to be alright.

But of course, it wasn't. There wasn't anybody to tell her those things. Not even from Pastor Carmichael and his kind wife, Rosalita. After her father had pleaded with them to watch over her during his absence, they had graciously allowed her into their home. Those first days had turned into several weeks; now, the time had stretched into months.

Huan tightly clutched her mother's favorite jade pendant in her hand. It had become a fading tether to a family that she now realized had been permanently broken by death.

While the Army had yet to proclaim her father's demise, nearly six months had gone by since the day he'd left with her grandfather's map. Pastor Carmichael said that because the mission had been top secret, he believed that the standard military protocol in these situations wouldn't be observed.

But late one evening, long after Huan was supposed to be asleep, she had listened to a whispered conversation they'd had through her bathroom vent. It turned out what they really thought centered around politics, not protocol. Then, they had made a hushed vow to God to protect her from those who would want to take her away.

In some people's eyes, she would always be two halves and not one whole. Huan understood that, and knew that it was only a matter of time before the inevitable happened. She was a young Chinese-American girl without papers or legal guardians. Eventually, the government would send her away from her home and deport her to China.

The thought brought with it an ocean of fear.

Now, Huan's small hands trembled as she placed a sprig of sage on her mother's grave. Her fingers brushed the sage, its sharp scent mingling with the damp earth.

"Mama?" she whispered. "What's going to happen to me now?"

A warm voice broke the silence behind her. "While I never got the privilege of meeting Major Quinn personally, I've heard such wonderful things about your father from a very dear friend of mine."

Startled, Huan spun around on the damp grass, heart hammering. She immediately recognized the man speaking to her from all of his pictures in the newspapers.

It was President Theodore Roosevelt. He stood a respectful distance away from her mother's grave. His square jaw was softened by a gentle smile, and his suit appeared to have been kissed by the dust from a long journey.

Huan felt her breath catch in her throat. Anxiety flared through her like a brushfire. Her voice trembled. "Mr. President, why are you here?"

Roosevelt took a step closer, face awash with kindness. "No need to be frightened, Huan. I'm here because of your father's bravery." He reached into his suit pocket and produced two large envelopes, their wax seals glinting in the light. "These are for you."

Huan's eyes widened with confusion. "What are they?"

Roosevelt held up the first envelope. "This is a Presidential Proclamation of Exemption, signed by my hand. It declares you as being a rightful resident of these United States, born on this soil and granted full rights to stay on this soil."

Huan felt tears welling. "I can really stay, sir?"

"You can, and you will," Roosevelt said. "Here. There's more." He handed her the second envelope. "This is an acceptance letter from Mills College in California. It's a women's institution where students of all backgrounds and ages can study, grow, and thrive. You'll be attending high school and college there. In fact, all of your tuition and board have already been paid for the next ten years."

Huan's hands shook as she held the letter. "Paid by whom?"

"Chenoa Winterhawk."

"Who's that?"

Roosevelt smiled. "She's a Nez Perce warrior who fought valiantly beside your father. Chenoa's bravery saved countless lives. She made Major Quinn a promise about you before he was killed."

Huan had already accepted that her father was never coming home again, but the finality of President Roosevelt's words still stung deeply. Her father *was* dead.

She wanted to be brave in front of Roosevelt and not cry, so she focused her eyes down on the envelope, instead.

"I really don't understand, sir."

"Chenoa knows how important it is to honor a father's legacy. She paid for all of your schooling because that's her gift to you: a future."

Huan's chest tightened with a mixture of gratitude and anxiety. "Eyes and ears," she finally said.

"Excuse me?"

"It was something my father used to say." Huan bit her lower lip in that peculiar way of hers. "Poppa said that as long as we use our eyes and ears, we can always see the people that God puts in our life to help us."

"Major Quinn was right."

Huan stared up at him for a long moment. "I'm scared."

Roosevelt carefully knelt down until he was at her level.

"Of course you are, Huan. You have every right to be scared. Your father was a brave soldier, but I know there were times when he was scared, too. But I know what gave him strength during those hard times: your mother. Well, you're their daughter. That means that even though your parents are no longer with us, you're both of them; the best parts of them, I think. And you know what? That makes you strong, too."

Huan felt tears begin to roll down her cheeks. "I'm not two halves, but one whole."

President Roosevelt nodded and slowly stood. With a smile, he reached down and offered her his hand.

Huan once again felt the gentle stirring of the wind. Glancing down, she saw the sage sprig dance off the grave and land on her feet.

Thank you, momma, she thought.

Taking a deep breath, Huan took Roosevelt's hand, and they began walking out of the cemetery.

"Chenoa is very excited to meet you someday," Roosevelt said.

"I would like that a great deal. What's she like, sir?"

"She's the warrior daughter of Chief Jolon Winterhawk. Chenoa and her father fought monsters, you know."

Huan's eyes were like saucers. "Monsters?"

"Indeed. We've got a long train journey ahead of us, Huan. I'll tell you all about their adventures during the trip."

Huan nodded at him enthusiastically. She liked hearing about adventures.

She felt a surge of hope in her soul as she thought about what her future held. She thought about how proud her Poppa would be of her right now. She thought about how beautiful her mother was, and she hoped that she'd grow up to look exactly like her.

And then, Huan suddenly realized something.

She wasn't afraid anymore.

THE END

ACKNOWLEDGEMENTS

British superstar Robbie Williams once remarked that songs are only valuable if they cost you something. While writing "In the Wrath of Legends," I found out that novels can be like that, too.

After my publisher contracted me to write a sequel to "In the Lair of Legends," I began to work on it immediately. Although I had never planned for the story to continue beyond a single book, I knew instinctively that the next adventure needed to rest on the capable shoulders of Chenoa Winterhawk. I had fallen in love with this character in the first story (the flashback chapter between Jolon and Chenoa was my favorite part of the first book), and I was excited to explore more of her character in the sequel.

As I was doing the research and plotting out the story, I kept in mind something director Renny Harlin had said during a promotional interview before the release of CLIFFHANGER. When a reporter asked him why he'd chosen this particular film, Harlin answered: "After DIE HARD 2, I was looking for a movie that would give me the same kind of thrills, but offer me more in terms of character and relationships."

That became my daily mantra while working on the second book: same thrills, more character. While it was absolutely the right approach, Chenoa's amazing journey brought out unforeseen creative difficulties and emotional challenges within myself that felt nearly as insurmountable as the Wen'ey'ti themselves.

As always, I owe a huge debt of gratitude to Reagan Rothe (who has been incredibly patient and understanding with this second book) and the team at Black Rose Writing for believing in my potential. Thank you Mary Ellen for the frequent pep talks, and once again to David King for his spectacular cover design.

Along this creative journey, I've been blessed to associate myself with an incredible group of encouraging and supportive authors: Eric Bishop, Sheila Young, Tobin Elliott, Steve Stark, Cam Torrens, Jeremy Engel, Nick Horvath, Janelle Schiecke, Tom McCaffrey, Brian Kaufman...and so many, many others. Thank you for everything!

Extra special thanks to Lena Gibson. She's been such a wonderful friend (and incredible author) who has lifted me up so many times over the last three years. I simply cannot thank you enough for all of your kindness.

I have so many friends who offered endless support after the release of my debut: Becca Zander, Maggie Crawford, Michelle Cox, Marine Hill, Lindsey Stark, Tapi Gibson, Serena Hunt, Tina Harding, Hannah Knotts, Tara Smith, Amelia Burton...and again, so many others. THANK YOU!

Thanks to the continuing support from my amazing Buzan and Hughes families. And to my incredible mom and dad, who are the biggest heroes in my life.

My beautiful wife, Deborah, who continues to amaze me with the unlimited depths of love, patience, and support. I love you, Snuggie!

And thank you to the wonderful readers who so greatly embraced the fantastic world of Jolon Winterhawk. The book was a success because of your enthusiasm and continued word of mouth.

And yes, books can cost you something. But in the end, they give you something a lot more: hope.

And hope dies last.

No Surrender,

Dave Buzan (August, 2025)

ABOUT THE AUTHOR

David Buzan is a novelist and screenwriter. His bestselling debut novel, *In the Lair of Legends*, became a multiple award-winner, including the 2023 Best Thrillers Book Award for Historical Thriller of the Year. A graduate of the Vancouver Film School, Buzan also holds a Bachelor of Science Degree in Psychology from Liberty University. *In the Wrath of Legends* is his second novel.

DAVID BUZAN
IN THE LAIR OF
LEGENDS

NOTE FROM DAVID BUZAN

Word-of-mouth is crucial for any author to succeed. If you enjoyed *In the Wrath of Legends*, please leave a review online—anywhere you are able. Even if it's just a sentence or two. It would make all the difference and would be very much appreciated.

Thanks!
David Buzan

We hope you enjoyed reading this title from:

www.blackrosewriting.com

Subscribe to our mailing list – *The Rosevine* – and receive **FREE** books, daily deals, and stay current with news about upcoming releases and our hottest authors.
Scan the QR code below to sign up.

Already a subscriber? Please accept a sincere thank you for being a fan of Black Rose Writing authors.

View other Black Rose Writing titles at
www.blackrosewriting.com/books and use promo code
PRINT to receive a **20% discount** when purchasing.